# Praise for P L

'His stories will take you to the edge of your seat and
beyond ... so sit tight!'
**Paul Finch, author of *Strangers***

'Original, engaging, unique. A fine read'
**Joe R. Lansdale, author of *Cold in July***

'Scarily original'
**Peter James, author of *Dead Simple***

'An exciting new voice on the crime scene'
**Elly Griffiths, author of *The Crossing Places***

**P L KANE** is the pseudonym of a #1 bestselling and award-winning author and editor, who has had over ninety books published in the fields of SF, YA and Horror/Dark Fantasy. In terms of crime fiction, previous books include the collection *Nailbiters* and the anthology *Exit Wounds*, which contains stories by the likes of Lee Child, Dean Koontz, Val McDermid and Dennis Lehane. Kane has been a guest at many events and conventions, and has had work optioned and adapted for film and television (including Lions Gate/NBC, who picked up a story for primetime US network TV). Several of Kane's stories have been turned into short movies and Loose Canon Films/Hydra Films have just adapted 'Men of the Cloth' into a feature, *The Colour of Madness*. Kane's audio drama work for places such as Bafflegab and Spiteful Puppet/ITV features the acting talents of people like Tom Meeten (*The Ghoul*), Neve McIntosh (*Doctor Who/Shetland*), Alice Lowe (*Prevenge*) and Ian Ogilvy (*Return of the Saint*). Visit www.plkane.com for more details.

# Her Last Secret

## P L KANE

ONE PLACE. MANY STORIES

HQ
An imprint of HarperCollins*Publishers* Ltd
1 London Bridge Street
London SE1 9GF

First edition published in Great Britain by
HQ, an imprint of HarperCollins*Publishers* Ltd 2020

ISBN: 9780008372224

MIX
Paper from
responsible sources
FSC C007454

This book is produced from independently certified FSC™ paper
to ensure responsible forest management.

For more information visit: www.harpercollins.co.uk/green

Printed and bound in Great Britain by
CPI Group (UK) Ltd, Melksham, SN12 6TR

*For Marie, who encouraged me to write this book,
and Jen, who thankfully was a joy to bring up.*

# Prologue

As the girl stumbled forward, she had one name on her mind.

She'd lost her mobile back there on the street and didn't have time to stop and search for it; didn't have the strength. She just needed to get to some help, maybe make it to the clubbing part of town – though that seemed like a very long way away. And she was getting tired now, breath misting in the autumn air, hardly able to focus. Little wonder – because as she touched the wounds on her chest, brushing the handle of the knife that was still sticking out, that had been left in there as she'd attempted to escape, her hands came away wet. Totally black in the moonlight.

Blood ... so much blood.

Pain that had been unbearable only minutes before was dulling now, making her numb. She clutched at a wall, leaving a handprint behind her. There'd be someone soon, she'd find someone who could help her. In fact, yes, there up ahead the street was opening out. Even in her confused state, she knew where she was: the market square. Ahead of her were the stalls, empty now at night-time – not that many were used in the waking hours, either, apart from on certain days – rows of wooden skeletons, looking like the carcasses of long-dead monsters.

Monsters like the ones she'd been so afraid of when she was little. Silly really, being scared of imaginary things like that, when there were so many real things to be frightened of after you grew up. She wished more than anything at that moment – as she slipped on her own blood, righted herself and lunged towards the stalls – that she could go back in time to those days. Back when make-believe creatures under the bed were the only things to worry about. Back when life was so much simpler.

She used the stalls to drag herself along, still searching the space for ... there! Someone was waiting in the middle. Or at least she thought it was someone, only to get there and realise it was just tarpaulin hanging down on yet another frame. Things were getting hazy now, her vision blurred. Time was running out. If the monsters here were dead, then she wouldn't be far behind them. And wasn't there a part of her that felt relief at that, because living was so, so hard? She'd always assumed it would get better, but it never really did; always thought there would be a brighter day to come. Instead, it was getting darker by the second.

She flopped onto that stall with the canvas sheeting, pain shooting through her again and waking her up momentarily. Forcing her onto her back, because the knife wouldn't let her lie down on her front.

*If I could just go back. If I could just see him one more time.*

The man who'd always chased away those monsters back when she was tiny, who'd picked her up and put her on his shoulders when they'd go for walks in the park. Who'd tried to teach her right from wrong, set an example. And whom she'd treated so, so badly.

That's why the name that had been on her mind, the name that came out – as she finally went blind, as the last of her vital lifeblood seeped out – wasn't that of the person who'd done this to her. Their name was as far from her thoughts as possible.

No, the name she uttered with her last breath was that of the man she thought might come, as if they shared some kind of psychic bond and she was sending out a distress call. It was the person, when all was said and done, that she still trusted most in this world; the irony being that he probably didn't even know that anymore, regardless of how true it was.

No, the name on her lips was simply this, uttered as if she was 5 again: 'Daddy.'

Then all she knew was the dark.

# PART ONE

The historic town and borough of Redmarket is situated thirty miles west of Granfield, and is so called because of its association with the meat trade, dating back to its founding in 70–100 AD. Originally the site of a Roman fort, later on an Anglo-Saxon village grew up around the area. However, it wasn't until the early thirteenth century that it received its official market charter. Known for its friendly locals, Redmarket is surrounded by beautiful countryside and yet is only a stone's throw away from a number of other thriving towns and cities.

# Chapter 1

It always had been, and remained, the worst part of this job.

Some coppers called it the 'Death Knock' or delivering the 'Death Message' – but whatever name you gave it, the result was the same. You were delivering news that would devastate a family, changing their lives forever. Once the words were out, there was no taking them back again. The knowledge would have an impact on everything, from doing the groceries to whether you even wanted to get up out of bed in the morning.

So, DC Mathew Newcomb paused before rapping on the wood of that door. It wasn't simply the gravity of what he was about to impart, although it was the worst thing anyone could ever tell another human being; the worst thing they could possibly hear, as well. It wasn't even the effect on him; that wasn't – *shouldn't* be – what this was about. He'd done this dozens of times, although selfishly on this occasion he knew it would upset him more than any of the others. For the same reason he'd volunteered to come here in the first place, along with the Family Liaison Officer Linda Fergusson. Because he owed this family, knew them personally.

Because he knew the victim.

Linda was looking at him, those brown eyes of hers questioning. Mathew couldn't put the moment off any longer. He

7

brought his knuckles down on the wood, hard, a couple of times. It was ridiculous, but he didn't want the knock to sound flippant – he wanted it to somehow convey the seriousness of his business. Wanted it to have told them some of what he needed to impart even before the people inside had answered the call.

Sadly, when the door opened, and standing there was the one person he would have gone to the ends of the earth not to see, she only frowned momentarily, then was suddenly smiling. 'Matt?' said Julie, and it was as if the decades hadn't really passed at all. They were still at school together. She had been his first crush – those freckles and that flaming red hair. Both had faded in the intervening years, the latter to an auburn colour. But in spite of a few wrinkles here and there, the beginnings of crow's feet at the eyes, she was still beautiful – even in those jeans and a loose shirt. She was still Julie Brent ... Jules. How could he have thought he'd ever stood a chance with her? She'd only had eyes for one bloke, right from the start. 'I can't believe it. What are you doing ...? I haven't seen you since the reunion a few ...' Her gaze flitted from Mathew to his companion, but now she was frowning again. 'Mathew, what ...?'

He opened his mouth to speak, but nothing came out. Mathew realised he was standing there like an idiot, yet there was nothing he could do about it. The words simply wouldn't come.

*This had been a bad idea*, he said to himself. He'd wanted to ... what, break the news to Julie gently, make sure it was delivered in the right way? *Was* there even a right way? Didn't feel like it at the moment. Not at all. Wanted to be there for Julie, then? Even after all these years. But he was making such a cockup of it, leaving the poor woman just standing there, wondering what was going on. Looking from him to Linda, then back again. All Mathew could do was shake his head.

'Matt? Matt, you're scaring me.'

*You* should *be scared*, he couldn't help thinking. He opened and closed his mouth again, looking for all the world like a ventriloquist's dummy whose owner had laryngitis. In the end, he managed a strangled, 'I'm so sorry.'

But, as it turned out, he didn't need to say any more than that. She'd already realised he was here in an official capacity, from his expression, from the fact he wasn't alone; knew what his job entailed. There were really only three people this could be about – and Mathew had heard that Julie's dad was in a home somewhere, so if something had happened to him, she would have received a phone call from there. That left a choice of two, and probably only one of them hadn't been in the house all night. Wasn't an uncommon thing, if what he'd heard about the girl was correct – which was why Julie hadn't been worried …

Until now.

It was Julie's turn to shake her head, going into denial: 'No … no, it can't …' Mathew had seen this on more than one occasion as well. Julie's hand was going to her mouth, tears were already welling in her eyes.

'Who the bloody hell is …' The voice drifted through even before this newcomer followed, dressed in a vest and pyjama bottoms. Mathew recognised him as Greg Allaway, Julie's husband. Hair closely cropped to hide the fact he was going bald, and with a well-cultivated beer belly – even more so than the last time he'd seen the man – he was totally the opposite of what Mathew would have expected Julie to end up with. Mathew might not have stood a chance back in school, but he could run rings around Greg Allaway as it stood today. If he hadn't been married himself, of course. The thought made him uncomfortable, and wasn't welcome in any way, shape or form. But when Greg snapped, 'What the bloody hell is all this? I was just getting ready for work!' it surfaced again momentarily, and just for a second Mathew wanted to punch him squarely in the face.

Julie couldn't speak, was having trouble even standing. She toppled sideways against the open front door, and it was only when Mathew moved forwards to try and catch her that Greg

9

did something to help – getting there first and grabbing her by the arm to steady her. Grabbing a little too forcefully for Mathew's liking.

Greg looked from his wife, back to Linda and Mathew. And was there a hint of recognition now that he could take the latter in properly? Did he remember him from the last time they'd met? Remember his vocation? Even if he didn't, Mathew had been told after all these years on the force he definitely looked like a policeman; didn't even matter that he was plain-clothes. 'What's happened now?' Julie's husband asked gruffly.

Linda spoke up this time, doing the job that she'd been trained for. 'I think it might be best if we came in off the street to talk about it.'

Greg looked back at his wife, who was on the verge of collapsing altogether – her green eyes rolling back into her head – and nodded.

*  *  *

Twenty minutes later, and they were all sitting in the living room: Greg and Julie on the couch, him with his arm around her; Mathew and Linda on the chairs opposite. Linda had made them all a tea, after asking where the kitchen was. An especially sweet one for Julie because she was in shock, although the woman hadn't touched a drop yet, kept staring at the mug in front of her on the coffee table.

'I just … I just can't believe it,' she kept on saying. 'Not our Jordan.'

All Mathew could do was shake his head in reply. Not that he hadn't done all the talking he needed to for now, hoping that what he'd said had helped a little. Of course, hearing that your daughter had been stabbed to death was never going to be easy to take in. But the fact that they had a suspect in custody, that he'd been picked up covered in blood not too far from the crime

10

scene, must have been some sort of comfort to her. He left out the fact that they'd found fingerprints on the handle of the murder weapon for now, because it was currently being tested, but Mathew had no doubt whatsoever that they would end up belonging to one Robert 'Bobby' Bannister: Jordan's boyfriend.

'But ... but why?' Julie asked again, gazing up at him with eyes that looked like they'd been scrubbed raw. All he could do in answer to that was give another shake of the head, because Mathew Newcomb didn't have the first clue. What he did know was that it was only a matter of time before it all come out in the wash. Things usually did.

'That young lass was always getting herself into some kind of trouble,' was Greg's reply. 'I've ... *we've* done our best to try and help her, but, well, some people just don't seem to want to be helped, do they?' Before anyone could say anything to that, he added, 'Oh, Christ – work! I need to give them a call and tell them I'll be late in.' When he saw the look Julie cast him, he changed that to: 'Tell them I *won't* be in, I mean.'

He let go of his wife then and went out into the hallway to use the phone on the table there. It was only now that Mathew got up, went over and sat down next to Julie as she broke into another fresh bout of tears. 'Hey, hey ... it's okay, Jules. Everything's going to be okay.' Hollow words and they both knew it. Nothing would ever be okay again as far as Julie Allaway was concerned.

The sound of Greg's voice on the phone wafted through to them and it was suddenly as if a light bulb had gone on in Julie's head. 'Has ... has anyone let him know?'

Mathew was puzzled for a second or two, then realised who she meant. 'Someone's contacting him, from the station.'

As Julie nodded slowly, Mathew caught the look of confusion on Linda's face. 'Greg is Jordan's stepfather,' he told her, and she nodded.

'He ... he'll be in bits,' Julie mumbled, as if she hadn't even heard Mathew's words to the FLO.

11

'I know,' said Mathew, patting her knee. 'I know.' She broke down once more, leaning across and sobbing into his shoulder. There were words, but he couldn't really make them out at first. Then Mathew realised what she was saying.

'What are we going to do?' Julie was repeating over and over. 'What are we going to do?'

* * *

Jacob Radcliffe yawned as he sat waiting for the other members of his team to get their act together, to get *there*. It was like trying to herd cats, getting the producer, reporter and sound person all in one place at the same time so they could set off to their destination – this time to do a thrilling piece about an old married couple who'd been together for seventy years. Lucky them. Typical kind of thing for the local news sections on TV. Jake was *so* looking forward to pointing the camera at them and listening as they gave sage advice like: 'Never go to bed on an argument' or 'Try not to worry about things you can't control'. Jesus.

*Where was all the big news?* he had to ask himself. He'd been on more exciting gigs when he'd been a photographer for *The Granfield Gazette* back in the day. There was even that report about mob boss Danny Fellows and his operations that Jake's old colleague Dave Harris had been lining up until it got squashed. It had been exciting though, going round and taking pictures of the places Fellows owned, like that casino or the strip joint. Felt like they were doing something important, something worthwhile...

Probably a good idea it stopped where it did though, if Fellows' rep was anything to go by, Jake often thought to himself. At least when you were interviewing old married couples there was no chance of ending up at the bottom of the river wearing concrete slippers.

He looked at his watch again, then out across at the newsroom at the various people who were in at this hour: only a handful so far, checking emails, answering or making calls. Jake yawned again. What was the point of arranging a time to set off on their long drive when nobody was going to show up but him? He had been hoping they could get this in the bag and out of the way before lunch, so he could sneak off and do some more editing on the short film he'd been making in his spare time. It was just something he was doing for fun at the moment, not really thinking it would go anywhere – and certainly not thinking along the lines of BAFTAs or Oscars – but maybe if he could get it up to scratch he could hit the festivals with it. Jake had mostly recruited students from the local unis and colleges to help with it all, people who'd work just for credits over several weekends. And it wasn't shaping up too badly at all, if he said so himself: a film about young people today and their thoughts about the future, where everything was heading. Fiction, but in a documentary style.

But he was never going to get it finished at this rate, not if Sarah, Phil and Howard didn't get their arses in gear so they could get this over and done with. 'For God's sake,' he said, stifling yet another yawn.

They were lucky he was in at all, the restless night he'd had. It had taken him ages to actually get to sleep and he'd only been in the land of nod a short while when he'd woken up, panicking and sweating. He could have sworn someone had been calling out his name, but when he turned on the light he felt quite silly for answering. Jake had struggled to get back off, tossing and turning, rolling onto his front, his sides. Thank Christ he didn't share a bed with anyone anymore, because they probably would have kicked him out onto the couch. In the end, he'd got up at stupid o'clock and made himself several cups of coffee – which was probably why he'd got here so early that morning, and why it seemed like he'd been waiting ages. Couldn't blame the others for staying tucked up in bed a little while longer, he supposed, but all the same …

Jake was relieved when he saw Sarah, their reporter, come

through the doors, looking immaculate as usual (he'd once joked that she probably got out of bed looking like that, and she'd scowled and filled him in at great length about all the prep it took). She held up a hand in greeting, then pointed to indicate she was going to grab a drink before coming over. He sighed ... but then neither of the others had even shown their faces yet.

Phil and Howard turned up together, laughing and joking as usual – not a care in the world – and Jake was just rising to go and join them when someone actually did call his name. It was their IT person, Alison, holding up a phone for him to come over. Jake touched his chest and she nodded, face quite serious.

'Who's calling me here?' he asked her as he trotted over. He had his work mobile on him, so why not use that? 'What's it about?'

Alison shrugged. 'Wouldn't say. Sounded official, though.'

Jake took the phone from her, his brow creasing. 'H-Hello?' He nodded when they asked if they were speaking to the right person, before realising they couldn't see him. 'Yes, that's me.'

Then, as the words came through the receiver, it was as if time stood still. Jake tried and failed to process them. Instead, he dropped the phone which hung down the side of Alison's desk by its cord. Then he walked away, leaving Alison and everyone else mystified, ignoring their calls.

He had somewhere to be.

He had something to do.

14

# Chapter 2

How Jake got to his Silver Toyota, got on the road, and made it to the motorway was something of a mystery in itself.

There were just too many thoughts racing through his mind. Memories especially, winding back time to the day he'd first seen Julie at school, and they'd shared that moment – the one that told them both they'd be together forever (hadn't made seventy years, though, had they). Hanging out with her and Mathew after hours – the Three Musketeers – then him and Matt getting into all kinds of trouble as they started to gravitate towards the wrong kind of company. Graffiti, bit of pickpocketing, joyriding; the usual juvenile stuff. In Jake's defence, he'd lost his father back when he was only 10 to bowel cancer and his mother was so busy working all the hours God sent, she couldn't keep a proper eye on him. That was the excuse those lawyers had used at any rate. Then they were caught with a stolen car, and Jake had carried the can for Matt. It had seen him get away with a suspended sentence and community service, thank Christ, though it had probably contributed to his mum having her heart attack a couple of years after that.

None of this had put Julie off him, though. In fact, it only seemed to make her want him more, despite the fact he'd dropped out of school and she was trying to get her A levels. Maybe it was the bad boy thing a lot of young girls went through? He hadn't been *that* bad, though, not really. In any event, they'd ended up spending more and more time together – at the local skateboarding area, at the park after sunset, at the woods nearby. Her parents, the Brents, who to him were like something out of the 1950s, definitely didn't approve. But it was getting to the point where they couldn't really tell her what to do anymore. He and Julie started sleeping together, and it was amazing … right up until the point that the condom they were using one night split; Julie had been too scared to go to the doctor's and get the pill, so that had been their only method of birth control.

Jake remembered the night she'd told him, having hidden it from everyone for months – right up to the time when it was too late to do anything about it but have the baby. Not that they'd have done anything differently, he didn't think. So there they were, not even 18, green as grass, and they were looking at being a family. Naturally, Julie's parents had freaked the fuck out – her dad even handing her an ultimatum, to give Jake the heave-ho or get out, much to her mother's distress. He hadn't meant it, he'd told her later, just hadn't known what else to do to get her to see sense. Stubborn Jules and that fiery temper, which matched her hair. She'd been his little girl, and the man had seen it as a violation (Jake didn't get that until much, much later). He wasn't exactly a catch anyway …

However, Julie had chosen to be with him – put her faith in Jake even though it scared the crap out of him. It had forced them both to grow up overnight, for Jake to take some responsibility and get whatever above-board job he could (and now he could finally understand what his mum had been doing to put clothes on his back, to put food on the table). He'd done all kinds of work back in those days, from manual labour on building sites to packing goods on a conveyor belt in a factory.

Julie had to give up on the A levels, of course, abandoning her ambitions of becoming a vet. But oh, it really was worth all the struggle in the end. Because when Jules gave birth that afternoon in January, it was like their lives had only really started. The love they'd felt for her ... for this girl they'd named Jordan – becoming The Three 'J's now – well, it was just indescribable. Like he would do anything for her, anything at all. Step in front of a bullet, a train ...whatever, gladly.

She'd been Jake's pride and joy, had brought so much happiness to their tiny little home: a two-bedroom flat, in quite an undesirable part of town. They didn't have much, but they had each other, they had love. More love than some folk had with mountains of cash.

And, in time, Jake had found himself in better – more regular – employ, while Julie had gone to work part-time at a local vet's, just while Jordan was in school. Jake began to think about bettering himself, and Jordan had made that happen. He wanted to be somebody she could look up to, not just 'Daddy' but a guy who had a vocation. That was when he'd taken the night-school classes in photography, something he hadn't thought about in years but had been quite keen on as a young kid. He soon found he had an aptitude for it – composition and framing came as second nature to him (this was back in the days of single lens reflex and developing fluids, back before digital photography became the norm). Some of his work had even been sent with the classes' offerings on a touring exhibition abroad.

It gave him the encouragement he needed to apply for work at all the newspapers in the surrounding areas, especially now they'd finally managed to afford a small car. Julie's parents had started to chip in as well, not vast amounts but at least they were trying – probably so they could gain more access to their grandchild. By then, Jake's mum had passed away, so really they were all Jordan had in terms of grandparents.

He'd got his job as a junior at *The Granfield Gazette*, and worked his way up, becoming one of the most trusted photographers on the staff. They got a house, a real house with stairs and everything. Jordan was doing well at school, showing signs of Jake's own creativity – especially painting and drawing, some writing too – but also a love of animals that she got from her mother. Always wanting to take in strays, look after them. Things were good, life was good.

But then came the teenage years.

In the space of just a few months – so little time – when Jordan was coming up to her fifteenth birthday, her whole personality had changed. She'd always been so sweet, so thoughtful, but the kids she'd started hanging out with at school were just idiots, plain and simple. Jake and Jules had tried to instil in her a sense of right and wrong, a moral core, but that was soon eroded away by the need to be popular – to not look like one of the eggheads who were always studying. And those fucking smartphones, bloody social media ... They'd been able to police it to some extent when she first got one, which they'd thought was a good idea to begin with, a way of keeping in touch. Jake had even bitten the bullet and got one himself at the same time, just to try and hang on to some of that closeness they'd once had as father and daughter.

Gradually, and inevitably it seemed, guys showed up on the scene. Jordan went from not really being interested, to plastering herself in make-up when she was heading out, even just down the road to a mate's, or staying over at a friend's (which they would later usually find out was male). Photos would appear all over her online pages: Jordan with groups of both girls and boys, some they didn't even know from other schools, or older lads from college. Some of the comments beneath them were absolutely disgusting. They'd confronted her about it on several occasions, but her answer was always to point to their own teenage years. And, no, Jordan hadn't got pregnant, but there had been a couple of scares at least that they knew about. All of which had Jake pulling his hair out.

It was also putting a hell of a strain on his marriage, the constant worry and the arguments. Each relying on the other to try and sort this mess out before it was too late.

By the time he'd decided to go and do more night-classes – now in camerawork, an attempt to move sideways into that field – Jordan had already failed most of her GCSEs and was looking to attend college herself for resits. That only made things worse, increased her contact with boys. A string of them stretching back and every single one interchangeable; same shit, different day, all because of the influence of her man-mad friends. Apparently, it was okay to jump straight into bed with someone, they were part of the so-called 'hook-up generation'; try before you buy, before you put a label on it … all of that bollocks. Even with those guys who threatened to hurt her, that Jake had wanted to pummel on a regular basis – ride in like some kind of half-arsed knight on a white charger or something, when it was the last thing in the world Jordan wanted; she'd made that plain.

She'd started dressing in what he thought were totally unacceptable clothes, swearing and smoking like a chimney. Talking to her became all but impossible, the generation gap obvious, and she would disappear for days on end. They'd even called the authorities on a number of occasions, fearing the worst, only for her to crop up or call them to say she was okay and just staying with friends again. What could they do? She was lost, but she was also practically a grown-up. He'd lie there in the dark at night, time ticking away so slowly, wondering if his daughter was okay; his contact with her amounting to a green dot on a screen to show if she was online, to indicate whether she was alive or dead.

And yes, if he was honest with himself, he was jealous that she had this whole other life that didn't involve him; that she actively kept away from him because she knew he wouldn't approve. It seemed a million miles away from the relationship they'd once shared as dad and daughter, the time – the years – between them stretching out further and further.

There had been more rows, Jake's imagination running wild and accusing her of all sorts – drugs were a particular suspicion – not that Jordan ever realised, because she wasn't around. Her mother would always give her the benefit of the doubt. 'What do you want me to do? We have no proof about any of this!'

'By the time we find out the truth, it'll be too late,' Jake would always argue. Chicken, egg. Egg, chicken.

The other thing Jules would say time and again was: 'She's not doing any of this to *get* at you, it's not personal. She's just trying to find her way ...' So why did it all *feel* so fucking personal? They'd spent all that time trying to bring Jordan up right, and she was basically throwing it back in their faces.

It had all hit the fan one night when she returned, having missed her eighteenth birthday. This time she'd pushed Jake too far and he'd offered a few home truths, which had made the girl cry but also ended with her telling him that she hated his guts. 'I never want to see you again!' she barked into his face.

Jake had taken one look over at Julie for support, but she'd turned away. And then so did he. Turning and walking out through the front door, going off to stay in a hotel that night. He'd returned the next day, of course he had – but Jordan hadn't been around, and he could tell by the frosty reception he got from Jules that things would never be the same with them again either. He'd tried a few more times, to make their marriage work, to talk to his daughter, but in the end, he had just headed off because he thought that was for the best. Julie's parents had been delighted by the news, naturally; probably thought it was his fault in the first place that Jordan had gone off the rails and they would now get her back on track. They never had been able to see what was right in front of their eyes.

Contact with the two ladies who'd been in his life, who'd *been* his life, had turned out to be minimal since the divorce. The odd strangled phone conversation, calls on birthdays or at Christmas – nothing more. Jake hadn't seen Jordan in almost three years now, he got the feeling she preferred it that way. He'd deleted his social media accounts as well, got rid of his old mobile so he didn't have to watch the continued self-destruction of his baby girl. He'd moved away, found a job at the local TV company and was doing all right … At least that's what he told himself. He hadn't even been fazed – much – by the news that Julie had got married again. Maybe at some point they could all sit together again in a room and talk like adults. At some point, that's what he'd thought. His daughter's twenty-first was fast approaching, so maybe …

But then the phone call. The news.

Another landmark birthday they'd miss. (No, it wasn't true!)

He'd dropped the receiver, he remembered that much. Had to get in the car, get back – just to make sure it wasn't real. Some kind of practical joke, it had to be. It couldn't be right. Just couldn't be!

*Where's all the big news?*

*You had to ask, didn't you? Well, it's here, this is it,* his conscience taunted.

In any event he had to get back there, to the town he'd once called home. Get back.

Get to Redmarket.

* * *

In his haste to reach the place, pulling off the motorway but barely slowing down, he'd almost had a collision with a blue Sierra.

Jake heard the blast of the motorist's horn, but it was muted. This whole journey had been like driving through a fog. But now he was emerging out of the other side, driving down that familiar dual carriageway, spinning off the roundabout that had only been small when he was growing up, but was now controlled by a lights system. Then up and into town proper, where the traffic was slowing to a crawl.

He craned his neck to see what was going on, but this scene was also familiar to him. He'd filmed ones just like it, with the police flitting around, tape flapping and crowds gathered. There were even TV crews setting up in the distance, vans with logos on the side that he recognised – some of them competitors. How long before his station showed up? he wondered. And he thought briefly then that he should have let someone there know where he was going, what he was doing.

But he didn't really know what was happening, did he? Not for sure. Had to find out for definite – that's what all this was about. Something had clearly happened here, but that didn't mean it was Jordan. Let it be someone else's daughter, he thought, then felt terrible for even contemplating such a thing.

Enough. Time to get this over and done with, get rid of the lump in his throat and the fist that was opening and closing in the pit of his stomach. It was time to *really* go home.

Except it wasn't his home anymore. The house he pulled up outside, when he'd finally got past the jams that were snarling up the centre of Redmarket, belonged to other people now. He remembered coming here with Julie, looking around with the estate agent: a simple three-bedroom semi, but it seemed like a palace to them after their flat. It had not long been built back then, but looked so old and tired now, maybe reflecting all the sorrow it had witnessed over the years.

Nothing as sad as this, though. Not if it was true.

It couldn't be. Just couldn't …

Even as he was getting out of the car, another door was opening. The front door he'd entered through and exited from so many times; once permanently. It wasn't Julie standing there, however, it was Mathew Newcomb. A blast from the past, an old mate he hadn't seen in …

A policeman.

That was when he knew for sure, when the lump and the fist became permanent additions.

That was when he knew it was his little girl they'd found dead in the market square last night.

# Chapter 3

The darkness was his friend tonight, he welcomed it.

That was one of the reasons Jake was sitting with the lights off, hadn't bothered to even turn them on when he crashed in through the door. There was still enough light coming in from the window to see, to make his way to the edge of the bed, casting off his jacket as he went. He'd thought about one of the chairs, but reasoned – while he was still capable of doing so – that he would end up on the bed at some point anyway. Sooner rather than later, he hoped; he'd put the whole of this wretched day behind him and wake up the next morning to find it had all been some horrible nightmare. An anxiety dream, didn't they call them?

Jake took another swig from the full bottle of whiskey he'd opened back in the corridor, pulling it from its plastic bag and ignoring the filthy looks some of the other people staying in the hotel were giving him. A place that hadn't even been there when he was young, back before he and Jules had …

That was why he needed the darkness, because unlike those memories, unlike the past – dulled by time, by heartache – the ones from today were so, so bright. Like they'd been seared into his brain, would probably never, ever fade. And they hurt. By Christ, did they hurt, worse than anything physical he'd ever endured. These were wounds that wouldn't, couldn't ever heal as far as he could see.

And now, in spite of the way he was working his way down that bottle – having already been in the hotel bar the last few hours – those memories were playing out in front of him like a projector throwing out images on the cinema screen. Or a home cinema, like he had back at his own place: hi-def, the sound crystal clear. Maybe it helped to think of all this as a movie ... No, he decided, shaking his head and almost falling off the end of the bed, it didn't help at all.

That was still Matt, his old friend, now a copper, waiting for him when he pulled up outside his old home. Not some character in a script, not an actor playing a part, but his actual best buddy. Waiting there in the doorway to confirm his worst fears. That there hadn't been some kind of mistake, a mix-up; you heard about those all the time in cases like this. Mistaken identity, people getting the wrong end of the stick. Families suing because of the trauma of getting it wrong.

But no. Matt's face said it all. He knew this particular family, knew Jordan as well. He wouldn't be putting them through this if there wasn't just cause.

Jake couldn't remember getting out of the car, or even closing the door again, locking it – that didn't matter anyway, not in the great scheme of things – but suddenly he was at the door with Matt, who was just shaking his head. Didn't have the words, clearly.

So Matt was stepping aside instead, letting Jake pass through. It felt weird to be back, and if this really had been a film he was directing or something, he would have noted how the carpets had changed; the wallpaper and pictures, photographs hanging from those walls. All reflecting how things had moved on, how it was no longer a place he shared with—

Suddenly there she was, in the living room: the woman he'd spent so many years with. The love of his life, he would have said at one time – still was, probably, there'd been no one else who'd been serious since her anyway. She was rising, albeit shakily, getting up off the couch. He was aware of someone else in the room, another woman standing, Matt saying something behind him, maybe trying to introduce her, something about liaising? Jake wasn't really listening, because all he could see and hear was Jules.

Standing there, as striking as he remembered her with that auburn hair falling about her shoulders. Those freckles on cheeks that were still wet with tears, reminding him again why he was here. Her green eyes doing the same, moist, cloudy; looked like they could barely focus on him. Yet she knew who he was, instantly, just as he had when he walked in. There had always been that unspoken connection between them, they could always tell when the other one was nearby.

If he'd needed any more proof that she recognised him, she provided it by saying his name, though it came out as more of a squeak than anything; a noise that would have been comedic in any other circumstances. 'Jake ... Oh, Jake.'

She was shaking her head as well, just as he was back in that hotel again now – mirroring her actions, playing them out with her. Jake drank deeply from the bottle and watched as more of it unfolded, as he was about to go to her. About to take her in his arms and try to comfort her, if that was at all possible, drawn by that look on her face he'd seen many times before (not least when she'd told him she was pregnant), scared and in desperate need of a hug.

But then realising that there was yet another person in the room with them, someone who'd come through from the kitchen or even upstairs; yes, the sound of a toilet flush. Someone who'd shoved past Matt and caused Jake to start. Someone who'd skirted around this newcomer in *his* house. Who was stepping between them, ensuring that Jake could not reach Julie. Someone snaking a hand around her waist, not to try and tell her that it would all be okay, but telling everyone else that this woman was his property... that's very much how Jake saw it, anyway.

The action made him feel physically sick and his eyes flicked away, coming to rest on another new addition to the décor of this house: their wedding photograph, Julie and Greg Allaway, the happy fucking couple. About two stone lighter in that, there was a meanness to the man's face even back then. Jake had to ask himself again, as he did when he first heard the news: what the hell had Julie been thinking? And the answer, not that it was anything to do with him anymore, was that Greg had been there for her when Jake had not. But he also knew that in times of stress, people act hastily, act without thinking, and he had to wonder whether she regretted her decision now.

Especially when he forced himself to look back at them again, Greg still holding her in a vice-like grip. Her pleading face.

Jake steeled himself, then replied to her, his name still hanging in the air. 'Jules. Is it ...?'

She closed her eyes, squeezing more tears out, and nodded. His ex-wife also leaned in more closely to Greg, though whether that was because he was pulling her in Jake couldn't tell.

'It can't be,' said Jake, a part of him still unwilling to believe it. 'What ... what happened?' He knew the broad strokes, though he'd had trouble taking them in over the phone. Jordan found on the market square, stabbed in the chest.

Dead.

That was when he was aware of Matt behind him again, moving into the room and joining his colleague ... Linda something? Had that been her name? Everyone was standing now in that room, everyone paired up – except him.

'All I can tell you at this time is that we have someone in custody who was fleeing the scene. Jordan's boyfriend.'

'Her *what*?' Jake shook his head. 'She had a new ... I didn't know.' There had been a couple of guys she'd mentioned the last time they talked, but then there always were. Always had been.

But nobody serious that Jake was aware of. Nobody she'd put that label on.

'Why would you?' This was Greg, grunting out the words.

Jake ignored him. 'And ... and he did this? Why?'

Matt shrugged. 'We don't know yet. He claims he didn't do it, but ...'

'I ... What was she even doing with this bloke, if he was ... What was she doing out *at all*, at that time of night?' It was a general question, speaking out loud, but without thinking he directed it towards Julie.

Then he saw it, the strength there as her face changed, as she straightened up and dried her tears with the back of her hand. Saw the feistiness that had been so attractive once, but could be lethal if you were on the wrong end of it – as he so often was towards the end. 'What was she doing *out*? She was nearly 21 for heaven's sake! Jordan could come and go as she pleased, she had her key.' Twenty-one, key to the door and all that, though Jake knew she'd had one of those for a long, long time. She had been an adult, or acted like one anyway, for a good while. 'And we don't vet who she sees, Jake!'

'Maybe you should have.' The reply was out of his mouth before he could stop it. He couldn't help it, a knee-jerk reaction.

'Maybe you should keep your big mouth shut.' Greg again, letting his wife go and moving forwards. In spite of himself, Jake was doing the same, teeth gritted. He needed someone to take all this out on; it might as well be the twat in front of him. His fists were already clenched, and now he couldn't see anyone else apart from Greg.

Not even Matt, as he stepped between the two men and placed a hand on each of their shoulders. It wasn't a tight grip, but there was strength there as well – enough to stop Jake and Greg in their tracks. 'Maybe you should *both* calm down,' he suggested.

Jake looked from Matt to Greg, and then gave a nod. He backed off, but it was a moment or two before his opposite number did the same, shrugging off Matt's hand. It was only then that Jake glanced over at Julie again. She was looking daggers at the pair of them, didn't need anyone to fight her battles for her. When she said her next words, she held Jake's gaze and didn't blink. 'This wasn't my fault,' she said simply.

He sighed, and even after everything, he couldn't help himself. Jake said, 'No, it's *ours*.'

She looked away, drawing in a breath and trying not to cry again. Trying not to let him see that she was crying. Love, hate. Two sides of the same coin.

'Again, not really helping,' Matt whispered to Jake.

He'd like to know what would at that precise moment in time.

There was silence for a few long minutes, then Linda suggested they all sit down again. Maybe have some more tea? But nobody did either of those things. In the end it was Matt who spoke again, breaking that silence which felt like it had gone on forever.

'I hate to bring this up, but it's probably as good a time as any.' He paused before continuing, as if realising there would never be a 'good' time for whatever this was. He took in each of their faces one by one, putting off what he was about to say next. 'There's ... folks, there's still the matter of a formal identification.'

Julie let out a small wail at this, while Greg just stared at Matt. Jake frowned, processing the information, and then realised this was actually good news. If they hadn't made an identification yet, didn't that mean there was a chance – however slim – that it could still be someone else? Someone else's kid? Once more, as he had done on the journey here, he felt that guilt at thinking such a thing. 'I can do it,' he said, eager to put this whole nonsense to bed. So he could take a look for himself and prove that it wasn't Jordan.

Julie was gaping at him, probably wondering why he was in such a rush to see the dead girl, but he couldn't explain it right there and then. That might ruin the hope building again inside, particularly if Matt was to say to them: 'It's just a formality, we're

99 per cent sure it's her.' He couldn't afford to hear that right now. Didn't *want* to hear anything that might ruin the fantasy.

'There you go, then,' said Greg.

Julie was facing her husband now, still staring. 'What?'

'Let him do it, love. No need for you to get any more upset.'

'Get any more ...' She couldn't finish her sentence, Julie's mouth was hanging open.

Greg obviously realised he'd said something wrong, but couldn't figure out quite what. 'You know what I mean.'

'It's okay, Jules ... Julie,' said Jake. 'I've got this.'

She shook her head, first at Greg, then Jake. 'W-We should both do that. Together.'

'Julie,' Greg said; it sounded more like a warning than anything. She flashed him another look that told him she was doing this, no matter what.

'Okay,' said Jake. In his own way he'd been trying to spare her the pain of this, if it did turn out to be Jordan – but she had the right to come along. More right than him, if anything.

Greg sighed. 'Right, fine. Well, I'll come too.'

'Actually ...' It was Matt this time, chipping in. 'It might be better if this was just family.' Jake could see Greg was going to say something, going to point out that he was family, when Matt added, 'Immediate family.'

Jake didn't know whether those were actually the regulations – he didn't think they were; not judging from the way the liaison woman's eyebrows were raised – or Matt was just trying to avoid more trouble at the hospital, though it might cause trouble for Julie later on ...

'We can drive them,' Matt said finally. *No*, thought Jake, *it's just that he hates this bloke as much as I do.* Who could blame him?

Greg sighed again, though it came out more like a snort. 'Right. Well, I suppose I'll head off to work after all. If I'm not needed anymore.' He looked to Julie and she didn't say anything. This probably would all come back on her later, but Jake had to admit he was glad Greg wouldn't be tagging along. 'I'll go and make sure they haven't burned down the factory.'

Made it sound like he owned the bloody place, rather than just being an 'operative' as they called it at GWR Plastics just outside of town. Not that he could talk, Jake had worked his fair share of crappy jobs to help keep his family together back when they still *were* his family. A family that had included his wife and...

Julie still didn't answer, just folded her arms.

'Off to work it is, then,' said Greg, and gave Julie a kiss on the cheek, like it was a normal weekday and their world wasn't really falling apart. Jake couldn't be sure, but he thought he detected the merest hint of a smile on Greg's face as he left the room to get ready. Probably one of relief that he'd been let off the hook, that he could go and do something practical instead of having to deal with all this emotional shit. He would prefer to be at work with his mates anyway; wasn't really his kid they'd found, at the end of the day.

Once Greg was out of the way, they waited for Julie to get her purse and coat, then Matt gestured for them to follow him. Julie was the last one out, with the liaison woman by her side, watching her like a hawk as the woman locked up; an automatic thing, done in a zombie-like way. Wasn't a bad thing, they didn't want the place burgled on top of everything else. But Jake couldn't help thinking about the key to the door stuff again. How Jordan would never be using that again when she came home.

If *it was her*, he reminded himself. *That's what you're going to find out for sure.* Going as a family; the only one he'd ever really known since his mum had gone.

In the present, Jake drank more of the alcohol, feeling it burn as it went down his throat. Back then, in the car, they'd been in a little bubble and he could still pretend it wasn't his little girl on that slab. He hadn't yet seen her likeness. Once he had, and

31

once he'd seen those marks, those scars, there'd been no denying it ...

But he hadn't been able to tear his eyes away from that face. That pale, blue face. It looked for all the world like she'd just wake up at any moment, like she used to do sometimes when she was little and he'd look in on her after a long shift at work. She'd open her eyes and blearily say: 'Da ... Daddy?'

'Hey pumpkin,' he'd reply, then kiss her on the head and tell her to go back to sleep.

He wanted anything but now. No more sleep, just *wake up!* People had been known to do that, right? There was a case not that long ago where a woman woke up in one of these drawers in a morgue. That could still happen, Jordan might still ...

But Jake knew that all the straws were gone. No more clutching.

And still the tears wouldn't come.

Time seemed to work so strangely that day, somewhere in the back of his mind he observed. Like the journey to Redmarket, which was quite a distance away but went by in the blink of an eye, with Jake lost in thoughts and remembrances. Lost in regrets. Then that walk up to the doorway, towards Matt, would only have been seconds in reality, but to him it took forever, because he didn't really want to arrive at his destination. Didn't want to know what – in his heart of hearts – he was already certain of. Similarly, the identification couldn't have lasted more than five, ten minutes, including arguing with Julie (who'd come right out and said it: 'You left her when she needed you the most!'), but was stretched out into a lifetime. And afterwards, in that hospital café, that went by so quickly as well, but by the time they'd left the hospital most of the afternoon had been eaten up, even if none of the food Matt bought them had.

They'd ferried Julie home again where the female police officer was going to stay with her. Probably make sure she had yet more tea. For his part, after he and his wife had said a cool goodbye to each other, Jake felt like he could definitely use something a lot stronger.

'Listen,' said Matt when his colleague had taken Julie back inside the house, turning to face Jake, 'why don't you come back to ours? Katherine would be fine with it, I'm sure.'

Jake was struggling to understand, to remember. Katherine was Matt's wife, right? And … and didn't they have a little kid? A boy? That was the last thing he wanted, to be around someone else's happy family. He shook his head but managed to thank his friend for the offer.

'You could have some dinner there or something and—'

Jake held up his hand. 'I'm good thanks. I'm still not really that hungry.' The thought of that sandwich Matt had placed in front of him back at the café had turned his stomach, let alone a full meal.

'I just don't think you should be on your … Hey, where do you think you're going?' Jake stared back, unblinking, the passenger door open. 'You're definitely not driving, mate. I don't want to be getting called to a traffic accident today as well.'

Jake thought back to the journey here again, his mind elsewhere – on anything but his driving – and his near miss. Maybe Matt had a point.

'Let me take you somewhere, a hotel for the night. I assume you'll be sticking around for a while?'

He just continued to stare at Matt. He hadn't been thinking further ahead than identifying Jordan, if he was honest.

'Okay, listen. I know a good place on the outskirts, quite reasonable. I'll take you there.'

Jake locked up his car and then placed a hand on Matt's arm. He knew above everything else what he needed the most right now. 'Can … can we make a stop off along the way?' he asked.

Matt nodded, a little reluctantly – almost as though he could hear what Jake was thinking. He'd slanted it that they were stopping off at the supermarket for a toothbrush, perhaps some pyjamas – he obviously hadn't had time to pack anything – but Matt knew what the real agenda was here, and although he looked on disapprovingly when Jake returned with just the one thing in the bag, there was no way on earth he was going to blame his friend for buying what he had.

Jake took yet another swig from that very bottle he'd purchased, that he promised not to start until he got to his room ... and he'd pretty much stuck to that promise, hadn't he? Matt hadn't said anything about not making another pitstop in the hotel bar beforehand, had he? Had simply urged him to get some food inside him first, even if it was just a bag of crisps or two from a vending machine inside.

But Jake's appetite still hadn't returned by the time Matt was called away, a summons from the station he'd had to answer straight away apparently. Maybe something to do with the case? He hadn't been allowed to say, but told Jake he'd be in touch again tomorrow.

'Now, are you sure you'll be all right?' he'd asked, then from the look on his face he'd realised it was relative, that phrase. *All right.* 'I can get someone out to come and stay with you if you—'

'I'll be fine,' Jake had told him, knowing exactly what Matt was worried about – that he might do something stupid, especially after a few drinks. Stupid ... that was also relative; he might do a lot of stupid things, but not *that* stupid. And when they locked eyes one final time, Matt could see Jake was still Jake. That wasn't his way, even when things were at their lowest ebb he hadn't even thought about something like that. He wasn't a quitter.

*Oh yeah? You bailed on her, though, didn't you? Gave up on your only daughter when she needed you the most ...*

'I'll be fine,' he repeated again. 'Just need to be alone for a while. I need sleep, need this day to be over.'

Matt nodded, gave him his card in case he needed to reach him, said goodbye and drove off, leaving Jake to check in (Matt had brought him to some generic 'Lodge' or another) and then hit the bar. He was two or three pints down, having enough sense to start with lagers first, ease his way into oblivion, when he remembered his phone. Remembered that he hadn't let work know where he was or what he was doing, although they'd probably figured it out by now. Had probably been camped out here all day, doing reports.

He'd turned it on and immediately found several voicemails from colleagues, Alison, Phil, Howard – even Sarah. And Trev, his boss – the media studies graduate who looked about 12. All concerned about him, wanting to know if he was okay and if he needed anything. Jake had sighed. Yes, he needed for things to go back to the way they had been. Not yesterday, or the day before, but many years ago when they'd all been happy: a happy family. Could they possibly sort that out for him please? Or perhaps that weird time thing that was happening could wind itself back instead of playing around with the speed … do some editing of the movie.

Jake had turned the phone off again, not wanting to speak to anyone at the moment, but vowing to put them in the picture tomorrow.

He'd been well into his mission to drink the hotel bar dry of their house whiskey, however, putting double after double on his room tab, when the TV had been turned on in the corner and the local news had thrown back pictures of the market square, of presenters who looked like Sarah doing their piece to camera. On any other day, it would have been him pointing that camera, but not today. He'd squinted at the television set, then at the barman who was looking sideways at him, looking at him funny like he was making that connection with the drinking.

The thin man, whose uniform was hanging off him like washing on a line, looked like he was about to say something. It would have been the only thing he'd said in all this time, if he had, apart from 'What'll it be?', with a kill-me-now expression on his face …

*Kill me ...*

But he'd wandered off to serve a couple of other customers instead. People were starting to filter in, because it was early evening now, and Jake knew that it wouldn't be long before the TV people who were camped out in Redmarket started to check into hotels themselves.

Light was giving way to darkness, and it was time to take this 'party' back to his room. Time to welcome in the dark to get rid of those bright memories of the daytime. So Jake had levered himself off the stool, gripping his carrier bag tightly, and begun his trek to the lifts, swaying slightly as he went. He'd stabbed at the button for his floor once he was inside, then waited for the lift doors to open again. He'd reached into the bag, opening up the full bottle he still had and ignoring the glances from people who were just on their way out to start their evening proper. He didn't give a shit, just needed to get to the room. Needed to get to the bed, needed to start on this bottle now, bring on the real darkness.

Because this was no good; the dark in the room wasn't chasing away those bright memoriesthe movie still playing out in front of him. Only the booze could do that. More and more of it, with Jake wondering if maybe he should have picked up a couple of bottles rather than just the one.

Especially when he started having those telepathic conversations, not with Julie, but with Jordan. The kind he'd play out mentally whenever she wasn't listening to him or wasn't even around. Asking those questions again:

'*Why were you out on a weeknight, and with that guy?*'

Getting answers like: '*That's my business, it's got nothing to do with you, Dad. You wouldn't understand.*'

'*Try me ... I was young once.*'

'*I love him!*'

'*No, you just* think *you do. Like all the others that ended up causing so much trouble.*'

36

'What, like you thought you loved Mum? That why you left and never came back, why she had to turn to a guy like ... like him.'

'I left because she didn't want me around. You *didn't* want me around, remember? Christ!'

Some part of him knew it was his own mind filling in the blanks, but it was based on knowing her like he did. Based on previous arguments they'd had, which he could trot out word for word.

And finally, that last one which neither of them could ever answer: 'How did we get to this? How did we become strangers?'

Both at fault, neither giving any ground. He thought they'd have time – there it was again, that word, the strangeness, the trickiness of time. He thought they'd be able to fix things once enough time had passed. But time also had a way of running out.

Just like he was passing out, losing consciousness. His friend, not Matt, the other one – the darkness – embracing him.

Only to let go again in the middle of the night, the darkness outside almost matching the oblivion he was rising from. Waking up when he heard noises, sounds that his rational mind would have told him were people in the next room, or in the corridor...

Except, when he looked over into the corner of the room he thought he saw someone there. A shape.

'Who ...who're ...?' he managed, but there was no reply. His hand, still wrapped around the practically empty bottle of whiskey, tightened its grip. If this was someone here to rob him, they'd really picked the wrong night.

However, as the figure moved closer, further into the room, he recognised its delicate features. A mixture of him and Jules, the figure holding out her hands – a different kind of darkness staining the middle of her chest. Opening her mouth, though he didn't want to hear what she had to say:

'You left me when I needed you the most. You left me ...'

Not him putting words in her mouth now, but Julie's from earlier, recycled.

'*You left me,*' she kept repeating over and over. '*You left ...*'

Jake put his hands to his ears, still holding the bottle in one of them so that it stuck out at an odd angle. 'No ... No!' he shouted, then when the voice wouldn't stop, he threw the bottle at the opposite wall. But he couldn't even get that right, and instead of smashing it just bounced off and hit the floor.

'I'm sorry,' he said for each accusation. 'I'm sorry.'

'*You left, you left, you left ...*'

'I know, I'm sorry.'

The darkness, or this darkness at least, wasn't his friend at all. It was showing him things he really didn't want to see. His dead daughter getting closer and closer, so close he could see marks on her outstretched arms, and imagine the knife there sticking out. There was no getting away from today, from the memories, nor from what had happened.

'No ... please God, *no!*' The tears were finally coming now, thick and fast. There was no holding them back at all. 'No, I'm sorry. I ... I can make it up to you,' Jake said quickly, as if that would will the vision away. 'I ... I can ... I can be there for you now, sweetheart.'

What was he saying? How could he be there for her when she was lying in that cold drawer with all the other corpses. What help could he be now? What use?

But that was the thing, he hadn't been around when she'd needed him; hadn't been a real dad to her. Hadn't been there in the run-up to this, nor on the night of the murder itself when he should have been protecting her. (how, how could he have done that? She would never have let him!) It was all getting tangled up in his drunken mind, her words, Julie's words, his; all mixed up and jumbled.

Except for one thing – how he could do something now. How he could help ... Not to save her, because it was way too late for

38

that – was probably too late even before he walked out of that front door … But to get to the bottom of this, find out what happened. Perhaps even avenge her. No, back to that stupid image of a knight on a white horse, riding to the rescue … not rescue, not this time.

It was there, though, that germ of an idea. Something he could do that wouldn't leave him feeling completely useless. Something he could … And almost immediately, the image of his daughter faded, and he felt more at peace than he had all day – than he had in a long while. The worst thing he could have possibly imagined had happened, he couldn't do anything about that now – there was no winding back time. So, moving forward, he had to get his head around what had happened. Knew what he needed to do, even though the police, even though Matt, had told him they were doing everything they possibly could.

And that thought, the thought that there was something positive Jake could do, sent him off to sleep again. Gave him the oblivion he sought.

Made the darkness his friend once more.

# Chapter 4

Julie felt numb.

There was no other word for it, she was simply numb. Still cold from visiting the hospital, frozen solid: as if she'd brought some of it back with her. She was sitting there on the couch where she'd been since she returned, the FLO having made her a cup of tea which had also probably gone cold by now because she hadn't even touched it.

She knew she shouldn't be doing it, but she was going over and over the events of that day in her head. Like picking at a scab, except even if she left this one alone it would never, ever heal. And she felt cold, numb, like it hadn't really happened to her but someone else.

Opening the door and seeing Matt there, a figure from the past. Then realising what it meant – some kind of trouble, definitely – and finally realising just how big that trouble was. Not being able to hold herself up, Greg catching her. Strong, solid. Supportive.

She just hadn't been able to take it in, couldn't believe it even as they were talking about it in that living room. Not their Jordan, it couldn't be. They'd made a mistake. And Bobby? No … it couldn't be. He'd seemed so …

And it had popped into her head at that point, his face. The other person who needed to know. No sooner had she asked whether he'd been informed than he was there, at the door and in the house. A ghost of relationships past.

Still as handsome as she remembered him, the man she'd fallen in love with when they were just kids themselves. Who she'd loved even when he walked out through that door after that final massive row that had broken everything. The row to end all rows, and she was glad of that at least because she was so, so tired of the circular arguments over Jordan. Why couldn't he just see that she was going through what so many girls of her age went through? That one day it would all be over, she'd get her head together and they'd be the best of friends again? Instead of which, they'd hardly spoken to each other in all this time: *so much* wasted time. And now it was too late.

It was the reason he was there, standing in front of her.

'Jake... Oh, Jake.' She could barely get the words out, couldn't make her voice work properly. All she'd wanted then was for him to take her in his arms and tell her it would all be okay, that it wasn't really happening at all. That it had been a bad dream and they were still together and their daughter wasn't really...

There'd been a moment when she thought he was actually going to move forwards and do that exact thing. But he wasn't moving because of that, he was moving out of the way of her husband, who – quite rightly – was joining her. Who wanted to be with her for this, knew she'd be even more upset once Jake arrived. Greg was there, holding her close again, making sure she was all right. Probably wanted to make sure she didn't keel over again.

Jake was doing the same thing as her, couldn't believe what had happened – and it wasn't long after that the accusations had begun, same as before. Interrogating her about Bobby, wanting to know what she was even doing out, for Christ's sake! Like she was still a child. Why did everything always have to be *her* fault,

41

Julie had thought. Jordan was a grown woman, she made her own decisions; had done for a long time, if Jake would just wake up and see it. Telling them they should have been vetting who Jordan saw? Absolutely bloody ridiculous!

Matt had done his best to referee, but her back had been up. She'd wondered then, and not for the first time, whether it was possible to love and hate someone at the same time. In equal amounts. 'This is not my fault,' she'd told Jake, locking eyes with him. But did she even believe that herself? Perhaps she *should* have been keeping a closer eye on her daughter; those seeds of doubt Jake was always so good at planting. Making her feel like shit, as always.

'No, it's *ours*,' had been his reply, which actually had been a fair comment. They hadn't been able to make it work, and she had to wonder if they'd stayed together whether this would have happened. Impossible to know, and one of those things that if you thought about it too much would drive you stark, staring mad.

Just when Julie thought things couldn't get any worse, Matt had raised the subject of the 'formal identification'. That's what he'd called it. Identifying the body was what he meant, as if there could be any doubt about whether it was Jordan or not. If it wasn't and the police had put them through all this torment, she might just scream until there was no air left in her lungs, though that would also mean their daughter was still alive.

Jake had offered to do it so eagerly, like they were keeping him from something. As if he had a prior engagement somewhere – and she realised then that she knew absolutely nothing about his personal situation. Was there someone waiting back home for him, worrying about him? Strangely she felt a twinge of jealousy at that.

Greg had wanted to spare her the pain of going, was all for just letting Jake head off alone, but Julie *needed* to be there. Needed to see this, for her own sake. Needed to find the inner strength from somewhere. She hadn't wanted to sit with Jake though, so had asked the liaison officer to come as well; with them in the back of Matt's dark blue BMW and Jake in the passenger seat.

No one really spoke on the way to the hospital, except for when Jake's mobile buzzed in his pocket and he'd reached in and switched it off. Work trying to reach him, he explained, but he didn't want to talk to them. He wanted to get this done, it seemed. Get it out of the way ... That just made Julie even angrier.

Matt had steered them up one familiar road and down another, spinning off on another roundabout that would take them to The Royal. Even up to the point that they were let into the morgue, let into the ice-cold room where the body was being kept, Julie had dared to hope. But not once the body had been pulled out of one of those huge things that looked like giant filing cabinets, drawers containing not papers and documents but frozen corpses. Julie had even expected the man in the white clothing to walk down the length of the wall of drawers rubbing his chin and saying: 'Now where did we put her? O ... P ... Q ... R! Here we go, R for Radcliffe!'

Jordan had never taken Greg's name, had been too old for that really, adoption – if she'd even wanted it. R instead of A for Allaway ... Putting off the moment once more, in her head at any rate. But there had been no denying anything once that drawer had been opened, the slab dragged out on those wheels which somehow kept the body horizontal, like some kind of magic trick where you dragged a hoop down the floating woman.

Then the man was ready to pull down the sheet, the one last barrier to the truth. Julie had moved closer to Jake, was at the side of him, couldn't have been closer, and – without even thinking – she'd snaked her hand into his. Holding it tightly, so tight she was practically cutting off her circulation, then reaching across and grabbing his arm with the other one – squeezing that too.

Praying, as he probably was, that this wasn't Jordon splayed out in front of them.

And even when the sheet was down, the magician's curtain swept back, revealing her face – even as Julie's hands released their grip and went to her mouth, a stifled scream emerging – for a moment or two Jake looked like he refused to believe it. As if this was a special effect from one of those movies he liked ... Prosthetics, life-casts, weren't they called?

Jesus, she was so, so, pale: creamy-white skin, verging on blue. The lips definitely blue. Hair dull, eyes closed.

'I-Is it Jordan?' asked Matt, knowing the answer already.

'It's her,' replied Jake, because Julie couldn't even speak.

Then suddenly she was in his arms, completing what they'd started back in the living room. Jake held her as she turned away from the sight, as each sob wracked against his body. Yet there had been no tears from him.

'Our baby.' She spoke it into his shoulder. 'Our baby!'

'What happened?' she heard Jake whisper to their child. 'What were you doing out there, sweetheart? Why? Why did this have to happen ...?'

Julie finally pulled her head away, saw that he was looking at something else and followed his gaze. One of Jordan's arms, the closest to them – her left – was uncovered also. The skin of the hand and arm matched that face: drained, lifeless. But he'd definitely spotted something. Something a little higher, past her elbow. On her upper arm were some scratches. No, not scratches ... cuts.

More wounds that had been inflicted during whatever struggle occurred? In her mind's eye, Julie pictured their daughter fighting for her life, maybe even gouging an eye or two ... she hoped. Only these looked a little older, more faded. They didn't look defensive, either.

'W-What are those?' asked Jake suddenly, his voice cracking. The hand that had been on Julie's back, rubbing and patting, fell away and he was pointing at the scars. Matt and the liaison officer

44

were rounding the table, as was the man in white. All craning their necks to see.

'I ... I'm not sure,' said the doctor, getting closer, then looking to the police officers in the room.

'We'll know more after the post-mortem,' Matt informed Jake. Standard detective patter.

'Are they ... They look self-inflicted,' he said by way of a reply.

Julie was frowning, sniffing back the tears, swallowing dryly.

'Did you know about this?' Jake asked her. 'Was Jordan self-harming?'

'Jake ...' said Matt. 'Take it easy.'

'*Was* she?' Jake asked again.

'I ... I don't know,' Julie replied honestly. If she had been, she'd hid it well, there had been no signs of it.

Jake was stepping back, rubbing his forehead. 'Good God. What could have made her ...?'

'I ... I don't ...' Julie was repeating.

'Well, something was clearly worrying her – quite a bit if she was doing that to herself.'

Matt walked around to Jake. 'Look, we don't even know that—'

'You can see it, as plainly as I can. Just what the hell was going on?'

Julie was getting mad again, glaring at Jake accusingly. 'You might have found out, if you'd been around.'

'Been around? Julie, she didn't *want* me around!'

Is that what he thought? What he'd thought all this time? 'That's ... That's not true. You're both as bad as each other. Both so stubborn, you're ...' Julie had realised that she was talking in the present tense about her daughter, when it should have been in the past. But then she changed tack completely and her last words were intended to hurt: 'You left her when she needed you the most.'

There was silence again, broken only when Matt said, 'I think we're about done here.'

45

About done. They were definitely about done.

Julie didn't remember a lot of the next bit, probably because there wasn't that much to recall. The pair of them being taken to a small café inside the hospital, away from the main drag and inside a little nook. Being furnished with more tea by the liaison woman, Matt insisting that they should eat something and when nobody replied buying them sandwiches anyway which Julie and Jake simply stared at like they no longer understood what food was, or how to process it.

How to process anything.

Every now and again they'd look up, at each other – accusatory stares saying everything that needed saying without words. A telepathic tennis match, words batted back and forth across the net.

Him: *I told you, I said this so many times. That something like this would happen if we didn't do something.*

Her: *And what exactly was I supposed to do? She was a grown woman ... Maybe if you'd tried listening to her, talking to her instead of at her!*

Then they'd look away, off to the side until it built up again. More arguments that would get them nowhere, because there was simply no winner of this particular match. They'd just go round and round in circles until there was nothing left to say or do.

And afterwards, when they'd dropped her off at home, she'd thought again about those scars. About what they'd meant, what had been on her daughter's mind that had made her do that? Something serious? Something about Bobby, or something else? How had she not known? How could Jordan not have told her? Not telling Jake, she could understand, but her? She thought they were closer than that? After all, she'd been the one who'd stayed – who'd done her best to look after her when Jake just upped and left. Who'd always defended her, seen her side of things even when it was a struggle to do so. Who'd always tried to sympathise.

What did it have to do with the murder of her child? she wondered. A murder she'd only found out about that morning, which brought her round – yet again – to the beginning of all this. Remembering Matt at the door, her reaction ... Going through it all again and again.

And sitting there, just feeling cold and numb.

Completely numb.

# Chapter 5

His friends had been on his mind all night.

How could they not have been? Jules, Jake ... Jordan. How could he just switch off and relax with the family, forget about it all, when they couldn't? Apart from anything else, he'd been needed back at the station until late – and Katherine had understood that. It went with the territory, though it wasn't usually as rocky as it had been yesterday.

Matt had swung by after leaving Jake (leaving him to get drunk back at the hotel!) and checked on Linda, who'd come to the door to talk to him in hushed tones, to answer his question about how Julie was.

'How do you think? Not great.'

'Yeah, I figured.'

'How's the dad? The *real* dad.'

''Bout the same,' he admitted, telling her which hotel he'd checked into so she could pass that on, but leaving out the bit about the bottle he'd bought to take with him.

'Poor sods,' said Linda.

'Yeah,' agreed Matt.

She'd told him she was sticking around for a while, maybe even until the husband came back, because at least then she wouldn't be alone – and Matt had thought about Jake again, who'd wanted, *insisted* on being by himself. How that probably wasn't a great idea, but how he'd almost definitely sleep that night. Probably better than Jules would, especially with that pillock of a partner by her side. They'd said their goodbyes, Matt telling her to ring for a squad car when she was done, and he'd headed off back to the station to answer the call.

Matt's boss, DS Channing, who looked like he should be selling used cars somewhere, or in a toothpaste commercial because he had far too many teeth and they were far too polished, had greeted him when he got there. With his slicked-back hair, and smile he kept flashing – which was very rarely genuine – he was a PR person's dream, and had spent most of the day talking to and 'handling' the press with regards to this case. He had a habit, especially where women were concerned, of introducing himself as 'Channing. Like Tatum …' (Not that he bore even a passing resemblance) 'Only better looking …' (He really wasn't).

'The big news is, we got the prints from the knife back,' he'd said to Matt, which surprised him because it usually took at least forty-eight hours. They'd been fast-tracked, Channing explained, and were pretty clean. They were also a perfect match for Bobby Bannister. 'Now all we need is a match for Jordan's blood on his clothes, and we're sorted. You don't see many open-and-shut cases on the force, Newcomb, but I think we're looking at one here,' Channing had concluded.

It certainly seemed that way. Wouldn't be long now before Bobby was officially charged, the whole thing done and dusted. That should be some sort of silver lining for the family, surely? Shouldn't it?

Matt couldn't help putting himself in their position, in Jake's position. Would it be a comfort to him at all if he were in that man's shoes? His daughter – his *estranged* daughter – was still dead. It had been on his mind the rest of his shift, on the drive home, and when he let himself in through the front door.

Katherine had been in the living room, watching the TV, watching the news reports that were still full of the story. They were bound to be, it had only broken today and was the most exciting thing that had happened in years around here. Wasn't exciting for Matt, though; wouldn't have been for any of those reporters either if they'd had to deliver the news to the family. Although some of them had rocks where their hearts should be, so maybe it wouldn't have bothered them one bit.

'Bad business,' Katherine had said. Katherine, not Kate, not Kitty; she hated abbreviations, his wife. Always called him Mathew, rather than Matt, and their son was Edward, not Eddie or Ed.

He'd nodded, then wandered over, loosening his tie and tossing his jacket onto a nearby chair as he did so. Matt picked up the remote. 'Do you mind if I ...'

Katherine, with her neatly cropped hair, still in her own work clothes – blouse and slacks, ironed to within an inch of their lives – rather than in pyjamas or whatever normal people might be chilling out in at this time of night, had nodded as well. She worked at a solicitor's in the finance department, which was where they'd met initially. Hadn't been anything police-related, but rather a hearing for his dad's will, sorting out the sale of the family house now that both his parents had passed away. He'd bumped into Katherine quite by accident, and quite literally, on his way out. They'd both laughed, looked into each other's eyes – like one of those crazy rom-coms he couldn't stand. She'd been on her way out too, for lunch, so he'd chanced his arm and asked if he could buy her something to eat. That had turned into drinks and dinner some other time, and before they knew it they were living together, then married, then along had come Edward.

After changing channels, finding some kind of inane quiz show where the contestants were answering questions to try and win a speedboat, he'd kissed Katherine and slumped down on the sofa beside her.

'Rough day, I guess,' she'd said.

'You could say that.'

'I saved you some lasagne, just needs heating up.'

'Cheers.' To be honest, all he was thinking about was the couple of bottles of lager still in the fridge from the weekend.

'You okay?' she asked.

He shook his head then. 'I ... I knew them. The family,' he admitted.

'Oh. I'm sorry, sweetheart. That's rough.'

Another nod.

There was a moment or two when he thought she was going to lean over to him, maybe put her arms around him and give him a hug – because, Christ, he could use one – but in the end she didn't. She wasn't the most demonstrative of people, Katherine, but she'd hid that well ... at the start.

'Eddie ... Edward in bed?'

Her turn to nod again. 'He wanted to wait up for you, but, well ...'

Matt understood, it was way past his bedtime and routine was important. So he'd been told. 'I think I'll just go and look in on him,' he said to Katherine.

'Do you think that's a good idea? He'll be asleep by now.'

'I won't wake him,' Matt promised and stood, making his way to the door. He looked back only once at the doorway, to see Katherine rising and picking up his jacket, brushing it down with her hands. And he thought again of Julie, her face – how she'd hardly changed that much. Then he thought about the tears she'd been crying, thought about her and Jake at the morgue, how they'd held each other, and his friend standing there at the entrance to the hotel where he'd left him. Then he'd carried on upstairs to see his son. Safe, in bed.

Alive.

As careful as he'd been opening the door to Edward ... Eddie's bedroom, the child had still stirred when he heard the noise. Not enough to wake up properly, which Matt was grateful for, just enough to turn over and face his father – something Matt was also thankful for. He studied his son's sleeping face, eyes closed, content, at peace. Eddie knew nothing of the world or its horrors yet, the things people did to each other on a daily basis. But the time would come when he did, and Matt wondered what he'd make of that. Would he be shocked or take it all in his stride?

And Matt thought then about the fact that Bobby Bannister had once been a kid in a bed like this one, innocent and at peace (or had he? Matt realised he knew very little about their main suspect's background yet). Flash forward a few years and, for whatever reason, he'd stabbed his girlfriend in the chest with a knife. Maybe she'd been cheating on him, a crime of passion – and Matt thought then how much of what was wrong in this world came down to love, to sex … either that or money.

They just had to make sure, somehow, that Eddie never went down that path. Teach him right from wrong, although there were some who said this kind of stuff was inside kids from the get-go; the whole nature vs. nurture debate. Looking at him here, his sweet, sweet kid, who wouldn't hurt a fly, Matt found it hard to image Eddie doing anything like that when he grew up. But given the right circumstances, the right push, couldn't anyone snap? He saw it all the time in his line of work, though never usually this dramatically it had to be said. If life threw enough shit at you, maybe one day you'd just lose it and …

Matt shook his head and closed the door. You could drive yourself mad thinking thoughts like those. Which was why he tried his best not to; he thought he'd gotten quite good at it, but …

Even as he warmed up his food and ate (he didn't bother with the lager) then attempted to watch a movie with Katherine – some political thriller about a president being in danger – what had happened to Julie, Jake, Jordan, was going round and round in his head.

Katherine was first in bed that night, and by the time he'd brushed his teeth and climbed in, she was sound asleep. It had been a long day for her as well, Matt understood that, working, then picking up Eddie from the sitter who took him after school, before cooking. But he could really have used some form of affection that night, even just a cuddle would have done the trick. It was like Katherine had this switch she'd flip when she went to sleep, out like a light – while he'd be there for hours staring at the ceiling or the clock, just trying to nod off.

Then, after it felt like he'd only just got to sleep, the alarm went off early for another day. Seconds later, Eddie was in their room, bouncing around on the bed. Matt felt like crap, but still laughed and hugged the kid to his chest – he never wanted to let go. Never wanted him to grow up.

'Come on,' Katherine said, already up and alert and holding out her hand for Eddie, 'we'd better get you some breakfast.'

And, even though they – his son especially – were only downstairs, Matt felt a sudden sense of loss. A fraction of what Julie and Jake must have been feeling that morning. All he had to do was follow his family to the kitchen, while they would never see their kid ever again.

He grabbed some toast and ate with them, showered, said goodbye – another big hug from Eddie, a peck on the cheek from Katherine who was dropping the lad off at school – and headed to work himself.

It was around eleven when he got the phone call. Jake had been on his mind again, and he'd been thinking about calling him at the hotel, or just going there to see how he was when his mobile had gone off.

'Matt?' the croaky voice said, then more clearly, 'Matt. You said to ring if I needed anything.'

'Jake? Hey mate, yes. Yes *of course*. I was just thinking about you.' Hadn't stopped, especially since most of his work that morning revolved around Jordan's case again. Organising uniforms to keep the press at bay around the Allaway house ... and it was only a matter of time before they found out where Jake was, as well. The fact the blood on Bobby's clothes had now come back a match for Jake's daughter's. 'How're you doing?'

Jake ignored the question and said, flatly, 'I need to see him, Matt.'

'See who?'

'The guy. The one Jordan was seeing. The one who ...' His words tailed off.

'Bobby?' Matt switched the phone to his other ear, lowered his voice. 'Jesus, I can't ... It's just not possible.'

There was a sigh at the other end. 'I just need to see him. Look in his eyes, you know?'

'I do, and I understand. Really I do, but—'

'You said whatever I needed.'

'Yeah, but I didn't ... Look, why don't I come to you and we can talk about this. About what a spectacularly bad idea it is.'

'I'm not asking to be put in a cell with him.'

'Good job, because that's never going to happen,' spluttered Matt.

'Just ... what do you call it, a supervised visit. I need to see him. Ask him a few questions.'

'That's *our* job,' Matt reminded him.

'I know, I know. I just ... Matt, I just need to do something.'

It was Matt's turn to sigh. 'Like I said, I understand. But it's impossible, Jake.'

'Matt,' the man said then, 'you owe me.'

Now that was low. Matt knew exactly what he was talking about. Not the fact that they'd done all sorts for each other, always been there looking out for one another ... at least until they drifted apart and then eventually Jake moved away. He was talking about that time with the car, taking the rap for it, covering for Matt. But to bring it up now ... 'Jake, you might want to think about what you've just said.'

'I know. I don't think I'm being left a lot of choice.'

'Might want to think about what you're asking. I could lose my job here.'

'You never would have had one, if it wasn't for me. Hiring a lot of guys with records these days, are they?' There was an edge to Jake's tone he hadn't heard in a long time, possibly not since they were rough and ready teenagers.

'Fuck you,' said Matt, all sympathy gone for a moment. 'I'm trying to help here.'

'I-I'm sorry ... but put yourself in my position,' Jake said then. It was exactly what Matt *had* been doing all day yesterday, all evening.

'Trust me, I am. I've been trying to. But it's really not fair of you to—'

'*Please*,' Jake broke in, his voice pathetic. 'I'm begging you.' Threats, then pleading. He had to remember what his friend was going through, what it was doing to him. But seeing the guy who'd done this, would that really help? Matt doubted it very much. 'For me, for Jules ... For what we all used to mean to each other. Just for a second. A glimpse. I just need to see him, I've never even seen the guy. I just need to understand.'

Matt was silent for a moment or two. Channing was out most of the day again, and he was pretty sure he could square it away with the sergeant on duty, Sharpe, who owed Matt a favour or two himself (it didn't hurt that Sharpe had a daughter about the same age as Jordan). Bring in Jake under the guise of asking a few routine questions, then slip him out to the cells for just for a few minutes. It was a small station, hardly Fort Knox, and their camera system wasn't exactly state of the art, was prone to glitches now and again. It could be done, wouldn't be the first time. But if they were going to do this, it had to be soon – before their prime suspect was charged, possibly transferred. Matt supposed he owed Jake that much, if it's what he wanted. Needed.

*Anything you need ...*

'I'm going to regret this, I know I am,' he said.

'Thanks, Matt. Really.'

'I'll come and pick you up,' Matt said, and he cut off the call. Then thought to himself: *and there I was worried that* he'd *do something stupid ...*

* * *

When Matt arrived at Jake's hotel, he was standing outside waiting for him, wearing the same clothes as the day before.

Or rather, he wasn't so much standing as leaning against the fencing outside; holding on to it for support. He looked dreadful. His skin was drained of all its colour, and his eyes were red, with dark rings around them. Just how much had he had to drink last night? More than one bottle, that was for sure, but it didn't look like it had helped any with his sleep.

When Jake saw the car, he held up a hand – which almost immediately went to his stomach. As he reached the vehicle, Matt wound down the window and said, 'I hope you got it all out of your system?'

'I'm fine,' Jake tried to assure him, the same crap as yesterday – but it sounded even less convincing today.

He opened the glove compartment, pulled out a pair of sunglasses and handed them to Jake as he climbed in. 'Maybe we should do this another time.' *Like never*, thought Matt.

'I said I was fine,' snapped Jake, putting on the shades. Then apologised. 'Please ...'

'Sure.' Anything but the begging again.

On the way back to the station, he thought about telling Jake the news: the fingerprint and blood match. Then he thought better of it. That probably wasn't the kind of thing you needed to hear just before seeing the person in question. So they rode in silence.

56

But then Jake suddenly piped up: 'Has ... has he said anything else?'

Matt looked across at his friend in the passenger seat. 'Bobby? Only that he's innocent. That he didn't do it.'

'Weren't there any ... I mean there must be CCTV footage of all this?'

'There's been a spate of vandalism attacks recently. The cameras were smashed in the square the previous weekend – haven't been fixed yet.'

Jake let out a slow breath, then asked, 'And what do you think?'

Matt faced front again, indicating left. He shrugged, thought again about telling Jake what they'd discovered, but didn't.

'You must have some sort of idea, some sense as to whether or not he did it. I mean ... you've been doing this a while now.'

'And I owe it all to you, right?' Matt couldn't help that one, picking up on what he'd said about people with records joining the force.

'I'm sorry,' Jake said again. 'I was desperate.'

The truth was he probably did owe it to Jake. Not just because he took the fall for stealing that car, but because he set an example. Got himself together and worked his arse off when Jules had fallen pregnant with Jordan, which in turn had made Matt realise he needed to get his own act together. Jake might not have steered him towards the force, but he'd made him see that there was more to life than just dossing around. And on the occasion he'd seen them all together, it had made him want a family as well. Had been one of the things he'd had in common with Katherine when they'd eventually met. 'I wasn't just covering my own back, you know. I'm not sure you're ready for this.'

Jake let out a bitter laugh. 'When am I *ever* going to be ready for it?'

'I just meant—'

'Matt, yesterday I saw my daughter for the first time in God

57

knows how long, and … and she was lying dead in the morgue. Today, I just want to understand. To know why.'

'You won't get that from just looking at him,' Matt promised.

'Maybe not. But it's a start,' Jake told his friend. 'It's somewhere to start.'

Matt thought about asking just what it was Jake thought he was starting here; after all, they were the ones conducting the investigation. If anyone was going to uncover the reason why this had all happened, it should be the police – and Jake had to trust them to do that. Had to trust *him*. Perhaps this was the first step in getting him to do that, a start in that respect as well.

And it had all been going so well.

Matt had got Jake inside, and in the cells – thanks to Sharpe's assistance. Then Matt had opened up the metal slot in the door to Bobby's cell, holding Jake back with one hand until he was sure it was okay for him to come forward – having made him promise not to do anything rash. 'I'll be there watching the whole time, and I'll rush you out of there so fast your feet won't touch the ground,' he'd said to him.

To be fair, Jake had kept that promise. It hadn't been him who'd caused the fuss. Bobby had been on his bunk, facing the concrete wall, dressed in a grey pair of sweats and top, having been relieved of his clothes the previous evening. He looked to be asleep – another person who'd had a bad night; the worst night … though not as bad as his victim, it had to be said. The timing for this little 'visit' couldn't have been more perfect, in fact. Jake wouldn't get to see his eyes, look into them as he'd mentioned, but he'd get to see the boy, and Matt would have fulfilled his promise to his old friend, not to mention built up that trust.

Matt looked at Jake and nodded for him to move closer, to look through the slot. Then he watched his friend, watching the boy. Sunglasses gone now, Matt could see just how bloodshot those blue-grey eyes were up close and personal like that, just how black the circles were that framed them. He looked like a shadow of the man he'd seen even yesterday, the toll of events – not to mention the alcohol he must have consumed – weighing him down. Jake's eyes were wide, staring, taking in the lump on the bunk. But he didn't say anything to draw attention, didn't rouse the boy.

Just watched. As if being in his presence might tell Jake whether he'd done the deed or not, some sixth sense that could detect a person's innocence or guilt.

*And what do you think? You must have some sort of idea …*

What *did* he think? Matt wasn't entirely sure. Open-and-shut cases like this appeared to be were a bit too … neat for his liking. Katherine would have loved them, tying everything up with a bow on top. But, like Jake said, Matt had been doing this a long time, actually did have a sense for these things. One of the first things he'd done that morning had been to go through the background on Bobby, who'd been adopted at the age of 5 – so there could be something to that, he'd have to look into who the real parents were – but to all intents and purposes had been brought up in a stable home environment. Had parents who loved him a lot, going by the way they were trying to get back from their holiday abroad to come and see him after they'd been notified. So what had gone wrong …?

The noise interrupted his thoughts and he followed Jake's gaze into the cell. Like his son the previous evening when he'd looked in on the kid, Bobby Bannister had rolled over when he sensed he was being observed. But unlike Eddie, Bobby had opened his eyes, had seen the figure peering into his cell, and he'd clambered to his feet.

'You're … I can tell, you … You're her dad,' said the boy, whose short black hair was sticking out at odd angles due to the way he'd been lying on it. 'I can see her in your face.'

Jake's eyebrows knitted together, breaths coming in short gasps. Matt looked down to see the man's hands balling into fists, then opening again. Clenching and unclenching.

Bobby was stumbling towards the door now. 'I didn't do it, Mr Radcliffe, I *swear*! I didn't do what they said I did.'

More heavy breathing from Jake.

'Easy,' Matt warned him, placing a hand on his shoulder which the man didn't even notice.

Bobby wiped his nose with the back of his arm, eyes wet with tears. 'It's like I've been trying to tell them, we just arranged to meet, see? To go clubbing ... I-I found her like that, I *swear*! I couldn't have done that to Jordan. I honestly couldn't.'

'Jake ...' Matt was squeezing that shoulder, knew he should be getting his friend away from there. That he'd done what he could for now, what he promised. Jake had even got to look into the lad's eyes.

'I tried to ... to pull it out, but there was so much ... I thought I might make things worse. I was about to call an ambulance, I was. But then I heard sirens anyway, only ... Only it was his lot. And ... and I panicked, I ran. I knew how it would look, 'course I did!' He stepped up closer to the open rectangle, voice rising. 'But I swear—'

That was it: the third time Bobby swore that he'd had nothing to do with Jordan's death was the trigger. Jake shrugged off Matt's hand and tried to reach inside the space, barely able to get his hand in and yet he was able to grab Bobby by the collar. Matt, in turn, grabbed Jake's arm to tried and wrench it away from the hole. But the man was stronger than he looked, even in his weakened condition, hatred and adrenaline obviously fuelling his attack.

How could he ever have thought it would end any other way, this encounter? How could he have been so naive as to think Jake just wanted to see the guy; obviously he was going to go for him, but as he was behind a thick metal door ... At this particular point in time, though, Matt wouldn't have put it past Jake to just ram down that barrier to get to Bobby. He was like a thing possessed, bucking and jerking to get a better angle, perhaps to try and wrap his fingers around Bobby's throat and get his revenge. Snap his neck sideways with a satisfying crack.

Matt was tugging and tugging, but Jake's grip on the boy was vice-like. In the end, what broke the spell, what broke into the moment, was the cry from behind them all. 'What the fuck do you think you're doing?' It carried weight that voice, authority, especially when it followed this up with: 'What the *actual* fuck is going on here?'

They both turned as one, and Jake finally let go of Bobby, who retreated into his cell, still pleading his innocence. Needing Jake to see that he hadn't done this terrible thing.

Matt and Jake stared at the figure of DS Channing standing there with his arms folded. You couldn't tell how many teeth he had now, because the fake smile was gone – replaced by a look of condemnation. He wasn't so much a PR person's dream right at that moment, as a DC's nightmare.

'Sir, I can explain,' Matt began.

'Can you? Can you now …' He unfolded his arms, leaned forward and cupped the side of his head. 'Well, I'm all ears.'

'Jake … Mr Radcliffe wanted to …' Matt realised how ridiculous his explanation would seem, even as he was saying it.

'It's my fault,' said Jake, looking down. 'Don't blame Matt. I talked him into it.'

Channing ran a hand over his face, then let it fall to his side. 'I can't believe this, I really can't! Do you know what you've done here? We were this close.' Now he held up that same hand, creating a tiny space between his thumb and forefinger. 'This close to it all being over.'

'It'll never be over for me,' said Jake.

Channing gaped at him, then waved his hand towards the exit. 'Come with me, *both* of you!'

As they began to walk out, Matt could hear Bobby one final time back in the cell, his voice barely a whisper: 'Wasn't me … I *swear*!'

* * *

61

Channing took them to an interview room, the one with a two-way mirror running the length of one wall, and told them to sit down – though Matt remained standing initially.

'I said sit down, DC Newcomb!'

Matt reluctantly did as he was told.

Channing proceeded to pace up and down in front of them as he spoke. 'Now, let me see if I've got this straight. You, DC Newcomb, thought it would be a good idea to let the father of our victim – and yes, I do know who you are, Mr Radcliffe – have access to the person we believe to have committed the crime? Is that about the size of it?'

'Well,' said Matt, looking at his folded hands in front of him, 'when you put it like that ...'

'When I ...' Channing banged on the table with his fist, causing them to start. 'And this was, what, because he asked you to?'

'Matt ... DC Newcomb was just trying to help,' offered Jake. 'I needed—'

'I don't care what you needed,' snapped Channing, face turning crimson. Then he saw Jake's mournful expression and relented. 'I'm sorry, I didn't mean that.' Matt couldn't tell whether it was because the DS was genuinely sorry, or he was just frightened of the repercussions; of what he'd said getting back to his superiors. '*Of course* I care, but you might just have ruined everything. We're readying to nail that guy to the wall, but now he could bring charges himself for assault – and all while under our noses! All because of you, Newcomb.' He rounded on Matt, jabbing a finger in his direction. 'All because of some misplaced sense of loyalty to a friend.'

'I ... I'm sorry, sir.'

'This could mean your job, you know.'

'I know.' It was what he'd told Jake when he'd been trying to persuade Matt; there was always a chance this could go south. That the ramifications would include his job, his career. Christ, how was he going to explain this to Katherine?

'And it happened on my watch, so it could mean my neck as well. Okay, damage control … damage control,' muttered Channing, concentrating. Then he stood up straight, leaning back. 'What if … what if none of this had ever happened, eh?'

It sounded like he was asking their advice, like he had a time machine or a way to wipe out the last twenty minutes, and was sounding them out about whether they should use it or not.

'I'm assuming there's no footage of what took place back there. You're definitely not *that* stupid, Newcomb.'

Matt said nothing, he didn't want to get Sharpe into more trouble than he clearly already was.

'So, it's just the kid's word against ours, right? Wouldn't be the first time. It's not like you were able to do any real harm … He's been screaming the place down about his innocence since he got here, has had hardly any sleep, probably imagined the whole thing – wanting to apologise to the father or whatever. Only natural, right? Maybe he even heard you were in the building, Mr Radcliffe.'

Again, Matt didn't say a thing; neither of them said a word.

'Yeah, didn't happen.' Channing clapped his hands together. 'And all is right with the world.' He saw Jake's expression once more, realised that his world would never be right again. 'That is … Look, Mr Radcliffe, can I give you some advice?'

Jake remained silent.

'I get where you're coming from, I really do. But I've seen this kind of thing before. I've seen that look you had in your eye before, and it never ends well. It ends with people waiting outside law courts with guns to shoot the person they want punished. Ends with those people in jail instead of the ones who should be, the bad guys. Let things take their course, let us do our jobs. Punk kid like that won't last long inside, particularly when they get wind of what he did. Killing a young girl? That's a big no-no.' Channing allowed his words to settle. 'Let us do our jobs, Mr Radcliffe. We might not be known here for dealing with fancy high-profile cases, but we do get things done.

63

What I'm saying to you is do us all a favour and leave it alone, okay? Please.'

Still no response.

'Or the next time I might not be so understanding, you see. Now, I think maybe it might be best if you leave to have a think about things. I'll have one of our uniforms drop you off where you're staying. I assume you're remaining here for the time being?'

Jake gave a slow nod.

'And as for you,' Channing continued, directing his attention towards Matt again, 'I'll be keeping a closer eye on you from now on.'

Matt swallowed, and also nodded, knowing he'd dodged the bullet ... this time. As Channing opened the door again and called for a uniform to escort Jake, his friend looked back at Matt, still seated.

His eyes said he was sorry, that he hadn't meant for him to get into trouble. But they also said something else. They still held that same look, the anger, the need to understand. A desire for revenge.

It told Matt all he needed to know. That there was no way he was going to just drop this, as Channing had told him to. Not that easily.

And Matt knew something else as well, that Jake, that all of this, was going to be on his own mind for some time to come.

# Chapter 6

He just couldn't stop thinking about it. Thinking about everything.

He'd let them drop him off back at the hotel, the couple of uniformed officers Channing had ordered to escort him 'home'. But Jake hadn't stayed there. Couldn't face going back to that room he'd woken up in, feeling rougher than he'd ever felt in his life. Half-dead …

*Better than totally dead.*

Though it was also the place he'd decided enough was enough. That it was time to concentrate on his mission, on what he had to do – which was dig out Matt's card and ring him. There were no two ways about it, he'd needed to see the boyfriend. He hadn't meant to cause problems at the station – or thought about the consequences for Matt if they were caught – but when the guy had got in his face, Jake had just seen red.

It was almost like he was watching a movie again, someone else reaching out and grabbing the boy by the collar, dragging him to the door. Jake wasn't a violent person, or at least he hadn't thought he was … until that moment. He'd assumed that once he saw the guy, this Bobby Bannister, he'd know one way or the other about Jordan. Had wanted to look him in the eyes, he'd

65

told Matt, but even just seeing him would be enough to know... But it hadn't really worked out like that, had it?

Jake still didn't know one way or the other whether this boy had actually committed the crime, although everything was pointing in that direction in spite of his claims of innocence. Claims that were actually pretty convincing. He should have felt something, sensed whether this was his child's murderer, surely? Instead, he'd just felt an overwhelming hatred towards him. But Jake wasn't just seeing his face, he was seeing all the faces of all the guys who – in his mind – had corrupted his daughter. Had turned her into something she really wasn't, something she shouldn't have been. Something that had got her killed.

And he'd snapped.

The rest, like a lot of things since he'd got that phone call the previous morning, was a bit of a haze. Matt trying to pull him away, Channing, the interview room. Jake was aware then of how much trouble he'd got his friend into, was sorry, but at the same time glad he'd got the opportunity – however brief it had been – to confront Bannister. It was only afterwards he'd thought about what that might have cost Matt: his job, his family ... He hadn't needed to stick his neck out for Jake, but had anyway. That was true friendship.

Luckily, Jake's actions hadn't landed him in too much hot water – Channing was more concerned about his own neck than anything. More than willing to cover things up.

*Wouldn't be the first time ...*

Which didn't exactly inspire confidence, made you wonder what else they'd swept under the carpet in this town. Jake guessed he'd probably never know.

It would be awkward probably at work for a while, but things would calm down. Jake would make it up to Matt, somehow. He wasn't sure how.

*What if ... what if none of this had ever happened, eh?*

If only.

But it left him right back at square one in figuring this all out. Figuring out *why* it had happened. The cops didn't seem that interested in the reason, they had their man (caught red-handed … yes, red as in Jordan's blood). It was like Channing had said to him, they were so close to nailing him now.

What had really happened, though, that night? Why had Bannister done it, if he even had? If he never admitted he'd killed Jordan, then none of them would find peace. *She* would never find peace.

Jails were full of convicts claiming they hadn't done it, swearing just like Bannister had sworn it.

*I-I found her like that, I swear!*

Nobody ever got to the bottom of those cases, nobody punished the truly guilty party or parties. Nobody really cared. There were people who cared about this one, though. Who had cared about Jordan. Who would find the truth, whatever that was.

Where to start, though? He had no idea. Where would Dave Harris have started? His old colleague from *The Gazette* … 'A story starts at the beginning,' Dave used to say. And even as he thought that, Jake saw a flash of Jordan as the happy little girl he'd known and loved (*still* loved, in spite of everything, but this was different). Before the world had swallowed her up, before social media, friends who led her down the wrong paths, boys. Back then, back at the beginning, things had been simple.

They probably hadn't been, Jake knew that – people always looked back with rose-tinted glasses. But they'd seemed it. Easier, happier. Happier than later on. Happier than now, that was for damned sure! There had been hope, anyway – for the future. That everything would turn out okay.

When he'd set off from the hotel, Jake hadn't really known where he was heading. He had some vague notion about buying a change of clothing, actually getting that toothbrush he'd told Matt he was after when whiskey was the only thing on his mind; plus a charger for his phone, as he'd left without one. And he'd done all that, found somewhere and purchased what he'd needed for now – had carried them around with him in plastic bags like somebody who'd just been to the sales. Or been made homeless.

But still he hadn't returned to the hotel, he'd carried on wandering. Realised at some point that he probably should eat; again, he'd be no use to anyone – especially Jordan – if he simply collapsed. How would he get to the bottom of anything then?

It wasn't the healthiest, but he grabbed a burger and some fries at a fast food place. Jake sat for a while just staring at the meal in front of him, felt like doing anything else in the world but this. The body was a machine, though, and like any other machine it needed fuel. So he picked up the burger, something he would have relished before, enjoyed on the hop between shooting gigs, and he forced himself to bite into it. Jake chewed mechanically, swallowing, fighting the sensations when he thought he was going to throw up again.

In the end, he wolfed the whole meal – he'd underestimated just how hungry he was – and washed it down with diet coke this time, alcohol the furthest thing from his mind.

Then he wandered once more, up and down streets so familiar to him but which now seemed alien and hostile. He barely noticed when the sun began to set; more darkness, which he could embrace. His feet hurt, but he kept going. Maybe if he walked long enough, far enough, he really could turn back time. Make it so this whole thing hadn't happened.

Had it been the noise that attracted him, he wondered afterwards. Redmarket coming to life and doing what it did best, welcoming the lost souls to bars and clubs. The one thing it was known for now, legendary nights out – bucking the trend of other towns and cities that found their streets virtually empty since the recession started to bite. Instead, Redmarket had blossomed; he'd seen that start to happen even before he left the area. A reinvention for this former market town that had once been known for its meat more than anything else, hence its name.

Now there were meat markets of a different kind, where young men could hook up with young women on any given night of the week. Jake observed some of them off out that evening: gaggles of girls wearing shiny skin-tight dresses that barely came down past their waists, clutching tiny handbags, already clearly drunk (not that he could talk after last night), tottering on high-heels, wearing make-up the Joker would have been proud of. Similarly, the lads out on the pull: skinny jeans and shirts open to their belly buttons practically. All they were missing were the medallions and flares and it could have been the 1970s rather than this day and age.

Jake heard the music being pumped out, the thumping bass that would have made your internal organs vibrate if you were close enough to it. Saw the flashing lights, all the colours of the rainbow. Mesmerising, drawing people in as effectively as those sirens used to do to the sailors of old – and there'd be just as many crashes later on. Perhaps not on rocks, but people crashing into each other. Dancing to begin with, then later in alleyways and in flats; bodies crashing against each other in another way. Kids who hardly knew each other, screwing like it was some sort of hobby or pastime, a new sport.

It was what Jordan had been doing all those years, coming to places like this, he reminded himself. It was where she'd been heading that evening, after meeting up with Bannister. Hitting the clubs, painting the town ...

Maybe the name of the place was still appropriate, Jake mused. Only in this instance it had been painted red with the blood of a girl, stabbed and dying on one of the market stalls.

And it was almost as if thinking of the thing had brought him here, to his final destination that night. Most of the vans had gone, the media and reporters having left the scene alone for the night. Nothing would be happening now, they figured; he'd have done the same if he'd been with his news team. They'd all have gone off to join the youngsters in the pubs, some in the clubs as well – the oldest swingers in town brigade. People who'd been in the industry a long time, but had never really grown up and probably never would.

The consequence of that was this particular part of the town was deserted. It was where all the trading had once taken place, people bartering for goods – not just pork and beef, either, but all sorts. Why the stalls were still here now, however, was anyone's guess. It wasn't as if anyone used them that much anymore, only on certain days. And at this moment in time, their only use appeared to be to hold the blue and white tape in place which told everyone this was a crime scene, that they shouldn't enter. Forensics would have done their jobs, though; samples taken. If Channing was to be believed all that stuff wouldn't even be necessary to convict Bannister. Wasn't an episode of CSI or anything …

Maybe it hadn't been the noise or the music at all that had delivered him here. Maybe it had been thinking about the murder, not being able to stop thinking about all of this. And the pull, to see the scene – just as strong as it had been to see her boyfriend in his cell. Thinking that this might hold a few answers, that he'd look at where it happened and suddenly have a revelation about why it had. Who might have done it if it hadn't been Bannister.

It was why he had to get closer, crossing that line of tape and making his way through the maze of stalls. He left his bags by the side of one of them, zeroing in on the stall he was looking for. Where Jordan had met her end. He could tell because of the white outline that had been drawn around the body – but just the upper half, on the part of the stall that had clearly been holding her up.

The wood was stained maroon, had sucked up the blood greedily until it was dry again. Jake stared at the stall, cocking his head. Trying to imagine Jordan there two nights ago, breath coming in ragged gasps … and then trying not to. Knowing that, like the rest of it, he'd never be able to wipe those images from his mind ever again.

He was bending, reaching out to touch the stall when he heard the cry: 'Oi! Oi, you there! What d'you think you're doing?'

Jake froze. To be quite honest, he didn't know what the hell he was doing. About to touch his dead daughter's dried blood to …what, reconnect somehow, to feel close to her again in a way he hadn't been able to in life of late? To feel her presence like some kind of ghoul?

'I asked you a question!' came the voice again, and now Jake straightened, turned, saw the torch before he saw the person who was holding it. Dark at first, shadowy behind the light, Jake soon saw it was a uniformed male police officer – probably left there to guard the scene at night-time.

'I …' Jake began, then hung his head. 'I just wanted to—'

'Get your kicks from hanging around murder scenes, do you?' said the copper, getting closer. He looked to be in his twenties, not that much older than Bannister … or Jordan. Looked like he should be in one of those clubs not that far away.

'No,' Jake replied. 'I … She was my …'

'Oh, hold on, wait a minute. I know you … You were at the station this morning. You're … Oh, I'm so sorry, sir.'

Jake shook his head. There was no need, he was the one who should be sorry if anything.

'But you can't be here, you know?'

He nodded. He did.

'It's against the rules. Not even …' The young copper paused, frowned. 'Why are you here, anyway?'

'I-I just wanted to see where …'

'Now then,' came the reply, the youth sounding older than his years. 'You'll only go and upset yourself more doing things like that.'

Upset himself more? How much more upset could he get than knowing his child had been taken from him, permanently.

'Would you like me to radio for someone to take you home?' asked the PC.

71

'Home?' To wherever he was staying the officer obviously meant. He shook his head, two of his colleagues had already delivered him there that morning but it hadn't taken. They'd wonder what he was playing at if they had to do it again.

'I'll ... I can walk, it's okay.'

'All right. Well, you mind how you go then. Can be a bit dangerous around here at ...' He realised what he was saying suddenly and clammed up. This man's daughter knew just how dangerous things could get. 'That is ... Take care, sir.'

Jake thanked him and went to retrieve his bags, then he made his way back outside the cordon. Began his long trek to the hotel, thoughts still jumbled and zipping around inside his head. The visit to the crime scene – not that he'd known he was going there – hadn't really helped in the slightest. No sudden epiphanies, nothing to give him any clue as to why this might have happened. So it was the same as the aftermath of seeing Bannister, just as fruitless.

What next? What next?

He pushed away the notion that he probably should grab another bottle of booze or hit the bar when he got back to the hotel. That wouldn't do anyone any good, would just muddle his thoughts even more. He needed to be clear-headed, needed to be able to think things through.

*You need to be able to sleep, as well,* said the little voice trying to lead him astray.

But he needn't have worried about that. All the walking that day had exhausted Jake and he was out like a light as soon as his head hit the pillow.

Unlike the previous night, he dreamed. Jake dreamt about Jordan, about when she was little – probably because he'd been thinking about that earlier on. It was a nice dream, they were happy, having fun. Julie was there as well, joining in. A holiday by the coast, on the beach, which somehow then morphed into a Christmas where they were all opening presents. He seriously hadn't wanted that dream to end.

But as dawn's early light streamed into the hotel room – through the cracks in the curtains he'd drawn – he had no choice but to wake up. As sad as this made him, though, remembering what had happened in the real world – when, only seconds ago he'd been in that blissful fantasy which seemed to go on forever – opening his eyes also brought with it that revelation he'd been looking for.

He knew, right there and then, what he had to do next. How to start, going back to the beginning. Jake wouldn't find that by gaping at Bannister, or the market stall where Jordan had died.

But he knew now where he would definitely find it.

Jake had to go back, once more.

Go back home.

# Chapter 7

He had a good excuse.

That's where he'd left his car, the day before last – when Matt wouldn't let him drive, had insisted on making sure he got to the hotel safely. Hopefully it was still there and that oaf Greg hadn't smashed it to pieces or something ... But that's where he was going anyway, back to his home, even if it didn't feel like one anymore. It was Jordan's home, though; had still been her home when she died. Jake felt sure he might find something there that would give him a clue about what the hell was going on.

He'd showered that morning, not wanting to show up on the doorstep smelling like he'd just rolled out of a skip, and he'd changed into the clothes he'd bought – a fresh T-shirt and pair of jeans. Jake had remembered to put the 'do not disturb' on the door the previous night, but turned this around when he left the room.

Then he went down to grab a bowl of something for the complimentary breakfast. It was only then, as a few people's eyes trailed him, that he realised what must have happened – and there it was, large as life on the TV in the restaurant. His face in a little square top right, as the newsreader silently carried on with his report, the sound off so it didn't disturb the other diners.

'Shit,' he whispered under his breath, making for a table in the corner with his cereal and coffee. He could feel those eyes boring into him, even as he faced away, kept his head down and ate.

It wasn't long before the first shadow spread across his table and he looked up to see a man in his thirties with tight curly hair standing there, hands open in front of him, his eyes digging holes into Jake.

'Yes?' he snapped, before he could help himself. 'Can I help you with something?'

The man's mouth dropped open, and he looked back to another table where a blonde woman the same age was sitting. When he faced front again, he said: 'We ... my wife and I, just wanted to say how sorry we were for your loss.' And Jake saw as the woman turned, that she was nursing a baby which couldn't have been more than a few months old.

He felt bad then, for thinking this was just someone poking their nose in – or, worse still, one of his own crowd on the hunt for a story. Jake shook his head, sadly, and said, 'Thanks. Appreciate it.'

'I-I'll leave you to it,' the man replied and went off, but Jake couldn't take his eyes off the baby as the wife cuddled and rocked it in her arms. It didn't seem like five minutes since Jordan had been that age, and he silently wished she still was. Keeping her safe back then had been as easy as making sure she had something to eat, changing her nappies and tucking her up in her cot.

But there'd been other things to worry about, hadn't there? Those rose-tinted glasses again ... Things like diseases and cot-death, or when she went off to school something happening like falling over playing and hurting herself. All concerns until she was old enough to look after herself ... *Should* have been able to look after herself.

Jake shook his head again; these thoughts were doing him no good. He finished his food and drink quickly, aware that the longer he stayed there the more people might come over who'd seen those news reports. The more risk there was of a journalist who was staying here clocking him.

When he was ready, he ducked out of the restaurant and went to reception, got them to order him a taxi. He had neither the energy after yesterday, nor the inclination to walk all that way into town again – or rather to that particular destination on the far side of Redmarket.

When it arrived, a black and white affair with numbers on the side, he'd slid into the back and given the driver the address. He saw the man, a thickset fellow who looked like he could have a second career moonlighting as a Sumo wrestler if he wanted one, looking at him in the rear-view as they set off. Saw that recognition there again, was expecting the cabbie to say something as well – as they invariably did – but was grateful when he remained silent throughout the journey. Perhaps he just couldn't think of anything to say. What *was* there to say, when all was said and done? If the roles had been reversed, Jake doubted whether he'd be able to think of anything that didn't sound trite or were platitudes tossed off which didn't actually mean a thing. This man didn't know him, the couple back at the restaurant didn't either – how could they possibly know the right words to say? Hell, even people who did know him like Matt hadn't been able to make him feel any better.

'This is as far as I can get,' the man told him when they pulled into the next street, and when Jake looked past him he saw the road to his old house was chock-a-block with media: vans, cameras and reporters flitting about. There were uniformed officers there, too, doing their best to keep those people away from the house, but there simply weren't enough of them to make much difference. He could just about see his Toyota, parked where he'd left it and mercifully intact.

Jake paid the driver, telling him to keep the change, and got out. How was he going to play this? he wondered. How was he actually going to get *in* there? Because he hadn't just come back

76

for the car; that was only the excuse. He'd come back for a specific reason, and it wasn't to end up on more news broadcasts throughout the day.

So, what to do? Rush through them, hurry past and hope that nobody saw him, nobody recognised him? Fat chance of that when his face had been all over the TV that morning, probably even the night before – he just hadn't caught it. Find a copper to guide him through to the house, create a safe passage if such a thing existed? Again, there weren't enough of them to hold back this tide. It was a funny thing being on this side of the fence. Being the subject rather than the one filming said subject ... Jake had never really camped out in front of someone's house like this, though. Was more used to filming Sarah as she did a piece to camera, or willing interviewees – not hounding people in their own ... in their own homes.

One thing was for certain – if he just stood there long enough someone would spot him anyway. Or maybe that was it? Maybe that was the way to ...

Jake coughed as he walked towards the neck of the road, trying not to make it obvious this was an effort to gain their collective attention. It didn't work, and so he coughed again more loudly. A female reporter on the periphery of the group finally noticed and pointed. It didn't take long for recognition to kick in after that, or word to spread through the ranks of assembled journos, who all began to move in his direction, run even if they could. So he ran, too. Jake knew these streets well, was betting that he could lead them a merry dance and then double back around and just knock on the back door.

But he'd underestimated their resolve – some even skirted round the other side, meaning that he was suddenly trapped in the street running parallel to his old house; a pincer move-ment approaching. Left with no choice, Jake aimed for the fencing at the back of that building and clambered up and over it before any of the media people could reach him. He was willing to bet none of them would risk trespassing to get their exclusive; Jake just hoped Julie would be all right with him doing that. Surely she wouldn't object, given what was going on out the front.

He heard a couple attempt to scramble over the wood, but then gave it up as a bad job. Jake couldn't help feeling triumphant, but at the same time was torn – those people were in his line of work, after all. Kind of. He flapped a hand to dismiss it, and began making his way up the garden towards the French doors at the rear. The curtains on the other side were closed, which was probably for the best as he didn't want to give anyone inside a scare, so he began to tap gently on the glass. When nobody answered, he knocked a bit louder. Then louder still.

When the curtains were yanked back suddenly, Jake started – stepping back onto the paving slabs that separated the grass from the doors. There, meeting his gaze, was an angry-looking Greg Allaway. Jake had been hoping the man had gone to work by now … Greg shouted something at him that Jake couldn't hear because of the double-glazing, then called back over his shoulder to somebody inside.

The next thing he knew, Greg was unlocking the French doors and swinging one wide. 'Well, look what the cat dragged in,' he said snidely. 'What're you doing skulking around in our garden, Radcliffe?'

Jake almost replied that it wasn't his garden – he'd planted the flowers in there, had mown the lawns for years – but instead he just answered: 'I wasn't skulking anywhere, *Greg*. I was knocking. On the back door. The front was a bit hard to get to.'

'What do you want?'

'Is Jules … Julie inside?'

'What's it got to do with you?'

'I want to see her.' Greg bared his teeth, then Jake heard a female voice calling from behind. The man in front of him closed his eyes and cocked his head back, then reluctantly stepped aside so that Jake could enter. 'Cheers,' he told Greg, but had never meant anything less in his life.

Jake stepped through into the kitchen, which he noted had been painted a different colour since he'd lived there – pale yellow having given way to a darker blue. Julie was standing in the hallway and he made his way towards her, only for her to back off and step sideways into the living room.

He followed her, with Greg bringing up the rear, crowding him. The first thing Jake noticed was that the liaison officer wasn't present. 'What happened to the lady? The female police officer?' he asked.

'I told her to piss off,' Greg snapped from behind. 'Couldn't stand all that tea and sympathy shit, could we?' He looked to Julie for support on this, but she said nothing. 'Getting under our feet.'

It was only now, in the light from the living room, that Jake could properly take in her face. She looked like she hadn't slept in months; probably felt that way as well. Her eyes were puffy and scarlet, and she wore the same jeans as the day he'd last seen her but a different baggy shirt which was half tucked in at the waist, half hanging out. 'What are you doing here, Jake?' she asked, echoing her husband.

'What am I ...' He realised he didn't know what to say, how to explain what he was actually here for – to say that he was trying to get to the bottom of this, for Jordan's sake. 'I ... I came back for my car, but well, I thought I'd see how you were while I was here. Had some trouble getting to the house, though.'

'Been there a couple of days. Parasites,' Greg muttered.

'I thought I'd give you a bit of time,' Jake continued, totally ignoring him. He realised that made no sense if all he was coming back for was the Toyota.

'Well, you've been a busy boy, haven't you?' Greg again.

'What are you talking about?'

Greg pushed past him and strode into the room, snatched up

a newspaper from the couch and then slammed it into Jake's chest. He tried to stand his ground, but wasn't expecting the push and stumbled back a step or two. 'Hey!' he said.

'Haven't you seen the morning editions? Well, go on then – now's your chance!'

Julie had lapsed into silence again, but he could see tears threatening once more, her eyes moistening.

'Congratulations, you made the front page,' sniped Greg.

Jake pulled the newspaper away and turned to the front. There he saw a grainy picture of himself and the policeman with the flashlight from last night, standing next to the stall where Jordan had died. The copper looked like he was either trying to get Jake to come away, or about to catch him if he fainted. The headline read: 'HEARTBREAK FOR FATHER AS HE VISITS SITE OF HIS DAUGHTER'S MURDER.'

'Jesus,' whispered Jake, wondering just where the photographer had been; he hadn't seen anyone.

'Yeah ...' said Greg. 'Go on, it gets better.'

Jake scanned the rest of it, which talked about how devastated Jake was – how he'd even been to the station to try and help the police. How in Christ's name had they known about that? Unless ... Yes, if the photographer had been that close, he might have heard the uniformed officer talking about seeing him at the nick. Either that, or there was some kind of leak there? Wouldn't surprise him in a place that bent.

Seemed like more of a possibility as he read on to find out details of the murder, how it had obviously been a crime of passion because Jordan's boyfriend was in the frame. How he'd stabbed her in the heart, picking up on the headline once more to drive the point home.

Without even asking, Jake made it to a chair and slumped down in it. 'I-I don't know what to say.' He looked up at them both. 'You don't think I've been talking to them, do you?'

'Why not? Birds of a feather and all that. It's what you lot

80

do, isn't it? Stick together.' Greg folded his arms. 'That's your job.'

Jake slapped the paper. 'No, this isn't *my* job.'

'Making money out of other people's misery. Why not your own, why not ours?'

*Yeah,* thought Jake, *you look real cut-up about all this* … Then he realised his poor choice of words. He found Julie's eyes. 'Julie, you know me. You know this isn't … I wouldn't do anything like that, not when it might damage Jordan's memory.' He sighed. 'I didn't even know my picture was being taken, for heaven's sake!'

'What gets me,' said Greg unabated, 'is the whole "father's grief" bullshit. You haven't been near her in God knows how long.' Jake could tell this was something that had been said quite a few times over the last couple of days, maybe even before the events in town. Stirring things up even more with Jules, as if they needed it. 'She fucking hated you, mate!'

'That's enough!' snapped Julie. Then, more quietly, 'That's enough, Greg.'

'But you were the one who—'

'I said that was enough.' There was still a spark of the old Julie left then, enough to tell this idiot to back off. He glared at his wife, though, in a way that said this conversation was far from over.

'I'm sorry,' said Jake. Now he was the one who didn't know what to say to make things better. It was something he seemed to be doing a lot of lately, apologising.

'You're sorry, I'm sorry.'

'What have you got to be sorry about?' Greg asked his wife.

'We're all bloody sorry!' she completed.

'I'm not,' growled Greg. 'Not sorry at all.'

'What are you doing here, Jake?' Julie asked him again, still ignoring her husband. It was probably for the best, thought Jake.

'I … Look,' said Jake, scrunching up the paper and shoving it down the side of the chair. 'I-I was wondering if I could have a look in Jordan's room.'

81

'You *what?*' Greg unfolded his arms now, throwing back his head again. 'You can't be serious?'

'What for?' Julie now, asking the more pertinent question of him.

Jake looked her in the eye. 'I-I dunno, I guess I need to feel close to her or something. It was why I was at the market square last night.' Only half a lie. 'I just want to feel some kind of connection to her again, find a keepsake possibly?'

'Whatever for? You weren't bothered about a connection when she was still alive,' spat Greg, then looked across at Julie. 'You can't possibly be considering letting him do this?'

'She was his daughter,' Julie said without hesitation. 'He has every right to—'

Greg threw his hands up into the air. 'Oh, I give up. I've had enough of this. I've got to go to work anyway, someone needs to bring in money to put food on the table.' He strode out again, shooting Jake a filthy look as he went. Jake rose when he heard the front door go, went to the window to watch Greg pushing past the reporters that had returned and were gathered once more on the street outside. He seemed to be enjoying shoving them, elbowing and generally forcing his way through, not giving a shit about hurting folk.

'Making friends and influencing people again,' Jake said, before he had a chance to self-edit. He turned, saw Julie had her arms folded now, or rather was hugging herself in the absence of anyone else who might be willing – Jake bit back the offer that was rising in his throat, the urge to go across and just hold her again like he used to do when she was this upset. Her mouth was a thin line.

'Don't let all that nonsense fool you, he's a good man.' Jake couldn't help letting out a sarcastic laugh at that one. 'Believe what you want, he's been good to us.'

Jake held his tongue. He'd get nowhere with seeing the room if Julie was mad with him, if she threw him out on his ear. So he said, 'Fair enough.'

'Do … would you like a cup of tea or something?' she asked without looking at him. That good old British tradition in times of crisis, Julie obviously picking up where the female liaison officer – who'd been told to 'piss off' because of it – had left things in that department.

'I'm good thanks,' he told her.

She nodded, then looked upwards. 'The police have taken a look at Jordan's room, taken her laptop. They already had her phone, she … she dropped that in the street when … Said it was standard procedure. I daresay they'll be doing the same with … with Bobby's.'

'I see,' said Jake.

'Would you like me to come with you?'

'Actually, is it okay if I go up alone?'

Another nod. 'Well, you know where it is … I'll make myself a cuppa, I think.'

Jake's turn to nod, but before he headed up he said, 'You do know I had nothing to do with that report, don't you? Nothing to do with any of them, Jules – or the stuff on TV.'

She met his eyes now and said, 'I know, Jake. I know.'

# Chapter 8

Julie had left him to it, heading for the kitchen where she'd fully intended on making that tea.

Instead she simply stared at the kettle, trying to summon up enough energy to fill it, to switch it on. She was trying desperately not to cry again; she was so sick of crying. She was sick of tea too, if the truth be known. That FLO, Linda, had made cup after cup of the stuff – all too sweet, when she'd eventually tried it, but apparently that was good for shock, for nerves.

She hadn't deserved the way Greg had spoken to her though, asking her to leave like that. Sometimes she wished he was a bit... calmer about things, wouldn't get so worked up. But he'd only done that because he could see the state his wife kept getting herself into. He was protecting her, in his own way.

Julie knew what people must be thinking, Linda, Matt... definitely Jake. Wondering just what the hell she was doing with a guy like that. But they didn't see the other side, the side she'd fallen in love with. The side that was just looking out for her, that had been looking out for Jordan as well.

Yes, she admitted she'd fallen quickly. She had for Jake as well... it was something she'd hoped she hadn't passed on to Jordan, but, well, if wishes were horses...

'*Act in haste, repent at leisure.*' That's what her mum had always said, and especially when she'd told her about Jake, about Jordan. Her dad hadn't said anything like that, he'd just delivered an ultimatum that had left her no choice but to leave home. She couldn't walk away from the father of her child, she just loved him too much.

So they'd struggled on by themselves, got by even though it was hard work at their age. But true love always won through in the end and they'd had some happy times, hadn't they? Jake had knuckled down and worked his arse off, she'd got a job herself after Jordan was born – okay, maybe not the career she'd always wanted as a vet, but close enough working there and helping out. Her real 'career' was as a mum anyway, and she put her heart and soul into that.

Things had got better, money-wise and with her parents as they went along. They'd put down a deposit on this place and moved in, made it a real home and been a real family.

For a while.

Then the stuff with Jordan. Julie had always been more tolerant of it than Jake, could understand it all more because she'd been there. Times had changed, certainly, but people were people when all was said and done. Girls were girls, women were women – and Jake had never really *got* either. Had taken it all so personally, when really those were things Jordan had to figure out on her own. Life lessons only she could learn ... if she'd let herself.

Julie would be lying if she said she'd understood all of it, and of course she'd been as worried as Jake about some of it. While he acted like he was the only one in the world who was concerned, acted sometimes like it was all Julie's fault (and sometimes had her believing it; so much so she thought she was going mad). Just because Julie didn't want to close off the lines of communication, didn't want to alienate her like she could see her husband doing. She'd seen that happen in other families with their children (seen it with her own dad, until they'd made up), watched how people had become estranged – moved to the other side of the world in some cases just to get away. Julie never wanted to lose her relationship with Jordan, even if they weren't quite as close as they used to be. She wanted to look forward to grandkids and family days out ... once all the dust had settled. Once Jordan and Jake had made things up again.

But he'd kept on pushing and pushing, hadn't he? Didn't know when to stop and that last blow-up had been the final nail in the ...

The tears were pricking the corners of her eyes, demanding to be free.

There would be no reconciliation now, no days out with the grandkids. Because her daughter was dead, brutally murdered by one of the guys Jake always said he was trying to protect her from – like she was still 10 or something. And Julie hadn't seen it coming. She. Hadn't. Seen. It ...

Maybe if Jake had been here, and still talking to Jordan – really talking, not just the pleasantries on the phone that never really sounded very pleasant to Julie – maybe all this wouldn't have happened. Then again, maybe it would have anyway; who knew?

The point was, their marriage had collapsed not long after that. Jake had left and Jordan had spent more and more time out with her mates, with guys. It had just made everything worse. Had even led to Julie losing her job because the focus just wasn't there anymore. Believe it or not – and Jake would probably refuse to – Greg coming along had actually made things better, given them all a bit of stability that they hadn't experienced in years. At first.

She'd met Greg completely by accident, through a friend of a friend. Introduced on a much-needed night out at the pub, he was a widower and had a kid around Jordan's age; a young lad. Here was someone who'd been through similar things to her, having to cope on his own; she'd felt relaxed chatting to him ... though she had to wonder now whether that was more the glasses of wine he'd been buying her. At the end of the evening, he'd asked if he could see her again – maybe coffee sometime. It was amazing how close they'd become after that, and so quickly.

It was so nice to have someone to share things with again, who actually understood her. Someone to help shoulder the load now that Jake was gone, now he didn't seem to give a damn about either of them (and she'd cried back then as well, night after night – often thinking about picking up the phone but too stubborn to actually do it after the way Jake had hurt her).

She hadn't needed a man, it hadn't been that at all – far from it. But it had been nice, it had been really nice. People weren't meant to be on their own, were they? And it surprised her more than anyone that the relationship moved so quickly, going from strength to strength; so fast in fact that Greg had moved in before the year was out, and they'd got married the following May. Registry office job, no need for anything fancy as they'd both been there before.

Jordan had got on with Greg, though it had to be said she wasn't around much to see him all that often, and she got on with Greg's boy, William – and why not, he was a nice, polite young man. They'd been a family once more, for a little while.

Naturally, once he'd moved in with them, Greg had had a few things to say about their daughter – usually when she needed to borrow money. But things had ticked along ... until they hadn't.

Julie didn't keep tabs on who her daughter was seeing or wasn't seeing, but she had met Bobby a couple of times when he called for Jordan at the house. Seemed a decent sort, although obviously she didn't know him that well. What could have happened between them that caused him to ... to do that?

Crime of passion, the paper had said ...

Crime of passion.

Jealousy? She could understand that, sort of. Just look at the way Greg was more of a dick now that Jake was around; the taunts and snipes designed to cause maximum pain. Not that Greg had any need to feel jealous ... did he?

Julie shook her head, to persuade herself more than anyone.

She did still have feelings for Jake, how could she not? He was the father of their ...

But all that was in the past; *had been* in the past. And then she'd seen him again, even under these circumstances, but she'd seen him – turned to him, fell into his arms so easily when she'd seen their little girl like that. Then been mad at him all over again when he started up with his bullshit. Even though she knew it wasn't his fault. She believed him when he said he hadn't talked to reporters or known the photo was being taken. Got angry with him because the media made it sound like there was only one person grieving over Jordan. The one person who'd not been there for her, who'd walked away.

*Was* it possible to love and hate someone in equal measure? she wondered again. Two sides of the same coin, hardly anything separating the two when you thought about it; both extreme emotions, provoked by actions, feelings.

She could hear him now upstairs, the floorboards creaking above as he moved around Jordan's room. He did have every right to be in there, as she'd said to Greg. But even that hurt after the way he'd behaved, the way he'd stayed away, cut himself off from Jordan ... from her. Hell, he'd crashed back into their lives the morning she'd found out about the murder, only to piss off again for two days without a word. What had he been doing? Wallowing like he always used to when he didn't get his own way? If she knew Jake, and she did, he'd probably got pissed to numb himself from the pain. It had crossed her mind as well, but someone had to be sober, to think clearly ... hence the tea. *So much* tea.

It was what she'd come in here to do, make herself a brew – and yet all she'd done was gape at the kettle for ... how long? Julie looked at the clock; Jesus. Trying not to cry, though as she touched her cheeks now she realised she'd failed. They were sodden with tears.

More footsteps upstairs, followed by banging noises. What the devil was he doing up there? Was he all right?

Was she? Julie began crying again, sobbing in fact. Rushed to grab the kitchen roll and ripped off a couple of sheets to dab at her cheeks.

*Just leave him to it*, she told herself – like he left you. Leave him alone now, he had to work things through on his own, just like Jordan had been trying to do.

But the banging ... She hated him even being in there; loved him for wanting to be in there. Hate, love. Love and hate.

With Jake planted firmly in the middle.

* * *

It seemed to take him forever to scale those stairs.

He'd spent ages at the bottom, just looking up – willing himself to put his foot on the first step. Then ascending, as if he was heading for another plane of existence or something. Jake swallowed dryly as he reached the landing, not sure, now he was here, whether he wanted to go through with this at all. Did he really need to be confronted with a room full of his dead daughter's stuff? A room where she'd laughed, cried, lived ... A room that would still be filled with her presence.

As he stepped onto the landing though, his mind was on other things. Like the door across from him, ajar and allowing him to see into the main bedroom. Throwing back a picture of the bed courtesy of a mirror in the far corner.

The marital bed.

The one he'd once shared with Julie, but she now shared with ...

No, it was a different bed, he could see that. The wooden posts at each end a different shape to the curved ones he'd come to know so well over the years. It made sense, Julie trying to wipe him out of her life. She certainly wouldn't have wanted to share that with another man.

And thoughts now invaded his mind, images of Greg and Julie.

Together. Scenes of them on that bed, the wood creaking, the springs protesting as they—

*No. Stop this! You're just torturing yourself.*

His eyes flicked over to what had once been the spare room, located right next door to the bathroom. An office of sorts where he'd first cut his teeth playing around with film, editing bits of video together he'd shot. Now he could see that also had a bed in it, the room where Greg's son – Julie's stepson – William Allaway stayed when he wasn't at university. It explained why he wasn't around at the moment, the autumn term having started a few weeks ago. Jake had never met the lad (when would he have had the opportunity?) but figured if he was anything like his old man then that was probably a good thing.

But he couldn't put off why he was here any longer, and his feet took him to that door. This one *was* closed, the only room up here which was. Making his job harder, to reach out and grab hold of the handle, turn it, open the door and walk inside.

He let go as soon as he'd gained access, like the handle was red-hot, and the door swung open of its own volition. And maybe it was his imagination, but it did feel very much like this was a different realm he was entering. Felt very much like Jordan was here, in this room – more so than it had back at that stall. How could it not, when it contained so many elements of her life?

Jake realised he hadn't taken a breath in a few moments, and suddenly felt light-headed. He sucked in oxygen so he didn't pass out – the last thing he wanted was for Julie to come rushing up here when she heard him slump to the floor, unconscious. He didn't want her up here with him, especially after seeing those images in his mind of her and Greg.

Jake shook his head; somehow those thoughts seemed disrespectful in here. Because it was almost like a religious experience. If he'd been looking for a connection, then it was most definitely here. A bridge between the living and the deceased. He wondered briefly if Julie would keep it this way forever, a shrine to their daughter – as some do when they lose a loved one. It hadn't really changed that much since the last time he'd seen it, or since Jordan had been a little girl really.

The posters on the walls, which used to be things like *My Little Pony* or *Teletubbies* back in the day, had been replaced with the most popular bands and film stars of the day as she grew up (he recalled a phase of her obsessing over the fellas from one particular generic boy band, and that guy from the *Lord of the Rings* and *Pirates of the Caribbean* movies; innocent crushes, nothing more).

Now those had been replaced with posters from more indie bands he'd never even heard of, music that was on the fringe and which if it ever became popular would suddenly lose its appeal for kids like Jordan and so many others. There were still movie posters, he was pleased to see – but instead of the more popular blockbusters, these were of classic black-and-white films or even foreign art house fare. He cocked his head, impressed.

Similarly, there was a bookcase not far away which revealed an eclectic taste in literature: Dickens rubbed shoulders with Ben Elton, Bronte with Niffenegger. Nowadays, it was quite something to see people of her age reading books at all – but they'd always done their best to encourage this. And it seemed it had paid off, the titles on the shelf wide-ranging and stimulating. Not just fiction, but non-fiction; history books and biographies.

Jake hadn't been aware of moving into the room, but now suddenly he was inside it. The bed on his right was covered in a white duvet with little circular patterns on it; might have been her choice, might have been Julie's. He wondered if Jordan had ever had any guys back here, snuck them in through the window or something like she was in a madcap American comedy? Hadn't happened on his watch, that was for damned sure, but once he was gone … Nah, he concluded; Julie wouldn't have been okay with that either. They were a bit old-fashioned that way.

But maybe she'd had friends over, staying in here? *Had Bobby ever been?* he wondered. Jake pushed the thoughts away that were souring the moment, and took in more of the room.

The dresser ahead of him, which had space for a chair in the middle and a high mirror forming its back, still had all of her make-up scattered across its desk. *Was this where she'd got ready before going out that evening?* Jake thought. He hadn't noticed any make-up on her when he'd been at the hospital, but then maybe the staff there had cleaned her up before they were allowed to see her?

How plastered in the stuff had she been when she'd gone out to see Bobby, off out all geared up for a night on the tiles? He liked to think she'd toned it all down since her teenage years, when at certain points there wasn't a bit of her face that wasn't covered in crap. How often had he told her that she didn't need it, that she was a pretty girl without all that stuff – but it had been the trend at the time, still was from the looks of those clubbers he'd seen the previous evening. Eyebrows plucked to within an inch of their lives, then drawn on again as if with marker pen; cheeks shiny, sometimes covered in glittery blusher; and lips that looked like a bee had stung them, coated in a shade of red that any pillar box would have been proud of.

If he'd ever wanted her to act on one piece of advice, it would have been not to be a sheep. Not to do shit just because your friends did it. Her taste in films, books and music reflected the kind of brain she had, so why she insisted on hiding that so much he had absolutely no idea.

*Why did* you *do the same?* a little voice asked him then.

He'd had a good head on his shoulders back when he was young and yet chose to hang out with those gangs, getting into all kinds of trouble. He'd learned eventually. It just made Jake sad that Jordan would never have that opportunity, to grow and develop. Who knows what she might have accomplished given more time?

Time … Jake was conscious now he'd spent a lot of that already up here just taking everything in, when he should be looking deeper. Searching for something, anything that might explain what had happened a few nights ago. Give him more options, leads to follow. Of course, Julie had no idea that's what he was doing up here, so he had to get a move on. Get this done.

Jordan was clever, she hid things. Always had done, especially when something was wrong. She'd done it literally when she was small, hiding away her favourite toys if there was any mention she might be too old for them (Jake would have given her all the toys in the world right now, if she'd wanted them ... if she'd been around to accept them), or comics, or even sweets – which she would stash about the place so she'd be able to eat them when she wanted to rather than just as a treat.

The police had taken her laptop, already had her mobile from the night of the attack (which she obviously hadn't had a chance to use). In any event, they'd find nothing on either of those, Jake was certain of that. Her social media messages would just be full of inane chatter, nothing of substance. Maybe exchanges between her and Bobby, but even then she would have been wary of someone seeing these at some point. Somebody hacking in or whatever ...

Someone getting in there after her death?

*Had she known that was coming?* Jake thought then. Had she been worried about being threatened maybe, but frightened to tell anyone – hiding things yet again? He thought back to those marks on her arms again, the self-harming. Nobody did that unless they were in an agitated state of mind. Hadn't he read somewhere that it was a form of control? That when other things were spiralling out of control in your life, it was the one thing you could keep a handle on yourself?

Thinking about that wouldn't help him find anything, so Jake started to search. The bookcases first, and then the drawers were another obvious one, pulling those out of the dresser and searching through. But he only found the usual: underwear, socks, jewellery

93

in boxes; earrings, necklaces and such. Jake pulled the drawers out completely next, checking underneath them, at the back of them. The police had probably done all this already – or at least a decent forensics team should have – but he had to be sure.

Hiding places ... hiding places ...

Jake looked back over his shoulder at the bed, then bent to look underneath. He got on his hands and knees, checked under it – and felt around to see if anything was attached to the underside of the bed, or between the mattress and the frame. Nothing. But then he remembered she would never go under there when she was little. Too scared of monsters, she used to tell him.

Instead, she would lock herself away in ...

Jake looked across at the old wooden wardrobe she'd had since she was about 7. Back then it would have towered above her (not so much these days), but she felt safe inside there. Always had done.

He pulled on both doors, expecting them to be locked but they tugged open easily. Inside, he found a range of clothes – some designed for a night out, some just for lounging around in like big, baggy sweatshirts, T-shirts or hoodies. And good God, there were so many shoes covering the bottom of the wardrobe. Seemingly one for every single occasion known to man ... So many heels, so many flats. Trainers galore, some he suspected were only bought because they were the latest thing. Absently, he wondered how she had afforded them all – and the make-up, come to that! Probably the bits and bobs of part-time work she'd had over the years, though the last time he'd spoken to her she'd been between jobs again.

The one thing he didn't find was what he'd been searching for all along, some hint of what had been going on.

Something hidden, just like Jordan used to hide herself.

Jake rubbed his chin, trying to think. Stepping back and glancing around the room again before coming back to the wardrobe. Looking it up and down, pausing again where Jordan kept her shoes. The base of the old wardrobe was two or three inches, and solid he'd always assumed. But he also remembered there being slats in the bottom of it, a couple of them that reached back, and that were at the moment covered up with the sea of footwear.

The police may well have had a look in there, moved some of the shoes around, but Jake had to wonder ...

He cleared a space, parting the shoes like Moses with the red sea. Yes, he was right ... slats. Screwed down, but slats nevertheless. He rapped on one of them. It was hollow. For the first time since he'd received that phone call the other morning, Jake smiled.

And hadn't he just seen ... He rushed back to the drawers again, rummaging through them. There it was, a screwdriver. He'd thought it strange at the time, but his eyes had glossed over it because that wasn't what he'd come here to find; the hidden thing, the secret thing. But it had been important nonetheless, a means by which to reach whatever was in that wardrobe.

Quickly, he went back and pulled out the shoes, got down on his knees and began unscrewing the slats, then levering them up. Jake sat back, panting with the effort of it all. Not daring to look inside the blackness there, in case he'd been totally wrong about this. In fact, even when he did summon up the courage, he couldn't see anything in there, and an initial sweep of his hand inside yielded nothing.

Then his fingers brushed something. The edge of a box in there, shoved up against the back on the far corner. Jake reached in, hooked it with his fingers, and began to drag it free. It took a few attempts, because of the awkward position he'd had to adopt – Jordan's arms being longer and thinner than his – but he finally tugged it free.

It was some kind of keepsake box, appropriately about the size of a shoebox, which opened with a latch at the front (thankfully not locked). After all of his efforts, Jake now hesitated to open it. Whatever was inside was not just secret, it was private. But, he had to remind himself, it might help. No one other than him – and Jordan – knew it was even here.

Gritting his teeth, he undid the clasp.

There were all kinds of things inside: shells; keyrings, foreign coins, a snow-globe, stones of various colours … Each one obviously had a particular, and special meaning for Jordan; and most were connected to her life as a child. Objects from holidays, a ribbon Jake remembered she'd wanted to keep from a birthday cake many moons ago. And some of those toys he'd been thinking about, the smaller ones like a stuffed mouse that looked like it would fall to bits if you picked it up; a penguin she'd been bought when they took her to the zoo, its colours – black, white and orange – faded with time. Tears were welling in Jake's eyes. Inside this box was his daughter. She *was* here, in every single object she'd saved all these years.

But there was also something else. Another book. It was only small, and leather-bound, but it was thick. Maybe even thicker than those books on the shelves not far away. Jake's hand was shaking as he reached for it, as scared as he had been to touch the door handle.

'Jake?' The voice wafted up the stairs. Julie's, full of concern, though he didn't really deserve it. He knew his wife … ex-wife; she'd given him some time up here, but now she wanted to know if he was okay. Even if he said he was, it would only be a matter of time before she came up here and saw for herself.

He had to make a split-second decision. Jake couldn't let Jules know about this, not yet. Had to keep it secret, just like Jordan had done. So he closed the box and shoved it back where he'd found it, tossing the screwdriver in there as well and replacing the slats as best he could, before bundling those shoes back inside the wardrobe to cover the base up again.

'Jake, what are you doing up there? What's all that noise?'

She was coming, he could hear her – up the creaking stairs. Then suddenly she was in the doorway just as he was scrambling to his feet. Her eyes were much redder than before; she'd been crying too. 'Jules,' he said.

'What's going ...' She looked beyond him to the open wardrobe, the mess he'd created. 'What are you doing, exactly?'

'I ...' He wiped his eyes with the back of one hand. 'I was ...'

'And what's that you've got behind your back?' she asked, eyebrows narrowing.

'Behind my ...'

'Yes, there! In your other hand – I can see it. Show me.'

'Jules, I ...'

He was stalling for time and she knew it. 'Jake, show me your hand.'

Slowly, he brought out the hand from behind his back. Jules let out an audible gasp. Because there, resting in his palm, was the toy penguin from the zoo. 'Oh ... oh my God. I remember that!' And suddenly she was smiling, laughing even. 'Where did you even find ...'

'It was ... it was in the wardrobe,' he told her. Wasn't a lie; not really. That was where he'd found it. 'Hidden, right at the back.' Again, not a lie.

'I ... I thought she'd thrown that thing away ages ago,' said Julie, the tears coming again, prompting more from him as well.

'I guess not,' said Jake. 'There was a part of her, you know, that was still our little girl. No matter what.' Julie nodded. She covered the distance between them, picking up the penguin and examining it like it was a priceless artefact. He supposed it was, in its own way – its value to both of them was priceless. He thought about asking if he could keep it, but then felt incredibly mean. Julie needed it more than he did. 'Tell you what, why don't you hold on to that.'

She looked up at him, confused. 'But I thought ... You wanted a keepsake, didn't you?'

He shrugged. 'You should have it, Jules.'

His ex-wife smiled again, and he thought then he'd never seen

97

anything as beautiful as that in his life. Jake missed that smile more than anything. Greg certainly didn't deserve to see it every day.

'I'll tell you what, though,' said Jake, drying his eyes again. 'If you're still offering tea, I wouldn't say no to a cup.' Julie couldn't help letting out a small laugh, and he laughed too. It felt good.

Julie kissed him on the cheek and turned to walk off to the landing. He followed, trying to ignore that open door to their bedroom, as he trailed her down the stairs and to the kitchen.

\* \* \*

It had actually been quite pleasant, like having a cup of tea with an old friend.

His best friend for so many years, even superseding Matt – it was a different kind of friendship, which the guy probably understood now he was married himself.

They talked about the past, recounted happy memories. Passed the time, until Jake told her that he really should be going. He decided to leave the car where it was after all, too much hassle with the press there, and rang for a taxi to pick him up in the street behind them and left the same way he came in – like a thief in the night.

Felt appropriate really. Because as he got into the vehicle (different driver, one who wouldn't shut up this time – but about some government bill or other, not that Jake was listening to him), he'd pulled the book out from where he'd tucked it into the back of his jeans, his jacket covering the top.

*'But I thought ... You wanted a keepsake, didn't you?'*

He'd held it in his hands, another piece of ancient treasure, but still hadn't opened it. Not yet. Felt disrespectful in that car. So he'd waited until he was alone, heading back to his room at the hotel again.

Then, and only then, had he turned to the first page.

# Chapter 9

*November 10th*

*I don't even know why I'm starting this. That's not true, I do know.
I need someone ... something to talk to. Something that won't judge
me. I need a way to get all these thoughts rolling around in my
head out of there, if only for a little while.*

*It's something that can be just mine. That no one has to know
about, and that they won't find out about because I'm going to put
it somewhere only I ...*

*I'm going to keep it safe, hidden. That way I can be honest. I
need to be honest, if only with myself. I can't talk to anyone else
about all this stuff, because they just wouldn't understand. Things
at home have been ...*

*I know Mum and Dad row about me, because I'm not the
daughter they thought I'd turn out to be. Even though I'm only
really just getting started in life, y'know? I just ... It's hard. I want
them to understand but I know they never will. They were young
once, but the world's changed so much since then. They've been
adults for so long, it makes them ...*

*I wonder if one day I'll look back on all this, maybe when I have
kids of my own, and laugh about it? Probably not. But maybe I'll*

*have been an adult too long then to make sense of all these scrib-blings I did when I was a teenager. Perhaps none of it'll be important then, but it is now.*

*It's not about fitting in. Not really. That's what they don't get. It's about feeling good about yourself, having some kind of identity that's not just about being at home, being their kid and all those expecta-tions. Though there are other expectations that come with being a good friend, of being ... Of being wanted, needed by someone.*

*I don't think that's making things any clearer, and definitely not to future me reading this back thinking 'stupid fucking child!' But that's the thing, I'm not a child anymore. Not really. It's like ... I'm in this kind of grey area, right? I'm in-between, like that show that's so popular.*

*Oh Christ, all this sounds so bloody wanky.*

*Maybe I'll try again tomorrow.*

*February 18th*

*Another party this week, Kerry's place. Her parents are at some resort in Spain all weekend, so she's throwing this big bash. I like Kerry, she can be a bit dense sometimes but her heart's in the right place. She wouldn't let you down ... I don't think – her and her mates, that I'm slowly getting to know. Some of them are a bit older than us, but only a bit.*

*I've kinda lost touch with some of my old friends since I've been hanging out with these guys, but hey-ho. I'm having fun! It's been a while since life was fun, y'know? And not some big hassle or thinking about careers or what you're going to do with your life like they keep banging on about at school. It's all ...*

*Lot of pressure to look right, I know. The right clothes, make-up. I think Von said Adam was going to be there, and he seemed really nice when we were talking the other week, hanging out at the bus stop, just mucking about. I know I shouldn't really smoke, that it's bad for you etc, etc, but, well, I don't want him or the others thinking*

*I'm some kinda twat. Enough people think that already about me, and it's ...*

*So, yeah, that'll be nice, I think. This weekend.*

*I'll tell Mum and Dad I'm staying over at Georgina's, studying. She'll cover for me, she still owes me for not blabbing about the clinic I went to with her when she thought that guy she was seeing had given her something.*

*Mum knows Georgie's folks, they'll buy it. I can't tell them where I'm really going, they'd go apeshit.*

*Just wouldn't understand.*

*March 25th*

*Christ, what a mess!*

*Adam's been spreading it around that we've been hanging out these past few weeks, telling people all sorts. I wouldn't mind but ... actually I do mind, we haven't been doing shit! Not really. Not compared to some people.*

*Now Von's not really speaking to me because she liked him as well, and apparently he's been seeing a few girls at college as well as the two of us and ...*

*I just don't understand it, why'd he have to be like that? We were having such a nice time, going to the pictures, he took me to a few clubs and that. Yeah, he could be a little ... insistent, but nothing too heavy. Nothing I couldn't handle.*

*And now this. I'm trying my best to sort it out, and Kerry's helping in her own way, but ... Christ.*

*If some of this gets anywhere online, I'm dead.*

*I'm properly dead.*

\* \* \*

Jake put the book down.

That phrase got to him every time he read it, and Jordan used

101

it a lot – usually within the context of them giving her a hard time, her parents. He let out a slow breath, glanced outside at the rain that was tracking down the window of his hotel room.

He knew he shouldn't be doing this, that it was a gross invasion of his daughter's privacy, but he kept telling himself it was for a good cause. Okay, a cause that might uncover what had happened in the run-up to events a few nights ago. But wasn't that what the police were supposed to be looking into? Surely he should be handing this over to them? However, the whole privacy thing worked both ways. These were his daughter's words, and if anyone should be going through them it was a family member – someone close – not a bunch of strangers.

Jake's eyes flicked over at the clock on the bedside table now, which told him he'd been reading into the small hours of the morning. In that time, he'd gone through the entries twice, come back to some – couldn't bring himself to look again at others, because it brought back memories of all this from the other side. Of being on the outside, looking in. How close was that, when you got right down to it?

She'd started the diary entries when she was around 15, obviously when she was struggling the most with where she fitted into the world. She'd doodle in there as well as write, sometimes flowers or animals – dogs and cats – if she was happy, things like spiders or lightning strikes when she wasn't. And what had seemed like fun at the time (though what was coming across to Jake was Jordan merely told herself that over and over to try and make it true) had quickly descended into round after round of the same old thing.

Faces and names interchangeable, especially where boys were concerned – and the ones who hurt her the most. She'd think she was in love with them, hope they were with her, only to find out time after time they were just using her. Then more often than not she'd end up on the outside herself of whatever social circle she was involved in at the time. Photos he'd seen himself crop up online, back when he was still looking, would only reveal half the story and in actual fact there were very few friends she could count on who wouldn't just drop her if they thought their own position in the social rankings was in jeopardy.

It built up a picture of a girl who was very lonely, had no confidence, was all raging hormones and worried about everything from her weight (which explained a lot of the meals she would skip) and appearance (the clothes and make-up basically like a uniform or mask, hiding her real self) to what was happening in the world. Someone who felt like she couldn't even confide in her parents, and who'd been let down by everyone ... including him. There were no specific entries about that time when they'd had the massive argument – in fact what he found was that she'd stopped writing in there for a while around then, probably too upset. But that in itself spoke volumes, didn't it? He'd hurt her with his words, with his absence.

'*You might have found out, if you'd been around.*'

'*You left her when she needed you the most.*'

Julie's words now, but she was right – Jake hadn't known how right until he'd taken this trip through Jordan's psyche. Though all this was probably only scratching the surface, because the more upset she got – and the more heartbreaking it was for him to read – the more confused about everything her writing became. No one understood; Jake had to admit he certainly didn't, but he had to wonder whether she included herself in that. What had originally been a tool for trying to order her thoughts became, at times, simply passages venting or reflections of some of the darker things she was thinking about, especially when guys cheated on her or slagged her off after they'd got what they wanted, leaving her nowhere to turn.

Essentially, she was lost.

And he'd let her down as spectacularly as he thought she'd done with him – the anger he was feeling at the time getting in the way of their bond. As she said herself, Christ what a mess!

Towards the end of the diary, she started to mention '*my new bloke Bobby*'. Meeting him, how she thought he seemed nice ... but wanted to be sure this time. Had been hurt on too many occasions. Then, in a series of quite worrying entries, she talked about mood swings:

*Sometimes BB scares me, he can be quite ... intense. Yeah, he makes me laugh and we can get on, then it'll be like a switch being flipped. He'll talk about how much I mean to him, how he just wants to protect me. How it isn't right the way guys look at me. Like I can do anything about that! They'll look all day and all night, I can't help that. It's kinda sweet in a way, protective, but at the same time a bit scary. I'm not really sure what to make of it. We haven't known each other that long, for him to be ... I dunno, I might be over-reacting to the whole situation.*

BB ... Robert 'Bobby' Bannister. A definite lightning strike! And no, Jake didn't think she was overreacting at all. The way she talked about him, '*Bobby was absolutely lovely today*' and then in the next entry '*BB's acting so weird and jealous*' ... They were surely the first signs of an insecure control freak, someone maybe with a personality disorder who couldn't stand any other man to be around. A good actor? Like he had been back in that cell when protesting his innocence? Jake didn't know what to think.

Was that what had led to the self-harm, which again he'd not been able to find any mention of in spite of the fact Jordan had said she'd be honest in this book? What had he been expecting to find, passages like, '*I began cutting myself today. Think I'll take it up as a hobby ...*'? Jake had been doing some checking and apparently instances of that sort of thing had increased massively in young girls, doubled in the last twenty years. Some people thought it was because more cases were being reported and treated (not in this instance it hadn't been) but while the figures had gone up regarding his daughter's contemporaries, they'd remained pretty much level for young boys. And as for abuse and attacks ...

*How much I mean to him ...*
*How he just wants to protect me.*
*How it isn't right the way guys look at me.*
*Crime of passion. Jealous. Stabbed in the chest; aiming for the heart.*

He'd wanted to find the reason for all this, and there it was in black and white, in his daughter's own handwriting. Even if they hadn't got all that other evidence, then there was enough stacked up in this diary to sink Bobby for good. Yet still something didn't quite add up. Something was nagging at the back of his mind, almost as if Jordan were speaking to him directly, trying to get him to see something he'd missed

She'd also made some really weird notes, including a couple of sets of numbers with no other explanation. More doodles? Or telephone numbers perhaps? Jake tried to call them, before realising they weren't long enough to be phone numbers anyway. Something else then, bank accounts? Or a secret code?

There was also a mention or two of the girls who were in her immediate circle at the moment, different names again – but Jordan did put down where they usually met. It was a place to start, and the weekend was coming up, so before Jake fell asleep from exhaustion, diary beside him on the bed, he'd already decided he would head out into town to find the place.

And that he was going to find out all he could from them, too.

# Chapter 10

She'd spotted the man even before he entered the place.

Laura was pretty observant like that. You had to be really, or important stuff passed you by. Her friends, Becky – sitting on her right, nattering away as usual, occasionally flicking back a dark-blonde curl or two that had flopped down over her brow – and Raju, short for Rajeshri, on her left, taking all the gossip in, didn't notice anything unless it was right on top of them.

There was only really one topic of conversation at the moment anyway, which made a change from the usual who was dating who, which clubs they were going to hit that night, and what was happening on whatever reality TV show was popular at the time … usually who was dating who on it, and what clubs *they* were going to.

But this week, and this weekend, there had only been one thing on everyone's mind – and their lips. Their social media had been full of it, both on their news pages and in the private messages. Even the mayor of Redmarket, that Sellars, had been on TV talking about how it was 'unfortunate' and 'tragic', but these kinds of things very rarely happened in towns like theirs.

Jordan Radcliffe's death. Her murder, more accurately.

What made it all the more surreal was that they'd known

Jordan. Okay, maybe not that well, but she'd been part of their circle for a short time, introduced by friends of friends of friends. Laura had liked her. Felt like maybe, finally, she might have found someone who could be that proper best friend you confided in. Perhaps even still saw when you were in your thirties and had a husband, kids and a mortgage. If you went down that route, of course. If you decided not to follow your dreams … or perhaps weren't encouraged to.

She'd been nice, Jordan. Easy to talk to, though she didn't really say much back. Quiet, maybe shy? When she did speak it was usually something worth listening to, though, decent advice; not like Becky who just liked hearing the sound of her own voice. Kept talking probably because she didn't want to hear her own thoughts.

Like she'd been doing when Laura had clocked the guy. She'd been looking at Becky's hair, envious of it if the truth be known, and then looking at Raju's perfect skin – so perfect half the time she didn't even need make-up when she went out – and had depressed herself thoroughly. That's when she'd looked away, seen him over the road, heading in the direction of the coffee shop they were in. The one they spent a lot of their free time in: 'Better Latte Than Never'. It had only been around the last six months or so, and was competing with several more in the streets surrounding it – including a couple from the bigger chains – but had the advantage at the moment that it was new. That would only give it the edge for a short while, though Laura had to admit the coffee – expensive as it was, but then where wasn't it these days? – was as tasty as it was elaborate, and the baristas were fairly easy on the eye. One in particular with skin the colour of the tanned drinks he was making, and short, velvety hair, would always give her a wink when he served her. He never did that to anyone else that she saw, which gave her a warm feeling …

The little things, the details. They were important.

Like the fact she'd seen this man's face before. It took a moment or two, because he wasn't like the photos they'd used. He looked like he'd been in a war, hadn't slept or eaten in weeks. He was thinner in the face, some might even say gaunt, and had dark circles around his eyes. The clothes he was wearing, and especially his shirt, looked new but unloved, like they hadn't been ironed; if there was one thing Laura and her friends knew about, it was well-loved clothes. They certainly had enough in their collections.

As Becky continued to drone on, now dissecting Bobby Bannister's relationship with their friend, while Raju nodded intently, the man entered the coffee shop, causing the bell to tinkle above him. He looked up with a start, as if wondering what it was. Here was someone living on his nerves, and Laura couldn't say she really blamed him that week. He made his way up to the counter to stand in the queue, looking about him as if searching for someone. They made eye contact then, but he looked away first.

He was not bad-looking – or wouldn't have been back when he was her age, and also before the week from hell. Someone she might even have gone for herself, maybe. Someone she thought she might trust, confide in. Someone her heart was going out to right now.

Her eyes trailed him as he got to the front of that queue, spoke to a different barista to the one who always winked, and asked him for a drink. Asked him something else as well, was talking to him. Laura watched as the man pointed across at the three of them – not that Becky and Raju had noticed yet. Didn't even notice as he made his way between tables, over towards them.

'... always said there was something funny about him, Bobby. Just something, oh, I don't know, that ...' Becky was wittering on. Laura didn't think the girl had met him more than a couple of times at most.

'Becks,' said Laura, trying to attract her attention. Then louder: 'Becks!' She was trying also to do the universal sign to stop, sawing her finger frantically across her throat – then realised how that might look. Realised what else that meant: to kill what you're saying …

To kill.

Luckily, the man didn't seem to notice, and Becky finally realised there was someone behind her when a shadow fell across their table. Raju looked up at the guy and was there just a flash of recognition? There should definitely have been, but you never knew with these two.

The man raised a hand to say hello. Laura glanced down to see that – in contrast to their Yuayang, Macchiato and Galao – he just had a simple black coffee. He looked like he needed it. 'Hi there, I was just talking to …' He pointed back at the man who'd served him. 'And, well, he said you might know my daughter, Jordan.' The man paused, then rephrased that: 'You *might have* known her. She … she passed away.'

Laura nodded. 'You're her dad, aren't you? Her real dad, I mean. Mr Radcliffe.' This was as much for Becky and Raju's benefit as anyone, in case they were still drawing blanks.

Now he was the one who nodded. 'Yeah. Jake. I … I knew some of her friends used to come here.'

There was an awkward silence then, before Laura asked him if he'd like to pull up a chair. Becky threw her a look as if to say, 'What the fuck are you doing?' but Laura ignored her. He placed down his cup between Becky and Raju – opposite Laura, as if he felt like he might be able to relate to her better than the others, perhaps.

'I was wondering if I could talk to you all, would that be okay?'

'Sure,' said Laura, again ignoring Becky. What was her problem? Usually she *liked* to talk. Couldn't shut her up! After she'd introduced everyone, she said: 'Talk to us about what?' She shook her head; that was stupid, it was about Jordan obviously. She'd meant what was it specifically he wanted to know?

'I …' Now he'd been asked, been put on the spot, the man looked like he was struggling to answer himself.

'I liked her,' said Raju, before he could say any more. 'She was nice.'

The man smiled, but his eyes were full of regret. 'Yes. Yes, she was. Thank you.' He took a sip of his drink. 'I suppose I'm trying to get my head around all this. Find out if there was anything strange going on, anything that might have led up to ... well, you know.'

'Strange?' asked Becky. 'In what way?'

'Was she acting strange perhaps, like something was on her mind?'

'Not ... not especially, so's you'd notice. We ... I mean, there are always things on people's minds, aren't there?' These pearls of wisdom from Becky, who'd finally chirped up. Laura begged to differ; sometimes she wondered if there was anything *at all* on Becky's.

'She seemed to have a bit more money than usual,' Laura told him. 'Bit more flush.'

'Oh?'

'Not sure where she got it, maybe a new job? Something a bit better?'

'Around here?' scoffed Becky. 'She'd not that long ago started going out with Bobby, it was probably from him. I was just saying, I wasn't sure about the guy, there was something about him.'

'Something ...?' prompted Jordan's father.

'You know. Just something. You know when there's something weird, don't you. Something ...' Becky shook her head. 'Shouldn't ... I mean, aren't the police already handling this? Don't they have ...? Bobby was arrested, right?'

Jake Radcliffe nodded slowly. 'I'm just trying to get to the truth, I suppose. Whatever that ... Have the police spoken to you guys?'

They all looked at each other, Becky and Raju especially trading blank stares. 'No one's talked to me,' said the latter. 'Have they you?'

110

'Not even the TV people,' said Becky, with a certain amount of bitterness. Laura knew that her friend had always harboured a hope that she'd be spotted by some TV exec and whisked off to star in something. She was constantly applying for the talent shows you saw on Saturday nights, but never got anywhere – mainly because she didn't really have any talents as such … Unless you counted being able to talk for long periods of time without drawing breath. 'How about you, Lor?'

Laura shook her head. She didn't really want to be interviewed by the media, and wasn't sure how much use she'd be to the police in the matter. But then there were those details, weren't there? Things that she noticed … Could any of them be important now?

'How about these, do any of you recognise these numbers?' He took a piece of paper from his jacket pocket; hotel stationery, by the looks of things. Probably where he was staying, because Jordan's dad was from out of town – Laura remembered that. The man passed it around, but all three of them said no. 'I was thinking maybe some ex of Jordan's,' he thought out loud. 'Someone who might have been … Or a reason for her current boyfriend to get jealous? Maybe even cause him to be violent.'

'Oh, I think we all know now how violent he could get!' Becky, queen of good taste as always, said with a laugh. Then, when she saw the guy's face said: 'I'm sorry.' It was the first time Laura had ever seen her apologise for anything.

'Did he strike any of you as that kind of bloke?' Jake Radcliffe asked.

There were noncommittal mutters and shrugs all round.

'There was just something …?' the man said, repeating what Becky had said.

Then suddenly Laura piped up. 'Oh, wait … There was that one time when he got upset, you remember?' She took in Raju and Becky one at a time, but again they both just frowned and shrugged. 'It was about Drummond. Oh come on, you must

111

remember it – wasn't that long ago, couple of weeks maybe?' The details, she was thinking. Never miss things if you can help it.

'Drummond?' said Jake Radcliffe, equally confused.

A look of recognition passed across Raju's face and she flapped her hand. 'Yeah, yeah. But that was just Drummond, right?'

'Who's Drummond?' asked Jordan's father with an edge to his tone.

'Drummond's just Drummond,' Becky explained, as if it told him everything he needed to know. It didn't; he just looked more puzzled than ever, and a little bit frustrated.

'He's sort of a local character,' Laura said quickly. 'At least he's become one over the last couple of years or so.'

'A little bit ...' Becky twirled her finger at her temple, chipping in and apparently eager to talk about it all of a sudden.

'I think he's creepy,' Raju said, giving her impression. 'The way he stares at you sometimes.' She shivered.

'Sounds like someone the police ought to be looking into anyway,' replied Jake, drinking more of his coffee.

'Hmmm, probably,' was all Raju would add.

'They know him of old.' Becky again. 'He's been picked up loads of times, they always let him go.'

'Probably because they have nothing to charge him with. Being creepy isn't against the law,' Laura pointed out.

'If it was then Stephen Mulhern would have been banged up years ago,' joked Becky.

'Anyway, we're getting off the point,' said Laura, trying to bring it back to the topic at hand. 'Bobby ...'

Becky clicked her fingers. 'That's right, now I remember! Something to do with Drummond following Jordan around, wasn't it?'

Jake Radcliffe leaned forward in the chair. 'Following her *around*?'

Laura pulled a face. 'I'm not sure he was exactly following—'

'Yes, yes! That's right. He was following her and Bobby didn't

112

like it.' Laura didn't recall anything about that, but then Becky did have a tendency to exaggerate. The number of times she'd told them tall tales about her exploits – particularly in the bedroom – only for them, mostly, to end up being false. 'Got all bent out of shape about it, wanted to know the ins and outs. He might even have shaken her.'

'This Drummond fellow shook Jordan?' asked Jake, seriously.

'No, no. Bobby shook her.' Laura stared at Becky, trying to work out if this was one of those times when she was making it up as she was going along, or had she really noticed something important for a change? One thing was for sure, Laura hadn't seen any of this. 'Yeah, yeah. That was it. When she said about Drummond following her. I don't think he liked it.'

'Didn't like the attention,' Jordan's father mused, and Laura felt like she was missing something now; some vital piece of information he knew that they didn't. 'Male attention.'

'I don't know if you'd call him a man as such,' said Raju. 'Just a creep.'

'A dangerous kind of creep?'

Raju shrugged.

Laura watched Jordan's dad suck in a breath before speaking, noticing the details again. Observant, knowing that this might be important at some point in the future and having a horrible feeling, like a lead weight in the pit of her stomach, that they'd done something terrible here today. That it would lead to something terrible.

'Okay, so where,' said Jordan's father, Mr Radcliffe, Jake, finally, 'does this Drummond character mainly like to do his creeping about?'

# Chapter 11

The more he'd sat and listened to Jordan's friends – acquaintances more like, as none of them had known her for very long, or even known her that well – the more Jake had disliked the person they were talking about.

This Drummond, known to the police, but never held for long, definitely sounded like someone they should be looking into, regardless of whether he had anything at all to do with Jordan's murder. At the very least, he may have been the trigger – the thing that had set BB off, flipped that switch Jordan had spoken about. The mood swings, guys looking at her. One specific guy, who liked looking at *a lot* of people by the sounds of it. Young girls in particular.

He'd asked whereabouts the bloke usually did this, and the answer he got back was anywhere girls like that would congregate. The popular choice was outside college when it started or finished, sometimes schools or parks. But as it was the weekend, there was really only one clear choice according to that lass Becky.

'He'll be at the leisure centre, perving over the swimmers,' she'd stated emphatically, folding her arms. And all the while her friend Laura, the one who'd actually seemed to have a clue, who'd remembered the encounter between Jordan and Bobby about

Drummond in the first place, had been biting her lip as if they shouldn't be telling him all this. Like she knew what he had in mind and that they were aiding and abetting him in this ... whatever it was. Something not good, that's for sure! Perceptive girl, nice girl actually. If Jordan had had more of those as friends, then maybe ...

None of them seemed to know where this Drummond lived, though. Perhaps he didn't even have a home, thought Jake. Maybe he was like one of those trolls, the monsters he used to read stories to Jordan about, the kind she would try and hide from. The kind that lived under bridges or what have you.

The kind that killed you, that ate you.

It was a comparison that seemed all the more appropriate when Jake finally came across him, exactly where Becky had said he would be: standing on grassland not far from the glass window of the swimming pool at the leisure centre, gawking away at what was happening inside; lots of families splashing around in the water, having fun; lots of young girls wearing nothing but bathing suits and bikinis.

They'd said he was a big man, Jordan's friends, a giant even – but that hadn't really sunk in until Jake had been this close to him. He had to be heading for seven foot, and solid with it. In spite of the fact it was cold outside, he had on only an ill-fitting T-shirt (Jake had to wonder what kind of shirt *would* actually fit him) and loose, faded jeans. Not the fashionable kind that seemed so popular these days, more the old kind that he'd had for years, and these met the tops of his boots just above his ankles. His hair hung limply in clumps on his head, with bald patches here and there that made it look slightly diseased.

Jake had approached from behind initially, then skirted around the nearer he drew. And it was at this point he saw the look on the man's face, the fixation on that pool. His eyes were narrowed, almost like pinpricks beneath a thick, swollen brow. His mouth was open in fascination, but from time to time, as Jake observed him, that mouth would break into a grin that was quite chilling. He hadn't thought past finding Drummond, what he was going to do when he actually did, but when Jake saw him lick his lips, openly gaping at one young girl as she got out of one side of the pool and trotted round it to the diving board, he suddenly found himself thinking about this guy ogling his daughter, what else he might be capable of. And he found himself striding towards him.

'Hey,' he shouted as he did so. 'Hey you!'

Drummond ignored him, continued to stare intently at the scene ahead.

Jake ground his teeth, carried on marching towards the man – zeroing in on his right side. 'Hey, I'm talking to you!' This time when he got no reply, he shoved on the guy's arm in an effort to get his attention, perhaps twist him around and make him see there was someone speaking to him.

He didn't even twitch, and Jake's shove pushed himself back more than it did Drummond. That gave him pause for thought if nothing else. What exactly was he doing, this man was huge! It was David and Goliath all over again …

But David had won on that day, hadn't he? Jake said to himself. 'Hey? Fucking well face me when I'm talking to you!' That seemed to do the trick, something in the tone of Jake's voice perhaps? But the man finally twisted his head, if not his body, around. It was like watching some sort of industrial machine, moving slowly as the operator punched in the commands.

Now Drummond was gaping at Jake, and he couldn't help but shiver in that same way Raju had when she'd been explaining it. *The way he stares at you sometimes …*

Jake knew exactly what she meant now it had been directed at him. Well, not exactly, because he wasn't a young girl – the kind Drummond clearly preferred to be looking at – but it was bad enough. Made Jake wonder how much more intimidating it would be if you were the opposite sex.

If you were Jordan.

116

Drummond's eyes, which had basically been slits a moment or so ago, were now wide. In surprise or anger, at being interrupted, Jake couldn't tell which, but they looked … dead. That was the only way he could think of to describe them. There was a deadness there, like nothing was going on behind them now – which said a lot for what he thought of this interloper and what he could do to this man mountain.

Here was someone who, never mind being run in occasionally, should have been put behind bars with the key thrown away ages ago. Assuming, that was, they could find any prison that could contain him. He was more than simply creepy, he *did* look dangerous. Looked like someone who might have scared Jordan, letched over her and possibly even followed her, as Becky said. Followed her that fateful night? That notion was bad enough, without her having to then deal with the consequences of telling Bobby about it.

*Got all bent out of shape about it, wanted to know the ins and outs. He might even have shaken her.*

Jake couldn't shake Bobby, though he'd given it a damned good try through his cell door. But here was someone he *could* shake. Verbally, if not physically.

'Jordan Radcliffe,' he said simply. 'That name mean anything to you?' Jake could see from the tiny twitch at the corner of Drummond's mouth that it did on some level. 'You were following her, spying on her. Weren't you?'

Another twitch.

'Like you're doing here today, spying on innocent young girls, their families.' Jake pointed across at the leisure centre window. 'What the fuck is wrong with you?'

Third twitch, still no words.

'Do you … Do you know what happened to her, probably because of you! Did you have anything to do with it?'

Drummond's mouth didn't even twitch this time, and somehow that made Jake angrier still. Made him want to hurt this guy.

117

'Answer me! Fucking answer me, or I swear to God ...' When the giant just kept on staring at him, something inside Jake just snapped. He ran towards him, ran round so he was in front – not even waiting for the head to swivel back in his direction this time – and he shoved the man again, with both hands. Hard.

This time there was movement, even though Jake staggered back himself a couple of paces. It encouraged him to have another go, just as Drummond's head was completing its second slow turn in order to regard Jake once more. Jake shouldered him now, jumping to connect with the man's chest – the added momentum helping. It still only saw him shift a couple of centimetres, while Jake almost fell back to the ground.

'Jesus,' he whispered under his breath. But he didn't stop.

Jake tried punching this time, blows to the stomach and then the face. If Drummond felt any of them he didn't show any indication. However, his left arm came up and – whether it was to stop his opponent or just protect his own head – the consequence of this sent Jake sprawling, after catching him on the jawline. He spun, losing his footing and toppling backwards. Not only that, Drummond's movements seemed to be speeding up, and he was heading for Jake – on the attack himself, it seemed.

Now Drummond was finally in the fight, Jake had to do something; had to find some advantage. The guy would pummel him into the ground otherwise. Jake put his hand on the ground to try and get himself up, and his fingertips brushed against something rough. He looked down and saw it was a rock, then remembered who he was in this fight.

*I'm David*, he thought to himself.

Instead of throwing his stone, though – and risk missing Drummond or losing it – he clutched the thing in his hand, and as he rose he used it as a weapon. The rock's 'punch' had more impact than his fists had; in fact, he'd nearly broken his knuckles trying to get some kind of reaction out of the giant. When it struck, it opened up a wound on the man's cheek. The tear was only small, but blood spurted from it – and it was only now that Drummond began to howl.

Then he lashed out, flailing around with his arms. Jake managed to duck the first lot of swings, but not the second. Those pitched him several metres where he landed once more on the grass, the rock falling out of his grasp. Drummond was going into a frenzy, touching his cheek and crying out, making again for Jake. He tried to get up but fell over sideways. Attempted it again, but instead of falling had to roll or be trampled by Drummond.

Jake half-rose, half-stumbled to his feet, checking over his shoulder for the giant – who was behind him. He was left no option, but to turn and face him, knowing he didn't stand even half a chance. So instead of fighting now, he dove at Drummond, wrapping his arms around the man in some kind of weird wrestling move. If the guy fell forward, then he'd crush Jake completely – as a flat as a card.

Jake could hear voices now, coming from behind them. People rushing from the leisure centre, and from the car park at the side of it. Some had their phones up already, a knee-jerk reaction in this day and age to something happening. Cries of alarm, panic, and even some of encouragement floated over. 'Go on, get him!' said one. 'You can do it!' Jake wasn't sure whether they were meant for him or Drummond, but all he could do really was hold on as the ride continued. As Drummond twisted this way and that.

Then Jake was flying again, thrown off this bucking bronco. The third time he hit the ground, he landed awkwardly, hitting the back of his head.

He remembered opening his eyes once, twice – seeing blurred figures and wondering if there were enough people here to stop Drummond finishing what he started ... Probably not.

Then it didn't really matter, because everything went totally black.

* * *

When he woke up, he was in a box.

Ceiling, walls on either side. *That's it*, thought Jake – *he killed me. The big brute killed me!* He wasn't frightened, though, because the next thing he thought was, *I'm going to see Jordan again.* He wasn't a particularly religious man, though his mum had tried to get him to attend Sunday School a few times. He'd never believed in men with white beards or pearly gates or wings and harps. But something told him that when he died, he'd see her. And it was bright here, not dark anymore like when he'd been out, or when he'd willed it to come … Or if he'd been stuffed in one of those drawers at the morgue. Or even in a coffin. No, it was bright … and getting brighter – the light his friend this time instead.

So, all that he felt when he realised he was moving, when he could feel the thrum of the engine of the vehicle he was in, and looked over to see the green of the uniform of the paramedic beside him, was disappointment. At not getting to see his daughter again, at not being able to apologise to each other and just move on, just be friends again.

The male paramedic, who had close-cropped sandy hair and was wearing thick-rimmed glasses, suddenly noticed his patient was waking up. 'Oh, hello there … Hold on a sec.' Things got brighter still then when he flashed a torch in Jake's eyes. 'Can you follow the light please, sir?' So he did, left and right, up and down. 'Now, how many fingers am I holding up?'

'T-Th …' Jake tried to speak, then realised he was still a bit winded, that the words weren't coming out as clearly as he might have hoped. 'Three,' he managed finally.

'Good. That's good,' said the paramedic, smiling.

'So, what's the verdict?' another voice said. A familiar voice. Jake lifted up his head, then regretted it, but he did catch a glimpse of the figure at the bottom of the gurney he was lying on. His face.

'Probably just a slight concussion,' the man in green answered. 'Best to get him checked over properly, though, just in case.'

'Right,' said the young policeman who'd been at the market that night. The one who'd also had a torch. The one from the photos.

'Wh …?' Jake began, then tried to rise again but couldn't. Slowly, it dawned on him that the reason wasn't entirely medical. His hand was attached to the metal railing at the side of him, or more accurately his wrist was. When he looked down at it, he saw the metal bracelet that was holding him there fast. He was going to ask what happened, but then switched it to: 'What's the handcuff for?'

'Oh, hello again sir,' said the policeman, realising he was the one being spoken to. 'Just a precaution.'

'A … I don't understand.'

'How to put this in the best way,' the young man answered, then just shrugged. 'It's like this, sir. I'm sorry to have to be the one to tell you this, but … Well, not to put too fine a point on it …'

'Yes?'

'You're nicked,' the policeman told him.

# Chapter 12

Matt hadn't been able to believe his ears when he'd been told.

Had needed to come to the station, even though it was a weekend and he was off duty, spending some quality time with Katherine and Ed. His wife at any rate, seeing as his son was at a party. There had been a time of day when having the place to themselves had meant one thing and one thing only, but Katherine had instead presented him with a list of things that needed fixing in the house; she said she was going to catch up on the book-keeping while she had a minute. Taxes ... how romantic was that!

To be honest, he'd been glad of an excuse to get away from the delights of oiling squeaky doors or making sure the gutters were unblocked. Domestic life, eh? You just couldn't beat it.

'I've got to go,' he said when he got off his mobile. 'Jake's been arrested.'

'Who?' was Katherine's first question, barely looking up from the paperwork and calculator in front of her.

'My friend ... You know, his daughter this week, she ...'

'Oh. Yes. Right ... Okay,' was her only reply. She barely looked up when he went over to her at the kitchen table and kissed her goodbye on the top of the head. Sometimes he felt like she loved those numbers more than she did him. Certainly wanted to spend more time with them today. Would it kill her to show a bit more emotion?

She hadn't even asked him *why* Jake had been collared. Wasn't particularly bothered, it seemed. If she had, he'd have replied, still shocked: fighting in public. Or, more specifically, disorderly conduct which had disturbed the peace. If it had been years ago, when they were in their teens, he might well have believed it. Would probably have been involved in whatever brawl it was himself. But not now, not Jake.

As he got in the car and drove to the station though, Matt was kicking himself for not seeing this coming. He'd known his mate was on the edge, was a hair's breadth away from lashing out at something ... someone. That much had been obvious from the business in the cells with Bobby Bannister. But on that occasion it had been personal, and he'd had his reasons. Should never have been near the prisoner in the first place, and Matt blamed himself for that as well. Had gotten a deserved bollocking from his superior, but luckily it hadn't gone further than that. Matt had only been trying to help, thought it might put Jake's mind at rest to see his daughter's killer locked away.

*What possible reason could he have had to be involved in this one?* Matt had thought as he'd listened to the PC on the phone back there. Had he been drinking again, and in the middle of the day? Just got into it with someone? Had it been one of the paps following him around again, trying to get more pictures? As the PC had continued, he'd reported that it happened just outside Redmarket Leisure Centre ... And the person he'd been scrapping with? Only bloody Drummond! Was he insane? Did Jake have a death wish or something?

Probably.

After this week, more than likely.

But there were easier ways to top yourself than picking a fight with that gargantuan, especially as he wasn't the full ticket. And if he was going to do it, wouldn't it have been the night Matt

123

had left him at the hotel after seeing his daughter's body in the morgue? Got drunk and just done it, no messing about? He was lucky the hospital had told him he only had mild concussion.

Then again, Jake might not have started the fight in the first place. Matt thought about this for a moment, thought about the large guy in question – who they knew hung around in certain places, just staring at folk. They brought him in occasionally, warned him if a complaint had been made – but technically he'd never really broken the law. Didn't seem to know what was going on, if the truth be told. Matt shook his head, couldn't see any reason why he'd go for Jake … It was all so strange. But the upshot was they were both in the cells now, alongside Bobby Bannister.

*I guess I'll find out what's going on when I get there*, he thought as he carried on down the road, turning into the next one. It was why he'd had to see for himself, go to the station and find out just what the hell was happening.

He hadn't been the only one, though. When Matt arrived and entered, he found out Channing was here as well. That man *never* came in on a weekend. Too busy selling his cars or doing those toothpaste commercials, Matt assumed. In reality, he was probably hob-nobbing it at the golf club with the higher echelons. It was how he was on the fast-track up the ladder, slated to make inspector before too long and in no time would be running this nick or another one just like it.

What was getting in the way of that right now was a fly in the ointment in the form of Matt's old mate. This whole affair – this 'open-and-shut case' as Channing had called it – was turning into a bit of a disaster, and a PR disaster at that. Channing was good at handling the press, but then he'd need to be to explain this one away – the father of murdered Jordan Radcliffe arrested only days after her slaughter, when all the news pieces were playing up the sympathy aspect.

It just depended on what they discovered, what had happened

to cause the fight in the first place. Which was probably why Channing was ensconced in the same interview room they'd gone to after the Bobby incident. Matt thought about just turning around and going back home again or waiting till Channing was done – but the curiosity was killing him. And the thought of returning home to that guttering, to Katherine and her number-crunching, wasn't exactly appealing either. He could go to the pub, he supposed, get drunk himself ... In the end, he bit the bullet and knocked on the interview room door.

'Come,' he heard through the wood, and when he stepped inside he saw Channing was alone with Jake – who looked up with the mixture of pleading and relief. They were seated across from each other in the usual fashion, interrogator and interro-gatee. 'Ah, it's the other member of our merry little band!' said the DS. 'We really should all stop meeting like this.' Then, to Jake, in all seriousness and with more than a threat in his voice: 'No, but *really* we should.'

Matt looked around the room, noticed the interview wasn't being recorded, that the cameras were off. Just an unofficial chat; it happened a lot in Redmarket station. There was an empty chair, but Matt decided to remain standing – and near to the door. 'Sir,' he said by way of greeting.

Channing folded his arms. 'I was just trying to get to the bottom of what happened today, DC Newcomb. Why your friend here was climbing all over that guy Drummond like he was piece of equipment from the leisure centre where they were picked up.'

'Climbing all over ...?' Matt was still having trouble picturing that.

'Bloke should be in prison somewhere,' Jake stated.

'Oh, found your voice now that your buddy is here, have we?' Channing didn't look particularly impressed. 'Look, Drummond's harmless enough. He's been hanging around some time, has never harmed anyone ... until today. He's a local figure of fun, the kids throw eggs at him come Halloween. He's a local character.'

125

'So I've been told,' Jake replied.

'Oh? By who?'

'Some of Jordan's friends, they said—'

'Your daughter's friends.' Channing threw his hands up in the air. 'And what were you doing talking to them?'

Matt had more of an idea about that. After the move, Jake had probably felt disconnected from Jordan; they weren't particularly close by all accounts. He'd more than likely tracked those friends down to get to know her again *through* them. Matt might well have done the same had the situation been reversed – and he thought again now of his boy, grown up. Of what losing him might feel like ...

'I ... I don't know,' was the only answer Jake gave, shaking Matt out of his reverie. 'She was my daughter. They were her friends. But you should probably talk to them too, because they've got quite a lot to say about this so-called "local character", Sergeant. Creepy was one of the words used.'

'Creepy? Of course he's bloody creepy! It's Drummond!' snapped Channing. 'Would you want to take him out for a drink? No. Would you want to take him home and introduce him to the family? Not in a million years. Would you want to get into a fight with him? Jesus God no!' Those last words echoed Matt's own thoughts about all this. 'But he's not—'

'He was following Jordan around,' Jake broke in.

'What?' said Matt, drawn further into the room by what his friend had just said.

'Following her,' he repeated.

'Says who, these friends of hers?' Channing again.

'Yes. You can check with them. In fact, please do. It caused an argument between Bannister and her apparently. Might have been the thing that led up to her death. Or maybe this Drummond—'

Channing sighed loudly. 'Listen Columbo, I thought I told you to drop all this the last time we were in here? Let the police do their job, and you do your grieving.'

'Sir,' said Matt, thinking the last bit could have been a bit more tactful – but then Channing was starting to lose what patience he had left for all this.

'Except you're not doing your job, are you?' Jake spat.

'Yes, we are!' Channing hit back. 'We're just not running every single detail by you, and frankly why would we? Isn't it enough that we have the guy who did this? All the rest will come to light in due course, I promise you.'

Jake shook his head, obviously not convinced.

'Well, if you're going to be running around causing trouble, then I see no alternative but to keep you here for a short while. Just till you cool down.'

'And Drummond, are you going to keep him here this time … for a change.'

'Hey,' said Channing, 'you're lucky that nutter doesn't know his arse from his elbow, or he'd be coming after you for assault.' Channing gave a grin that held no warmth at all. 'You think we don't know who started this? Especially after what you've told us here. You went after him—'

'I went to ask him some questions, to get answers,' said Jake, but even Matt could tell he was lying.

Channing pointed a finger at Jake. 'You wanted to pound on someone. It's understandable, though personally I'd have gone for somebody a bit smaller – who could feel it.'

'Oh, he felt it all right,' Jake assured the DS.

'That cut?' asked Channing. 'Didn't even need stitches. I'm telling you, the guy's like The Hulk or something. But when we do let you out of here, you'd probably best watch your back. He's never done anything violent before—'

'That you know of!'

'—But *you* might just have pissed him off enough to come after you, pal. Might just "Hulk smash" you!' Sounded more like a threat from Channing than Drummond.

It went quiet for a few moments, no one saying a thing. Then suddenly the DS piped up again. 'Oh, yeah, I meant to ask you about this.' He pulled a piece of paper out of his pocket. 'We found it on you when you were brought in. Care to tell me what these numbers are?'

Jake looked across and then down. 'I'm … I'm not entirely sure.' It was the truth this time, Matt felt – Jake didn't know. But it wasn't the whole story, Matt sensed that as well.

'So where did you get them, then?'

Jake shook his head. 'I don't remember.'

'Still playing the detective, eh?' Channing let out another long sigh. 'All right, back to the cells with you then. DC Newcomb, do you want to escort our prisoner? Maybe you can talk some sense into him on the way.' Matt nodded, waited for Jake to stand and beckoned him over. As they were about to leave, Channing stood too and covered the distance between himself and Matt, placing a hand on his arm. 'Oh, and no pitstops at Robert Bannister's cell along the way, you understand?'

Matt nodded again, glancing down at the hand – which Channing removed. Then Matt was out in the corridor with Jake, leading him down to the cells. Neither of them spoke for a few moments, until suddenly Matt said, 'You really do need to leave this alone, Jake. I've seen him like this before and it never ends well. He's been cutting you some slack, but …'

Jake didn't reply, just looked over at his friend and then back down at the ground in front of him again.

'I mean it, mate.'

'I'm doing this for Jordan,' Jake said under his breath.

'Jordan would want you to leave this alone too.'

Jake looked at him again now, eyes narrowing. 'You didn't even know her.'

Matt opened his mouth, was about to say, 'And did you?' but thought better of it. Instead, he said: 'I know she wouldn't want you to keep getting in trouble like this. No daughter would.'

Jake lapsed into silence once more.

'If nothing else, think about the people you're affecting. Jules, for example. All this publicity, it's—'

'Yeah, yeah. It was always about Julie with you, wasn't it?'

Matt stopped, tugged his friend's shoulder to pull him around. 'And what's that supposed to mean?'

'Come on,' said Jake. 'We both know how you felt about her, you even told me a few times when you'd had a skinful.'

Matt gazed at him. Shook his head. 'Yeah, but I—'

'She never felt the same way,' Jake said bluntly.

*Below the belt that one, way below. Okay,* thought Matt, *if the gloves are off* ... 'Yeah, I got it. She chose you. And then you walked away from her. From *both* of them, your wife and daughter.'

Matt tensed, wondering if his friend would go for him now – another punchbag to take this out on. *Go on, just try it,* he thought. But he didn't, Jake just looked sad. 'Yes, I know,' he said. 'Can we go now?'

He turned away and Matt let him, fell in pace alongside him. They stayed silent even as he escorted him to his cell, then Matt said, 'It was a long time ago.'

Jake nodded. 'It was. It was all a very long time ago.' Then he sat down on his bunk, facing away from Matt.

Nothing more was said, so Matt closed the cell door. He couldn't help looking through the flap one last time, but his friend hadn't moved, didn't even stir.

When Matt closed that again, he leaned back against the metal, head resting against it.

His turn to let out a long, slow sigh.

# Chapter 13

It was funny how things turned out, and how – in the space of a couple of days sometimes, not that he knew how long it had been – they changed.

Time was a peculiar phenomenon. He'd thought about that a lot again after Matt had closed the cell door on him, those last words they'd exchanged echoing in his ears.

'*It was a long time ago …*'

And yet it was no time at all. The blink of an eye, and they'd gone from idiotic teens themselves who didn't know what they were doing, to almost middle-aged … and still didn't really know what they were doing. Adults like to pretend that they do, but all it boils down to is more experience, thought Jake to himself. You've just been through more shit, and hopefully learned from it. Or not.

'*You walked away from her. From both of them, your wife and daughter.*'

They could have been Julie's words, and they were also correct. Time sped up, slowing down. But you couldn't go back – not even a little bit. Not even a few days, a week …

He'd deserved that response. Hadn't known where all that was coming from about Julie, certainly hadn't meant to hurt his friend in that way – rub in the way she'd felt about him, like a brother and nothing more. Just lashing out again, same as he had done when he'd left Julie and Jordan – hurting the ones you love. And you always hurt the ...

'*If nothing else, think about the people you're affecting*', that had been the trigger ... And he'd pushed back, as usual.

They'd taken away his watch, along with his other belongings and of course his belt, shoelaces. So he had no way of telling how much time was passing in this box; another box. Could see when the sun went down through his grilled window, had passed a fitful night without sleep that seemed to last forever.

They'd brought him meals, but he'd barely registered it. Should have had the presence of mind to ask what the time was then, but he'd only have forgotten it later. Would've lost track of it here on his own, with just his thoughts for company. Thoughts about the day he was told, about rushing to Redmarket, about Jordan in the morgue. About how time had worked then, and the first night in his hotel room ... drunk, seeing his daughter. Making that pledge he was still trying to honour.

Thinking about her room, the diary – those entries. Her friends, Drummond ... Getting arrested. Everything spinning round and round and round, until he felt like he was going insane. Was that it, was the grief sending him crazy?

'*Let the police do their job, and you do your grieving.*'

Round and round until finally he must have passed out at some point on the bunk from sheer exhaustion; mental and physical. He'd opened his eyes, woken up and it had been dark outside again, the second night (some part of mind could hold on to that, at least).

And there, in the corner of his cell, had been Jordan.

'Oh ... oh my,' he spluttered. 'Sweetheart, is it really ... I've been trying, really I have. I think I'm getting somewhere with all this. That guy who was following you, Drummond. I went to see him and ... well, that's how I ended up in here, you see. I got into a fight and ...' Jake was aware that he was rambling, excited and trying to get everything out that he needed to tell her, while he remembered. While it was still fresh in his mind and he hadn't tipped too far over the edge. 'Your friends said he caused argument between you and Bobby, that it might have been the thing that led up to ... I know he was jealous from what you said in your diary, sweetheart. I'm piecing things together bit by bit, it's slow but ...' He was also aware that he wasn't allowing her any time again to speak, no gaps in his verbal diarrhoea for her to come back to him on any of these points, so he closed his mouth. He'd got most of it out that he needed to say anyway, ordering his thoughts just like she'd wanted to do with her diary, only becoming more confused at the end.

Jake waited. But Jordan had just stared at him, her skin as pale as it had been in that morgue again. Stared like Drummond had been doing at the leisure centre, like he ... like *she* couldn't understand him. Maybe it had been too much to take in, all at once?

He'd started to speak again with his garbled report when she'd moved, had begun shaking her head.

'What ...? No? Is that what you're saying to me? Is that what you're trying to say? But to which bit, Drummond, the argument ...'

She'd continued to slowly shake her head. Was it disapproval? Was it because he wasn't going fast enough?

Just moving her head from side to side, from left to right.

'Sweetheart, I don't know what you ... You have to speak to me. *Please!*' Jake was down on his knees, hands clasped in front of him. 'Please tell me what I'm doing ... What I've *done* wrong!'

(*Do you have all day?* The thought just popped into his head ...)

But she kept on shaking her head, saying nothing. Until, eventually, he heard the noise. Metal on metal, screeching and scraping. From somewhere really far away to begin with, then closer. The

132

door behind Jordan. She was fading away now, obviously not allowed to be here if someone else was intruding.

'Go away!' he shouted at whoever it was, the guy bringing a meal, Matt ... Jake didn't care, they were interrupting this time with his daughter, scaring her off. Time ... not enough time with her.

More noise and the door slamming back on its hinges. 'Rise and shine, sleeping beauty! We've let you lie in long enough.' A voice he recognised, one he was beginning to hate. Channing's. That smug, superior voice, always telling him to leave things alone – when he couldn't, because that would be going against what he'd promised his daughter.

And it was only then that Jake realised he was opening his eyes for real this time, that he'd just been dreaming about Jordan. Not seeing her in the here and now like he had – like he'd *thought* he had – back at the hotel that night. So now he resented the fact he'd been woken up by Channing, that he'd ruined this opportunity of spending more time with Jordan, whether she was something conjured up by his subconscious or not.

He rose from the bunk, scowling. Glaring at Channing. 'Don't look so glum, you're being let off with a caution. And a warning. An official one this time to stay out of business that doesn't concern you, before you get yourself into a real mess.'

'Okay,' stated Jake.

Channing said nothing for a moment, trying to read him, gauge whether he meant it – which he so obviously didn't. 'Also, don't go thinking this is out of the goodness of my heart. You've got your new little friend to thank for it. Easier just to do this than have her kick up an official stink.'

Jake's scowl transformed into a frown. 'New friend?'

'*Have* her *kick up a fuss ...*'

'She's waiting for you at the desk, where you can also pick up your things.' Channing told him, then cupped and swept his hand in a motion that said, 'Come on, we haven't got all day'. Jake got up and joined him quickly, more out of curiosity than anything.

133

Who was this person who'd stepped up on his account? This woman who was apparently in his corner? Jules? He doubted it somehow, and the words 'official' made it sound like it was someone whose words carried weight around here.

When he arrived at the desk, he saw a woman sitting on the bench opposite waiting – someone he'd never clapped eyes on before in his life. She had dark brown hair, cut in a bob, was wearing a dark trouser-suit with a cream blouse beneath it and had a raincoat folded over her crossed legs. Resting on top of this was a shoulder bag, which was standing on end as if she was using it as a shield. He didn't get time to take any more in, as Channing ushered him across to be given back his belongings. This included his watch, and Jake noted that it was almost half ten on Monday morning.

Channing moved away without saying goodbye to Jake, but he did nod to the seated woman with a sort of grudging respect. 'Miss Ferrara.'

She nodded back, finally getting to her feet and wandering over to Jake – who'd finished tying up his laces, was taking possession of his jacket. She was about a foot or so shorter than him. 'Mr Radcliffe,' she said, transferring the bag to her left shoulder and draping the raincoat over that same arm, before sticking out her right hand.

'Yes?' Jake answered cautiously, taking the hand and shaking it. Her grip was gentle, but there was a firmness there too – and he thought to himself it could probably get firmer if the need arose and depending on who she was greeting. There was also a steel in those eyes of hers, in spite of the fact they were brown to match her hair.

'I'm Miss Ferrara, of Goodwin and McDonald,' she told him, breaking off the shake.

'A lawyer?' he asked, puzzled.

She nodded.

'But I didn't ... Who ...?'

134

'It's not exactly a secret that you're here. In fact, you're becoming quite the celebrity with your exploits.' She smiled. 'And I was visiting anyway ... to see my client. You might be familiar with him.'

'Your ... Drummond?' He was even more puzzled now. The giant didn't seem like the kind of person who'd have a lawyer onside, if indeed he needed one; the police didn't appear overly bothered about what that man got up to.

She laughed out loud. 'Oh my goodness gracious, no. He was let out yesterday anyway. No, I came to make sure my client was all right – seeing as they still haven't bothered to move him yet. Some nonsense about not being able to find space at the local prison. More like they just want to keep a close eye on him ...'

Jake finally got who she meant. 'Your client is Robert Bannister.'

'Indeed.'

He couldn't help his lip curling at that; so much for someone being in his corner. 'Then I don't see what ... Isn't this a conflict of interest, you just talking to me?'

She gave him a disapproving look. 'I'm not *representing* you, Mr Radcliffe. I was just doing you a favour because ... Well, I think you could use one.'

'And that's all?'

Miss Ferrara looked about her, then wrenched her head towards the corner – out of earshot of any officers who might be nearby. Jake reluctantly followed her. 'Okay, I'll level with you,' she said, keeping her voice down. 'I was hired by his parents even before they got back to the UK. I've had several meetings with both them and Bobby, and to be frank I don't think he did what he was accused of, Mr Radcliffe.' She held up a hand before he could say anything. 'Listen, just hear me out. He's said again and again over the last few days that he arranged to meet with your daughter at the market and they were going to head off clubbing. When he found her, she'd already been stabbed.'

Jake's lip curled again; he felt like vomiting at the words.

'I'm sorry, I know this is difficult,' she told him. 'But a young man's freedom is at stake.'

'I don't give a shit about his freedom!' snapped Jake, a little too loudly, drawing looks from a couple of passing uniforms.

'Yes, yes. I totally understand that. At the same time, you wouldn't want to see the wrong person punished, would you? Or someone else who did it go scot-free?' Miss Ferrara met his gaze and held it, and without giving him time to answer said, 'No, I thought not.'

'His fingerprints *were* on the handle of the knife, Miss Ferrara.'

She closed her eyes, then slowly opened them again. 'And what would you have done, if you'd found her Mr Radcliffe? Seen her in that state? He went to her, took hold of the knife to pull it out, then realised she was gone.'

Jake almost laughed at the absurdity of that image, pulling the blade out like some sort of bloody Excalibur – but from his daughter rather than the stone. Bobby's reward: instead of making him king, it had made him a criminal.

'When he heard the police, he ran. I'm not defending or condoning that ... It made it look worse than if he'd actually stayed, but he's young. He got scared. I can understand that.'

'Listen, Miss Ferrara, I'm not quite sure what you want from me. Does that boy want my forgiveness? Do you?' He shook his head. 'I can't give it. There's only one person who can do that, and she's dead. Do you understand *that*? She's dead!'

'Please ... Please, Mr Radcliffe, calm down. I'm not the enemy here.'

Jake looked at her, slowed his breathing. No more kicking off at people, no more knee-jerk reactions or he'd end up back inside that cell he wasn't far from right now – and he'd be no good to Jordan in there. Wouldn't be able to do a damned thing in that box, with ... with the key thrown away. So he repeated, more calmly: 'What do you want from me?'

'All right. I can see what you're trying to do, and I want to help. Strikes me we have the same goals here, Mr Radcliffe – and that's to get to the truth.'

'You want to get Bannister off,' he stated flatly.

'If by finding the truth, by getting to the bottom of this, the consequence is Bobby walks free, then I'll have done my job, yes.'

'Sounds like you have about as much faith in the coppers around here as me,' he said wearily.

'Well, they do have their moments, but ...' She leaned in, as if imparting something confidential that he didn't already know. 'They can play a bit fast and loose with the law, if you see what I mean. You shouldn't have still been in that cell, for starters – that was Channing proving a point, and he knows I know it. And Mr Drummond ...' It was the first time Jake had heard anyone use the word Mister with regards to that individual. 'He wasn't the first person you've assaulted this week, was he?'

Jake thought about the cells, about Bobby.

'I mean, he doesn't hold it against you or anything, he—'

'Hold it against *me*?' Jake couldn't believe what he was hearing. His daughter's murderer not holding something against *him*? Piss off!

'But the whole cameras being on the fritz routine? Come on, pull the other one.'

'I don't know what you mean,' he told her.

'You shouldn't have been allowed within a million miles of my client and you know it. I'm guessing you put some pressure on your friend, DC Newcomb? Nice bloke, bit wet for my liking.'

Jake shook his head. Just who the hell *was* this woman, and how had she ended up in his life?

'Sorry, sometimes I overshare,' she told him. 'Which is not always a good thing in a lawyer ... But anyway, here we are. What do you say?'

He was genuinely bewildered. 'What do I say to what?'

'Joining forces, working together? Or at least moving in the

same direction? Not strictly speaking on the level either, but ...
we can make allowances every now and again.'

'You're crazy,' he told her.

Without missing a beat, she replied: 'It has been said.
Hot-headed, impetuous – probably the Italian half of me.'

'I ...' He didn't know what to say.

'First things first,' she nipped in again before he could reply.
'Let's get you out of here. And not by the front door, either. Have
you seen it out there? No, what am I saying, of course you haven't
– you've been in a cell.' She smiled, placed a hand on his arm.
'Trust me, it's ugly. Okay, so, out the back way. My car's parked
round there, I can drop you off ... Where? Maybe get you some
proper food, breakfast?' She looked at her own watch. 'Lunch?
Brunch? Then we can talk. Where would you ...'

'I-I guess we could grab something back at my hotel,' he said.
What harm could it do? he thought. It might just give him the
inside track on Bannister. Besides, he was too tired to argue.

'Perfect. That's perfect. So let's go.' She led the way out through
the back, where Matt had brought him in the morning they'd
seen Bobby, and where he'd been brought after the fight; Jake
was guessing the media had been massing even then.

But as they got in Miss Ferrara's sleek red Audi – and Jake couldn't
resist pausing a moment to admire the vehicle – then drove past,
he saw just what she meant by 'ugly'. There were twice as many
vans and people as there had been camped outside his old house,
and he would have had to walk through that if it hadn't been for
the woman beside him in the driving seat. For a brief moment, he
felt quite grateful to her. As it was, a couple of more observant
reporters spotted him in the car and started to run over, but the
lawyer was already turning and speeding away from the scene.

'Can't have them scratching the paintwork,' she told Jake, then
asked him as they left the mob behind, 'How's it feel to be on
the other side, for a change?' When he looked at her blankly, she
clarified: 'Your job? You film stuff like this, right?'

138

It was the first time he'd thought about his job in days, and the battery on his phone had almost run out by the time he was arrested otherwise he might well have heard from work again. When he plugged it back in, he was willing to bet it would be crammed with messages about the weekend's events. 'Not ... not exactly like this, no.'

'Hmm. Well, you're flavour of the month I'm afraid – for better or for worse. Probably that late-night market photo; I have to say, my heart went out ...' She glanced over, then changed the subject. 'Even your own channel have been running stuff about you, work colleagues saying what a top bloke you are. And then the fight ...'

Jake shifted about in the seat uncomfortably.

'I know what you were up to, you know.'

'Oh, you do?'

She nodded and her bob jiggled slightly. 'You were chasing up a lead, thinking Drummond was maybe something to do with all this, right?'

'Well ... sort of.'

'So, come on – give. We need to start scratching backs here, Mr Radcliffe.'

He sighed. 'All right, if you really want to know. I spoke to some friends of Jordan's and they said he'd been following her. They also told me it had led to an argument between Bobby and her, that he grabbed hold of her because of it.'

Miss Ferrara stuck out her bottom lip, did a kind of Robert de Niro thing with her mouth and nodded, impressed. 'Not bad, not bad. Go on ...'

'Er ... that was it really. That and the fact this Drummond is just generally incredibly creepy.'

'Right, so you like *him* for the murder of Jordan, then?'

'I ... No, I didn't say that.' He rubbed his forehead. 'Maybe. No, no, it was Bannister, I really do think it was.'

'Yeah, I can see that. Why?'

'Apart from the prints, you mean?'

Miss Ferrara changed gears and dodged up a side-street. 'Which can be explained by what Bobby's already said.'

'Okay, I have reason to believe Jordan was scared of him, that he had mood swings. And he didn't like the way other guys looked at her.'

'You got this from the friends, too?' asked the lawyer.

'Not ... not as such. I kind of got it from her,' he explained.

'But I thought ... I mean, you were estranged, right?'

Jake turned in his seat. 'How do you know that?'

'Well, you moved away from the family home for a start.'

'A lot of families split up, doesn't mean that—'

'Look, I'm sorry to have to tell you this, but quite a bit of that stuff is out there now. Comes with the territory. You of all people should know that.' She gave a quick shake of the head and the bob swung from side to side. 'We're getting off-topic. How did you know about Bobby?'

'I ...' Jake clammed up. He was getting carried away, swept up in the fact that this was the first person who'd actually wanted to talk about this stuff – rather than demanding it from him. Demanding he kept out of it. But she was still a lawyer, defending his sworn enemy at that, and he *had* only just met her.

'What makes you so *sure*?' she asked again. 'Because I tell you, I'm pretty good at picking up on people's characters. Again, the Italian in me. I've looked into a lot of people's eyes who did things like this, whether they were crimes of passion or not, and I just don't see it in his. I see a scared, lonely boy. I see someone who's grieving possibly as much as you are. Who really did love Jordan.'

'Miss Ferrara,' Jake pleaded; he didn't want to hear all that. What did it matter, what she thought?

'Sam. Please call me Sam ... It's short for Samantha.'

He opened his mouth, ready to fire something back at her about her client, but all he managed now was, 'I'm Jacob. Jake.'

140

She knew it already, hell apparently the bloody world knew it now, but thanked him nonetheless.

'All right, Jake. You don't have to tell me how you know, that's fine. I believe you. Like I said, I'm a good judge of character. You're a father trying to do right by his daughter, I can see that. Christ, I wish mine had bothered as much!' She let out a small laugh. 'Oversharing again ... I really have to watch that, Jake.'

In spite of himself, Jake laughed as well. Then he said, 'All this first name stuff, it's not very professional.'

'Well, we don't know each other in a professional capacity.'

'We don't know each other at all,' he reminded her.

'Not yet, no.' Sam flashed him a smile and it was the most comforting thing he'd seen all week, perhaps in a long time. 'Maybe brunch will fix that?'

'Maybe,' Jake said and left it at that, noticing that they were nearly at the hotel.

Inside, the restaurant bit was practically empty and for that Jake was grateful as well. They were probably all at the station or still camped out back at the Allaway house. It would only be a matter of time before they twigged where he'd gone, but even the couple of folk who did spot him as they grabbed a table and looked like they were about to make their way over, were stopped in their tracks by Sam. He didn't hear what she said to them, but they listened and nodded; perhaps it had been a request for privacy, or she'd worded it a little more strongly than that ... Whatever the case, it did the trick and he suddenly felt more at ease here than he had at any other point during his stay.

That, in turn, made him feel hungry – and he surprised himself by ordering the eggs benedict after spotting it on the menu. Sam just ordered a muffin, and they both had black coffee. Jake tried to put it all on the room, but she waved that away and gave the waiter her card. 'And this is not to be construed as a bribe in any way, shape or form. Just so long as we're clear about that,' she informed him with a grin, and he smiled too; thanked her. 'If I wanted to do that, I'd let you drive my car.'

Now he laughed. 'I might even take you up on that.'

There was more chat as they ate, some exchange of what they knew – mainly Sam trying to get Bobby's point of view across again. Trying to persuade Jake that the lad might actually be innocent, though he warned her that was an uphill battle.

'All right, all right ... But can we at least agree to keep in touch, and if either of us finds out anything we tell the other. Deal?' she said, draining the last dregs of her coffee. Jake gave her a noncommittal shrug of the shoulders, which she said was close enough. 'Now, before I head back to the office is there anything else you want to tell me. Anything I might be able to help with?'

Jake thought about it, then shook his head. It was only as she was about to get up and leave that he remembered the numbers. He fished about in his pocket where he'd put the piece of paper after it had been returned to him at the station. 'Do these mean anything to you? I've been trying to figure out what they are – but I've come up empty.'

Sam took the paper and stared intently at it, then looked up at him. 'I don't suppose you're going to tell me where you got these from, either?'

'You suppose right,' he told her.

'But it's Jordan-connected, right?'

He nodded.

'Okay, well, nothing's jumping out at me at the moment. Might be some sort of code ... Leave it with me and I'll have a ponder.'

He thanked her again and she got up to leave, though not without giving him her card. Jake wrote down his own number on the bottom of the piece of paper, and it reminded him that he still needed to charge his phone, which he'd do when he got back to the room.

Then he sat there at the table for a few moments after Sam

had gone, thinking. Thinking about how things had changed once more, about how there was someone in this with him now – someone he could talk to about his 'investigation'. Who was helping him to get to the truth ...

Of course, she had her client's interests in mind first and foremost; Jake had to be careful to remember that. But for some reason he had a feeling, maybe the same one Sam said she got herself when she was weighing someone up, that she'd abide by whatever their findings were – whether they pointed to Bannister or not.

Jake was shaken from his thoughts when more people entered the hotel. He'd been lucky there were no more scenes, no more people coming across while Sam had been with him, or even afterwards, but it was time to head up to that other box now.

*Time ...*

At least it was a comfortable box, his room. A place where he could think, maybe even read the diary once more for clues.

A place where he could ponder the fact that it was funny how things turned out, how they could get a little better sometimes. And that in the space of just a few days ...

How things could change so much.

# Chapter 14

She'd done nothing but think about how things had changed.

Over the weekend, since Friday actually when she'd seen him again. Since Julie had sat down with Jake and had that tea. It had been just like the old days – well, not exactly like the old days, but close enough for Jake to have been on her mind since then.

In fact, she hadn't been able to stop thinking about him, about their time together when they were younger – and how it felt simultaneously like yesterday and so, so long ago. About how much they'd loved each other … Until the upsets with Jordan, the quarrels. She'd always stop before she reached that point, not wishing to relive any of that crap. Just focusing on the good times, like when they'd been to the zoo and had bought Jordan that penguin.

Jake didn't have to give her that, had been searching for a keepsake for himself, but she'd appreciated the gesture. Had stared at it long and hard, clutched it in her hands until Greg came home from work. Had hidden it away then, just like Jordan had clearly done, to avoid the questions. To prevent the past being dredged up when her husband was around; she knew how much he hated thinking or talking about the time before they met. The opposite of when they'd first got together, when she needed a shoulder, an ear, it was just a reminder now that she'd had an entire life before he showed up on the scene.

Greg had the weekend off and could spend some proper time with her, he said. Julie knew that meant he wanted to be close, show her how much he loved her – but she simply couldn't. Julie told him she was too upset and could he just hold her, and he'd seemed okay about that. Because yes, of course she was still upset – still in a state of shock really – about her daughter, but there was also the small matter that she kept seeing Jake's face, too. Couldn't stop seeing it, imagining they were his arms around her offering comfort just like they had been when they'd gone to see...

That wasn't healthy, she recognised that, but Julie couldn't help it. They'd been together such a long while, since they were kids themselves really. It was a bond that they might have put to one side, forgotten about temporarily, but would never break as such. Not that she wanted to get back together with Jake, God no! Too much had happened since they'd split up, too many accusations. Too many words said that couldn't be unsaid, no matter how much you wanted to wind back the clock. Too much that couldn't be forgiven, on both sides she was sure. She'd moved on, he'd moved on – had a whole other life she didn't know anything about, didn't want to (because it hurt too much, was easier to pretend he didn't exist anymore). He was only visiting her world, had been forced to come because ...

In the days, weeks after he left Julie used to have a recurring fantasy that he'd walk back through that door (the front door, not the back like he'd used on Friday). That he'd say he was sorry, they'd all say how sorry they were – and then he'd hug her, he'd hug Jordan. They'd be a family again.

But he never did, he never came back to them. If you talked to Jake, he would say it was because they wanted him to stay away; that he felt like they both hated him. Especially Jordan, she knew for a fact he thought that. And, indeed, the girl

145

had said it to him ... though hadn't meant it, Julie knew that. Neither of them felt that way, not deep down. They just wanted things back the way they were, or moving forward at any rate. Julie would have given anything for that. Too late now, of course. All too late ...

Yet she couldn't shake him, not yesterday nor the day before. She'd tried to stay away from the news as well, especially newspapers after that photo had been published. Julie understood it had been taken from a distance, that Jake hadn't had a clue he was being snapped. That he hadn't spoken to anyone from the media before or since (the old 'a source close to the family' bullshit), but still it had hurt seeing it. Seeing those words that made it look like he was the best dad in the world, that made the fantasy real. That he had come back and they'd all been together just before ...

However, she'd also heard about Jake's antics on Saturday from a friend who'd called. None of the details, because she didn't want to know the ins and outs – something about a fight? – and she should have felt mad about that, too, because he'd been on the news again. It just made her all the more eager to see him again, though. Find out what it was about, just him lashing out or ...

Find out more about his life, maybe even be involved in it somehow now they'd had contact again – as ridiculous as that sounded. Couldn't do it when Greg was about, so she waited till he headed off for work on the Monday and called a cab. She braved what media there still was outside to get to it, deciding she would just tell Greg she'd needed to head out for a bit if he got wind of it. Needed to get away from the house ...

But she'd had a destination in mind all along – the hotel she'd been told Jake was staying in. Even if anyone said anything about that, they had things to discuss. The arrangements for Jordan's funeral for one, once the ... the body was released. That would all need to be talked about at some point. Jake would need to be involved, would *want* to be involved. As the dutiful father again

... Julie pushed aside the resentment she felt at that again, remembering the good times. Remembering he had a right to at least be kept in the loop, to have a say.

It was one of the reasons she found herself at his hotel on the Monday morning, loitering and deciding whether or not it was a good idea to go inside. She'd tried calling his mobile, but it was going straight to messages. So she'd decided she would get one of the members of staff at the desk to call him up in his room, or get him to come down or something.

What she hadn't been expecting was that he wasn't even at the hotel. That he'd show up in an expensive-looking car with an attractive-looking woman whose hair was cut in a bob, chatting to her, heading to the front doors and through them. Julie had made herself scarce, skirting round the side of the building so she wouldn't be seen like something out of one of those spoof spy flicks from the 1960s. Peering round the corner until they'd gone in, an insane curiosity gripping her and causing her to sidle down, to get to a window so she could look inside.

And there they were, in the restaurant/café bit, ordering food and drink. The woman was saying something and smiling, then Jake reacted to that – smiling back at her. Who the hell *was* she? Someone from out of town who'd come to see him? Someone from back where he lived? Someone special perhaps?

Julie wasn't ready in the slightest for the barrage of emotions that flooded her system, chief among them – though she had no reason or right to feel it – being jealousy. Raging jealousy.

She shook her head, breath coming in heavy gasps. *What are you doing?* she asked herself. *What are you actually doing, Jules? You're acting like some fucking crazy stalker or something ... This isn't you. This really isn't you.*

In the first few months after they split, maybe – although even then her pride had prevented her from trailing him to his new home. Fear of seeing ... seeing something like this keeping the impulses at bay. It was why, she realised, he hadn't been near his old house since Greg came along; certainly since he moved in. Too weird, it was too …

*This* was all too weird.

Christ, she didn't even know who this woman was. Could just be a concerned colleague from work or something, who'd come to make sure he was okay. Was making sure he had something to eat, to drink – because, you know, somebody ought to. Somebody who wasn't already attached, who wasn't already *married*.

She needed to get out of there, now. Before someone saw her. Not just Jake, but someone else. Someone with a camera possibly. Their lives were being played out inside a goldfish bowl right now, everything under scrutiny. How long that would go on for, Julie had no idea – it was beginning to tail off at the house, because nothing very interesting was happening (today's news, tomorrow's history and all that) – she'd never had any experience of it. What wouldn't help any of them would be a photo in the papers of her crazy behaviour:

'MOTHER OF MURDERED GIRL CAN'T LEAVE EX-HUBBY ALONE … PEEPING THROUGH WINDOW OF HIS HOTEL AS HE HAS INTIMATE LUNCH WITH NEW LOVE.'

Intimate. Was it intimate? Did it look intimate? Julie risked another quick look. It did appear to be fairly pally.

*None of your business*, she reminded herself. *It's. None. Of. Your. Business.*

Another car pulled up nearby, and that's when she decided to move. To walk away as if nothing had happened, not draw attention to herself. Walk away and then call another cab when she got a suitable distance from the hotel. But instead of doing that, she continued to walk. Up one street and down another, not really knowing where she was going, where she would end up. Not really caring.

It was something she'd very often done when she was younger, following her nose, letting the wind take her where it may.

Something Jake had done as well, he'd often told her … Jake, don't think about Jake back there with …

Something they'd done together on occasion, when things had gone wrong. When they were trying to figure things out … They'd done it a lot when Jordan had announced herself.

Walking, walking. Inevitably, you had to end up somewhere. And, on this day, this Monday, she found herself turning the corner and facing a small, out of the way pub in the middle of nowhere, that obviously serviced the people local to the few streets surrounding it.

A far cry from some of those clubs her daughter used to frequent, it actually looked quite seedy. Looked like somewhere you really shouldn't be unless you knew how to handle yourself.

The Slaughtered Calf, it was called, probably named when this whole town still relied on the meat market. The sign was accompanied by quite a graphic artist's depiction of a baby cow being cut into with a knife (and how that had still been allowed to remain outside was anyone's guess).

Julie had a flash then, a vision of her daughter being stabbed with a similar weapon, her own baby being slaughtered.

It just made her want a drink even more. Nodding to herself, she crossed the road and headed for the drinking hole, pushing on the old wooden doors. The two customers that were inside, an old man in the corner wearing a cap and doing a crossword, a golden retriever laid at his feet, and a youth who didn't even look old enough to be in here, wearing trackies and playing the fruit machine, both looked over.

Seeing nothing of interest, or nothing that might interest *them* at any rate, they went back to their own business. If they recognised her, they didn't show it. The lady behind the bar, and Julie would definitely use the word loosely with her bright blue eyeliner, back-combed hair and ample cleavage on display, eyed her up and down before asking what she wanted. Again, if there was any hint of recognition, she hid it well.

'White wine please,' Julie told her, taking a seat on one of the stools at the bar itself.

'Large or small?' asked the woman, revealing hideously yellow teeth behind the bright pink lipstick.

'Large,' Julie told her. 'Definitely large.'

As it was brought to her, the best this place had to offer – which tasted vaguely of vinegar – Julie thought then again about time. About how much things could change again in the space of a few days (drinking before noon on a Monday morning, for one thing; that was new).

How, just when you thought things couldn't get any worse, they absolutely could. And how they could change, in such a short time.

How they could change so, so much.

# PART TWO

Much has been made of how Redmarket has reinvented itself over recent years. From a market town that relied more or less solely on its trade in meat, to a place known for its leisure industry and buzzing nightlife, the latter in particular. Young people especially flock here of an evening, guaranteed of a great night out with fun and laughter. But there is much to see and do for the entire family, from gyms and leisure centres – which boast state of the art swimming pools and climbing facilities – to cycle paths and visiting local landmarks. These include the market area itself, which is still open on various days (enquire with the local council, whether you wish to buy or sell), some of the oldest public houses in the land which serve a range of delicious real ales and wines, and the local church of the parish. This dates back to almost the founding of Redmarket itself, give or take a few hundred years, though it wasn't converted to the Christian faith until almost 740 AD. It is worth visiting for its stunning stained-glass windows, which depict a fantastic battle between angels and the forces of evil, led by the Devil himself. Some have joked in the past that it is not clear from the artwork in the windows which side is winning ...

# Chapter 15

Redmarket church wasn't that much to look at from the outside.

It was hard to tell what kind of architectural category it belonged to, as it appeared to be a mish-mash of various styles, almost as if different buildings were competing for the same space in different time zones. There were stories that it had been set on fire at several points in its history, and those bits had been rebuilt in the current prevalent style – which would explain the schizophrenic nature of the building. The most talked about feature of the church, however, couldn't be seen very well from the outside at all, but rather was best viewed from inside.

The stained-glass windows which ran the length of the building depicted a furious battle between the forces of Heaven and Hell, culminating with a rectangular showdown at the rear of the church between the Devil and the Archangel Gabriel, giant sword in hand, wings at his back. It was almost as if these warriors were fighting for the souls of the people who made up whatever congregation happened to be inside at the time.

As Jake sat in that space, looking up and around at this particular display (which should have been in widescreen, or deep focus) he couldn't help thinking that they'd definitely lost one soul that day. Or had they? If you believed in the afterlife, then the soul – assuming you'd led a decent enough life – would end up in Heaven anyway. Was no longer inside that body, which itself was encased in wood at the front: yet another box. The only box that actually mattered.

He liked to think Jordan was in paradise or headed there. But at the same time he couldn't help thinking she wasn't at peace yet. Could never be at peace until the truth about what happened was uncovered, whether that involved Bannister – and if you listened to a certain lawyer he knew, it didn't – or someone else. All he knew was that he'd vowed to find her that peace, had promised it to her personally.

Jake could barely believe the funeral had come around so quickly. That time thing again, speeding up and now slowing to a crawl in this place. Every minute like hours as he sat there trying not to look at the coffin they had carried from the hearse, one at each corner: Greg Allaway, his son William, Matt, and finally him. It had been Julie's call, so he'd gone along with her wishes. If he'd been strong enough, though, Jake would have carried it himself, alone, to the front.

She'd been in touch about arrangements a few days ago, after he'd stopped by for his car and found nobody at home. A curt phone call in which she had explained was what happening and where. He'd thought they were getting along better, but obviously not from the frosty tone of her voice.

'Just let me know … I mean, how much I owe for …' He felt so stupid bringing that up, like he was paying his share for a pizza delivery or something. But funerals were an expensive business, and he wanted to feel like he'd contributed.

'I will,' Julie promised him, voice softening but only marginally. 'Do you want to say anything?'

Jake thought about it for a moment or two, then declined. He didn't really feel it was his place, and Julie was getting up to say a few words anyway. She could do it for the both of them. She was always better at expressing herself than him, particularly when it came to the emotional stuff. That's what had got him into trouble in the first place.

The gathering would be small, Julie had told him; just friends and family really. And as Jake glanced around now again – anything to avoid his eyes settling on that coffin – he found he only recognised a few of the people present, all dressed in black or navy (during his latest shop for clothes, he'd picked up a black suit and tie himself). Had he been that out of touch with Jordan's life? He supposed he had ... Grateful to see a few familiar faces in the form of Laura, Becky and Raju at the back, he'd nodded to them and they'd nodded back.

Nearer to the front was the no-less-familiar form of Jules' father, Norman, in his wheelchair, someone from the home he was in accompanying him. The old man caught Jake looking and glared back, those beady pupils beneath bushy eyebrows making him look a bit like a vulture. Their one and only encounter outside while they waited for the black vehicles to arrive (Jake hadn't been invited to be part of that procession, as it had come from the 'family' home), had been less than pleasant.

'Norman,' Jake had said by way of a greeting.

'I'm surprised you had the balls to show up,' the man had wheezed.

He was shocked at first, then remembered just how much Julie's father had hated him. 'I-I ... Jordan was my daughter, Norman. How could I not?'

'You ruined *my* daughter's life, you bastard,' Norman had replied, and even the carer with him – a small but sturdy lady wearing round glasses – had balked at that one. 'And Jordan would still be alive if it wasn't for you!'

Jake had shaken his head, while the carer made noises about getting the old man inside and settling him in, like he was being put to bed or something. There was only one person that was happening to today, permanently, and according to Norman Brent it was all Jake's fault. He should allow for age and whatever form of dementia he had, but there had been no mistaking the anger and rage behind those words. And no mistaking the fact that Julie's father believed every single one of them.

Here, in the church, Jake broke off that gaze – a reminder of those accusations outside. A reminder that he might actually be right, and if Jake had been around …

'*You left her when she needed you the most.*'

And there she was, the person who'd said those words when they'd gone to identify Jordan. Sitting with Greg, who had his arm firmly around her shoulders, squeezing tightly in what Jake supposed was a gesture of support, but came across very much as another 'she's mine' gesture to him. He couldn't help feeling a pang at that, thinking how beautiful she looked in spite of the occasion. On Greg's other side was his son William Allaway who'd come back from university especially to be here. Jake hadn't really talked to him, but the lad looked nothing like his father, which was a tick in the right box. His features were quite soft, almost to the point of feminine, so Jake wondered whether he took more after his late mother than Greg. If so, maybe the young man had more of her in his personality as well. They could but hope.

Jake was on the opposite side to the 'family', which rankled if he was honest but he didn't want to cause a fuss. Not today. He looked over his shoulder, scanned back across the rows behind him and spotted Matt there, head down as if in silent prayer. Jake knew he wouldn't be, it was just that these places had always made his old friend nervous; probably still did. They still hadn't talked to each other since the cells, but Jake knew that he'd arranged for the police to keep the media at bay – and for that he was grateful. Next to Matt was a neat woman, sitting bolt-upright, who could only be his wife. She was wearing very little make-up but was quite attractive in a severe-looking way, hair pulled back so tight it stretched the skin around her eyes. She was, as his old mum would have put it, quite 'prim and proper'.

Not Matt's type at all, but then Jake reminded himself he didn't know the bloke anymore. Not really.

The hall had descended into a hush then, the vicar at the front in his dog collar rising to take his place at the pulpit. Rosy-cheeked, with mad white hair, he reminded Jake of that priest from the Nineties sitcom, but when he spoke it was the exact opposite of what you were expecting: a soft voice filled with a great gentleness.

'We are gathered here today to pay our respects to Jordan Abigail Radcliffe,' he began. Abigail after Julie's mother. 'We will start, though, by singing the first hymn on your sheet: "Abide with Me".'

Everyone got to their feet and when the organ cranked up, the smattering of people assembled did their best to get through to the end. Jake could feel himself welling up, having kept his tears under control till that moment. Lines like, 'When other helpers fail and comforts flee. Help of the helpless, oh, abide with me ...' certainly did not help. Other helpers, the people who should have been helping Jordan.

Him. That meant him.

But then he chastised himself. How selfish to be thinking of that on Jordan's day, to be pitying himself. She was the one who should be pitied, her whole life ahead of her and it had been cut short.

* * *

For Julie, most of the day so far – and much of the service – had gone by in a bit of blur. Readings, hymns, though she did stop to listen as the vicar read out the poem they'd chosen: '"God looked around his garden and found an empty place. He then looked down upon the earth, and saw your tired face. He put his arms around you. And lifted you to rest".'

That would be nice to think, wouldn't it? Jordan, a tired Jordan, now up there at rest. At peace. Which was more than could be said for anyone down here. Her eyes flicked over again to Jake, who'd had to sit on the opposite side to them, and she felt a pang of guilt at that. He should have been on this side; he was Jordan's dad after all. Regardless of everything that had happened, regardless of how furious she'd been since she'd seen him at the hotel.

Furious, bitter … jealous (*no, don't say that, especially not today*). But mainly furious. She hadn't been able to keep it from her voice when she called to tell him what was happening, and it had clouded her decisions about where people should be during the service. The fact was, she needed those closest to her around her, people like Greg and his son; the family she'd made for herself, that she'd *had* to make. And her own dad, her dear sweet dad, who she'd inflicted so much heartache upon, but had been there for her in the end. People she could rely on.

Jake couldn't even be relied on to get up and say something at his own daughter's funeral. Carry her, yes, but not that. Had dodged even that responsibility. She'd do it herself, Julie had told him: the eulogy. One of them should – and being angry at Jake had carried her through so far. Forced Julie to steel herself for the task. Yet, now the time was here, she wasn't sure she could do it at all. She was in bits, frankly, hadn't realised it but had got nearer and nearer to Greg until she'd practically collapsed into him. He was patting her shoulder, doing his best to console her, but nodding towards the front where she needed to be.

*No … I can't! I just …*

Jake was looking around at her, probably waiting for Julie to get up and get on with it, just like everyone else was. She fixed him with a pleading stare, hoping against hope that silent communication they used to share was still working, that she realised what she was trying to say to him. *Help.* If ever you were going to do something, then now would be the time. Please.

Jake gave a small shake of the head, showing that he knew exactly what she wanted. But still she stared, her eyes insisting.

He closed his own, took a deep breath, and rose. Began to walk to the front. Jake glanced back at Julie, who mouthed a 'thank you'. Greg was more vocal, half-rising and saying: 'Hey, what do you—' before Julie placed a hand on his chest to silence him, shaking her own head. Whispering that this was what she wanted.

Swallowing, and still trying not to look at the coffin, Jake made his way across to the pulpit where the vicar was hastily explaining there had been a change of plan. 'To talk about their daughter, in place of Julie Radcliffe' – she felt Greg stiffen at that – 'her father, Jacob.'

He nodded his thanks to the holy man, taking his place. As she watched, wiping away the tears in her eyes, Jake gazed out over the heads of those people. He was probably wondering what to say, wouldn't have had time to prepare anything at all. And he did so hate public speaking; it was one of the reasons he worked behind the camera instead of standing in front of it like some of his colleagues did day after day. Julie felt his confusion, his pain. Jake hadn't even delivered the eulogy at his own mum's funeral, because he couldn't face it. Yet here he was, doing this for her. Doing it for Jordan. He looked like he wanted to throw up, to just run from there.

Run, like he had done the last time things had got tough. When he should have stayed and fought for his family, tried to protect Jordan when it still meant something ... Julie shook her head, pushing those thoughts aside. Now really wasn't the time.

Then he looked like he'd spotted someone at the back, and his demeanour changed instantly. He suddenly appeared stronger, as if he was pulling himself together. Doing what she hadn't been able to. Julie lifted herself a little and traced his gaze. That was when she saw her, the woman from the hotel.

What was *she* doing here? Clearly Jake had invited her, had needed support of his own and knew it wouldn't come from her family. A friend, here to give him strength, or more? Why did that matter, why did she still care?

Julie watched as *they* locked eyes now, and the woman nodded in a way that said: 'You got this.'

Jake cleared his throat and Julie faced forwards again, leaning into Greg once more, holding on to him even tighter. 'I ...' Jake began, then stopped when his voice echoed throughout that chamber. It did sound strange, even to her. 'I'm not very good at this,' he admitted, then seemed to realise what he'd just said. Good at what? Giving speeches at funerals? Who was? Ghouls? *Nobody* enjoyed doing this, you just had to suck it up. *Yeah, right, like you did?* Julie said to herself. 'Sorry ... It's ... I'm finding this particularly hard because, well, regardless of what you've seen in the papers, on the news, I wasn't the best dad I could have been to Jordan. I-I think I used to be, I mean I did a pretty good job of it when she was little. But ... That is, in the last few years we've been ... we've not really had that much to do with each other. The truth is we had an argument, a big argument. We'd been rubbing each other up the wrong way for a while and the whole thing just ...' Jake looked around at people's faces, and Julie did too. Some appeared shocked, others just intrigued. 'I don't know if this is the right place to talk about all this, probably not. I think somewhere Jordan's laughing at her old man for making a pig's ear of it.'

That got a bit of a nervous chuckle, so Jake carried on. 'I think part of me really didn't want to let go, to see her grow up, y'know? It must have driven her mad. But she was always my little girl. My little ...' Tears were welling in Jake's eyes, and he paused to wipe them away before continuing. 'I think that was the problem, but it was also what was special about our relationship. In spite of all the words that were said, the hurtful things on both sides neither of us really meant – and don't matter anyway now – the love was still there. She was my daughter, and I was her dad. I should have been there for her, but I failed. I chose the easy option, walked away, because it's what I thought she wanted. But I didn't know, I never asked her. I just assumed it was easier for her, as well. Probably wasn't, not having your dad around ... I should know all about that.

'That's why I need to thank Jules ... Julie, who *was* around. Who was there for Jordan. Thank Christ someone was.' He gave the vicar a sideways glance. 'Sorry, didn't mean to ...' The holy man nodded. 'I just wish that ... Well, it doesn't matter. It's too late now. I just hope Jordan didn't suffer too much, and that she knows she was loved by everyone here. Especially by her mum. And I hope she knows I love her too, that I never stopped loving her. I really didn't. I ... I think that's all I ... Thank you.' Jake got down off the pulpit, almost tripping as he did so.

He made his way back to his seat, but caught Julie's eye as he did so. She was in floods of tears, her heart full, but smiling at him.

A genuine smile of thanks.

\* \* \*

Well, that had been one of the hardest things he'd ever had to do.

But actually, he was glad he'd been able to. Not glad his ex-wife was so devastated, but thankful he'd been given the opportunity to say all that. Julie looked like she was glad as well, though Greg was not smiling at all. However, when Jake glanced over at the back he saw Sam smiling, tears in her own eyes. She nodded; he'd done okay.

He was so glad he'd invited her, asked her when they'd last seen each other – a bite to eat over dinner that time, and he'd paid. Ostensibly to talk about how they'd got on with the case, but at the same time company for each other. Two lonely people staving that off for a little while. He'd made sure her name had been left with the police on guard, not a member of the press but legally connected with the case. And a friend.

Friends and family, right?

She'd definitely got him through it, and for that Jake couldn't thank Sam enough.

The ending of the ceremony seemed to rush by then, and before he knew it he was being called on once more to heft the box. To carry his girl through the graveyard of tombstones that looked like ragged teeth, the odd angel looking on in despair. To the hole they'd dug out the back, to plant her in the ground; hidden away like she'd done herself with so many things.

More words at the graveside from the vicar. 'Ashes to ashes, dust to dust', then handfuls of dirt being thrown onto the coffin which had been lowered into that space. Jake had joined Sam by the graveside, which drew a few looks from people – in particular Julie. But she had Greg and William with her, why shouldn't he have someone to lean on too?

*Someone you hardly even know*, he reminded himself, but that didn't matter today. He was glad to have her there and no mistake.

Most of the assembled crowd were moving away though now, even members of the family: Norman being wheeled down the grass, his carer helped by Greg.

'You're going to come to the wake?' Jake said to Sam, drying more tears that had been shed during the actual burial.

'I'm not so sure that's a good idea,' she told him. 'Even without my legendary powers of people reading, I think I can work out how your ex-wife feels about me.'

'Jules?' said Jake. 'But why should she—'

'You really don't know anything about women, do you?' Sam stated.

'But there's nothing to—' Sam kissed him on the cheek and began to move away. It was only then that Jake saw it, the figure standing on the other side of the graveyard. How he'd slipped past the cordon, Jake had no idea, but there he was, standing as large as life – larger even – and staring across at where the mourners had been. 'What the hell ...'

Sam paused, looking too. Then bristled. 'Jake. Now don't do

162

anything stupid.' Anything *else* was the inference. Like starting up where he'd left off with Drummond on the day he'd put his only daughter in the ground.

Jake made to move in his direction. 'I'm just going to see what he thinks he's playing at.'

'Please don't,' said Sam. 'It's not worth it.'

But Jake was already moving, barely felt the hand on his arm as he did so. Assumed it was Sam's, until it held him fast, stopped him in his tracks. He turned, to see Matt standing beside him. 'You should listen to the lady, Jake,' said the policeman. 'She knows what she's talking about.'

Jake looked from Matt, back across at the figure. 'But he's just …'

Matt's grip tightened. 'Let me sort it out.' It was what the cops had been saying all along, what Channing said practically on a loop so often it should have been his mantra. 'I'll get in touch with a few of the boys, they'll shift him.' Jake took in his friend again. 'I promise.'

He sighed, looked down at the hole in the ground and nodded. Saw the sense of what Matt and Sam were saying. Not today, he needed to leave it today.

'Come on,' said his friend, and Jake went with them. Down towards the church where the rest of the mourners were waiting.

# Chapter 16

The wake was held at a community centre, just across the road from Redmarket church.

An array of buffet food had been laid on, more than any of them could eat in a lifetime: a sea of sausage rolls and sandwiches, a variety of vol-au-vents, a deluge of desserts. But Jake didn't have any appetite at all.

Sam had stayed a few minutes, just to make sure he went there, Jake guessed, and didn't go tearing off after Drummond. But then she made her excuses and left. 'Your ex is giving me the evils,' she told Jake. 'Better if I make myself scarce.' She was probably right, but he had to say he missed her now she was gone.

At least Norman had gone too, headed back to the home because he was getting tired apparently. Sick and tired of being around Jake more like. He'd watched as Julie hugged the man, but he didn't really make any effort to hug her back. Norman had never been the most demonstrative of people in all the time Jake had known him, not with his daughter, not even with his granddaughter as such. There was as much bad blood with those two as there had been with him and Jordan, both down to him at the end of the day. He'd been the cause of so many of this family's problems.

Over the course of the afternoon, he'd made small talk with a few people, but not for more than a few minutes at a time. What did they want from him? He barely knew most of them. Greg had steered clear, but William made a point of coming over to talk to Jake. 'That was a very moving speech, Mr Radcliffe,' he told him. 'I'm sure Jordan would have been proud of you. She was a lovely girl.'

'Thank you,' said Jake. 'Appreciate it.'

When William had wandered off, heading in the direction of Jordan's friends to chat to them, Julie came over and joined him. 'Nice lad,' he told her.

'He is,' she said. 'Jordan and him were pretty close when he lived at home.'

Jake nodded.

'He's quite a sensitive soul, I think he liked having someone there to talk to if he had a problem or whatever.'

'Right,' said Jake, suddenly quite envious of that closeness they'd shared. 'And we're sure he's Greg's, are we?'

Julie looked at him, horrified, but couldn't help a twitch of the mouth that he was sure would have broken into a grin if she hadn't been fighting it. 'Jake, that's an awful thing to say.'

'Well ...' was the only reply he could muster. He wanted to say so much more, about Greg – about her and Greg – but held back. He'd need a lot more than the tea and coffee on offer here before he got into all that. Julie probably would have done, too.

'You just don't know him, that's all,' Julie said finally.

'I don't want to,' Jake replied honestly. When she pulled a face, he said, 'Jules, it's not like me and him are likely to be best friends, are we? That's never going to happen. Why would you even *want* it to?'

She remained silent for a moment, then said, 'So, are you going to tell me who your new friend is?'

The shift in topic was so sudden he had to think for a second who she was talking about. 'Sam, you mean?'

Julie nodded. 'If that's her name.'

'She's ...' Jake realised he didn't know what to say about her, how to describe her – or broach the subject of what she did for a living. Who she was representing. So instead he simply said: 'We're just ... There's nothing going on.'

Julie pursed her lips. 'I wasn't asking, Jake.'

She so blatantly had been – why else would she have brought it up? If there was one person Jake knew in the whole world it was Jules. He knew when she was jealous as well, like right now – and especially after Sam had flagged it. Was there a part of him that quite enjoyed that, seeing her envious of another woman? He shook away the thoughts; again, not today. 'Of course not,' he said, and meant it, though it came across as a veiled accusation.

'She's pretty,' Julie said then. 'You should ... It's about time you had someone in your life, Jake. Moved on. I mean, I've got Greg.'

Greg again. Fucking Greg. Jake paused, thought about those words, and an image of the bedroom back at his old home flashed through his mind. The bile started to rise and he pushed it back down, along with the unwelcome images.

Buried them ...

Buried.

'Yeah,' he said. 'You've got Greg.' And good luck with *that*. 'She's ... Sam's involved in the case,' he told her after another uncomfortable silence.

'Jordan's case?' Julie said, surprised.

'Yes,' he told her. Who else's? What other case actually mattered? But he was starting to regret having said anything at all about it.

'In what capacity?' asked Julie.

'She ...' If he didn't tell her, he'd look like he was hiding things (*you* are *hiding things, things that Jordan hid first*). But if he did ... 'Sam's Bobby Bannister's lawyer.'

166

A look of pure amazement passed across Julie's face. If she'd been expecting anything, it wasn't that. 'What?'

'You heard me.' Jake was suddenly annoyed and didn't even know why. The fact that Julie had been encouraging him to go off into the sunset with Sam? Or that he now had to defend her, because apparently it was some sort of betrayal? As if those thoughts hadn't crossed his mind as well.

'But ... so why are you ...' Julie shook her head. 'I really don't understand you, Jake. I'm not sure I ever did.'

'Don't be silly,' he said, then regretted it immediately.

'*Silly?* I'm silly now, am I?' She touched her chest, voice rising. 'I'm not the one who's seeing our daughter's murderer's lawyer.'

'I'm not ... Jules, *please*. She's trying to help.'

'I'll bet,' she snapped. 'Helping herself to inside information ... and whatever else. She should be reported.'

'Julie, it's not like that.'

'Jake, can't you see when someone's playing you. Whatever you say to her she'll twist it, use it to try and get Bobby off.'

'How exactly is she going to do that? The police have a cast-iron case, Jules.'

She shook her head. 'I just don't ...'

He placed a hand on her arm and she jumped a little. 'I haven't said anything to her, I promise. I wouldn't do that. If anything, it's the other way round. I'm trying to get to the bottom of all this, and she's helping me.' Julie's breathing was slowing down. 'I ... You're wrong, you know.'

'About what?'

'You've always known me, Jules. You've always *got* me. You're probably the only person who ever did.'

She looked into his eyes now, and suddenly the years were forgotten; the pain and misery were forgotten. Then a voice cut into the moment:

'What's all the shouting about? You all right, Julie?' Greg. Fucking Greg again. Standing next to his wife, slipping his arm around her waist – a movement that forced Jake to drop his hand from her arm.

She nodded, looking down, not looking at either Jake or Greg. 'I'm fine.'

'Didn't look fine,' Greg grunted.

'She *said* she was fine,' Jake told him.

Greg was raising his finger. 'Because if you're causing trouble again, I'll—'

'You'll what?' Jake took a step closer to the man, then suddenly there was another figure present.

'Fellas, let's calm things down, shall we?' Matt, putting himself between them. 'Remember where you are.'

'Well, tell him then,' sniped Greg, like he'd just been hauled up in front of the headmaster.

'I'm telling *both* of you,' said the policeman.

'Greg, come on,' said Julie, pulling him away from the scene. 'Have some food.' Jake was willing to bet it wasn't the first time she'd distracted him with that line, judging from his gut. Greg let himself be led over to the buffet but didn't take his arm from around her waist.

'Prick,' said Jake.

'Yeah, well …' Matt shook his head. 'That's twice in one day, got to be a record for you, hasn't it? You're going the right way to get banged up again.'

Reminded of the last time he'd actually spoken with his friend, Jake rubbed his chin and said, 'Look, I'm glad you're here. I wanted to say, y'know, sorry. For y'know …'

Matt flapped his hand, the blokeish apology accepted. 'Let's just forget about it, shall we?' He paused, then said, 'So, you and Sam Ferrara, eh?'

'Don't you start!' Jake muttered.

'I'm sorry, I'm sorry.' Matt clapped him on the arm. 'How're you holding up, anyway, mate?'

Jake shrugged. 'To be honest, I'm not all that sure.'

'You look to me like someone who could use a drink,' Matt told him, then nodded at the teapots and jugs on the table. 'A *real* drink. Can't say that I blame you.'

And there was he thinking Julie knew him better than anyone. 'Definitely,' admitted Jake.

'I've got the day off tomorrow, so what say we have a few jars tonight? We can drink to Jordan's memory.'

'That sounds ...' Jake peered across the room to where Matt's wife was talking to a woman with a blue-rinse. 'What about ... I don't want to cause any trouble at home.'

'Katherine'll understand. I'll square it away with her.' The way Matt spoke, it sounded like he could use the drink just as much as Jake.

'All right,' said Jake, returning the clap on the arm. 'You're on. Thanks.'

'My pleasure.' Matt made to walk off in the direction of his wife, no doubt to do that squaring away he was talking about, but stopped after a couple of steps and turned back. 'Oh, and do me a favour, will you?'

'What's that?' asked Jake.

'Try not to get into any fights between now and then.'

Jake hung his head. 'I think I can just about manage that.'

Matt smiled, then left him alone. Which was how he'd felt most of the day actually, alone, even when people had been around. Even with Sam there. It was how he'd felt for most of the last couple of weeks ...

Alone with his thoughts. Thoughts about Jordan.

Jake decided to try a sausage roll or two, see if they really were a good distraction.

# Chapter 17

It probably wasn't a good use of police resources, and if he found out Channing would give him another bollocking, but for once Matt really didn't give a shit.

After the funeral he asked Linda Fergusson if she'd swing by his house in a pool car and give him a lift to Jake's hotel, and from there to the pub. She'd been more than happy to, on her way home from dealing with a case of domestic abuse.

'How was the funeral?' she'd asked him as he got in. Linda had been keeping tabs on the case since she'd finished up at the Allaway residence. Or, more accurately, Greg Allaway had 'asked' her to leave.

'Had to stop Jake from starting a fight at the wake,' Matt told her.

'Let me guess, the new husband?'

'Yep.'

'Guy's a total prick,' she stated.

'Funny, that's exactly what Jake said.'

'How I've never been called out to a domestic at that place, I'll never know,' she said, glancing over.

'Julie seems happy with him,' Matt said, but he didn't know if he was trying to convince Linda or himself.

'Hmm,' was her only reply.

Jake was waiting outside the hotel, having changed into jeans, a maroon jumper and his jacket. 'Hop in,' Matt called through the passenger window he'd opened a crack. 'You remember Linda.'

'Hello again,' said Jake as he got into the back, but Matt could see he was trying not to think about the last time he'd seen the FLO.

'We were just discussing your favourite person in the world,' Matt told him, twisting round in the seat. When Jake looked confused, he said, 'Greg.'

'Oh,' breathed out Jake wearily. 'Him.'

'Jesus, whatever does she see in that guy?' asked Matt.

'She says he's different when they're on their own.'

'I bet he's not,' said Linda, pulling out into traffic. 'I've seen his type before. They're *never* different.'

'That's comforting,' Jake said to her.

'I ... Oh, I'm sorry. I didn't mean to ...'

'It's okay,' Jake assured her. 'Julie's a grown woman. She makes her own decisions, her own choices.'

'You'd be surprised how many grown women make the wrong ones,' Linda said sadly.

Matt thumbed across at their driver. 'Just come from a household where the partner's abusive.'

'Right,' said Jake, then lapsed into silence. Matt supposed there was nothing really to say to that.

'But anyway, I don't want to spoil your day ...' Linda closed her eyes and opened them again, remembering what they'd been doing earlier, where they'd been. 'Oh shit ... I ... I'm sorry ... I meant your evening.' She looked across at Matt, embarrassed, then flashed Jake an apologetic smile. 'I'm not usually this ... I'll shut up now.'

'It's okay,' Jake repeated. 'Really.'

She let out a sigh of relief. 'So, where am I taking you two gents?'

171

Matt directed her to a place a little out of town, somewhere a bit quieter than Redmarket itself and in the direction of where Linda lived so he wasn't putting her out too much.

'Oh yes,' she said when Matt told her the name of the establishment, The Peacock. 'Pretty new, that place. Nice family pub …' Linda stopped again, probably thinking she'd put her foot in it once more – Jake no longer had a family to speak of – then carried swiftly on, hoping nobody had noticed. 'They do good food in there. Their steak and ale pie is gorgeous.'

'I'll bear that in mind,' said Matt, who'd only been there a couple of times himself and never to eat; one of those places that was all pine and red velvet, and way too clean to have been around for long. From the back he heard Jake's stomach rumbling. 'I think we have one vote for it.'

'Yeah, sorry about that. I couldn't really face much of the food this afternoon,' Jake said. Another awkward silence followed, and Matt was glad when they finally pulled up at their destination.

'Here we are, then,' said Linda.

'Thanks again. I owe you one,' Matt told her.

'I'll hold you to that,' she replied with a smile. 'Have a nice … I mean enjoy your …' Linda gave up trying to reword it and just said goodbye, waving to them as they got out.

'She seems nice,' Jake said to Matt once she was gone.

'Yeah, she is.'

'There's not anything …' Jake let the sentence hang in the air and it took Matt a second to realise what he was trying to say.

'What, me and Linda? God, no. Not that she's not … I mean she's great, but … I'm happily married, thanks.'

Jake nodded. 'Just asking.'

'She is single, though,' Matt added.

His friend held up his hands. 'Cheers, but I'm good. Bad enough my ex is trying to pair me up.'

'You could probably do worse than Sam,' Matt told him, as they made their way to the door. 'Bit of a livewire, mind.'

172

'And Bannister's lawyer,' Jake reminded Matt.

'Yeah. But you two have been hanging out, right?'

'Sort of,' Jake admitted. 'It's complicated.'

'Always is, mate. Always is …'

'But we're definitely just friends.'

He held the door open for Jake to go inside first. 'Katherine works for her firm, you know.'

'Your wife?'

Matt nodded. 'Does their accounting and such.'

'And was she, y'know, okay with you coming out tonight?'

'Yeah, sure,' he answered, recalling the brief conversation about it earlier on. Katherine had been totally fine with it, saying that she had some work to catch up on anyway. Was she even bothered these days whether he was around or not? Depended on if the gutters needed doing, he supposed. What was that he'd been saying about being happily married again? He thought about Linda then, about what Jake had been asking … Wasn't as if it hadn't crossed his mind, was it? And was there more than just a friendship vibe there? Was that what Jake had been picking up on? It didn't seem to bother Katherine in the slightest that she'd been the one collecting him, but then would she even notice if Linda had turned up stark naked at the front door? 'She always is.'

'*She makes her own decisions.*'

'*You'd be surprised how many grown women make the wrong ones …*'

Men too. He wouldn't do that anyway, sacrifice his marriage, his own family just for a fling with Linda – not after everything.

*Julie, though. You might sacrifice it all for Julie …* Matt hated himself for even thinking that, on today of all days. And it wasn't true – his family was everything to him. He felt bad now for those thoughts about Jake's ex.

Jake, who'd been so quick to remind him that Julie didn't think of him that way – never had. Jake, who'd had it all and thrown

173

it away. And Greg, that knobhead of a man she'd chosen after Jake had left ...

He realised he was miles away, that his friend was actually speaking to him now they were at the bar. 'What ... Sorry?'

'I said what would you like?'

Matt flapped his hand again, trying to wipe the guilty look from his face; he'd always been quite good at doing that. 'First round's on me. It was my idea after all.' He clapped his hands together. 'So, what'll it be?'

* * *

It was almost last orders before Matt even looked at the clock on the wall.

They'd found a corner booth and had been steadily drinking for nearly four hours, sampling the finest real ale and spirits The Peacock had to offer. Relaxing in each other's company again, the years falling away. They'd even tried out those pies Linda had so highly recommended, which were as good as she'd claimed, they'd had to admit.

Matt had started out by asking if Jake's job were okay with the time he was taking off.

'Yeah, they said take as much time as I need here. I think they reckon they owe me; they've certainly had enough airtime out of me lately. Besides, I was due some leave. I can be a bit of a workaholic.'

Matt could understand that; just from chatting to him, he could tell there didn't seem to be much else in his friend's life.

'I was planning on spending it working on my short film.'

'Film?' asked Matt.

'Yeah, it's nothing much.' Jake went on to tell him the details of it, the subject matter about young people, the acting students he was going to use for it. His eyes lit up when he talked about it all, but also grew sad again when the link was made to his own situation. Matt had to wonder whether he was doing it to try and figure out the youth of today, or even support them in some way. What a pity he hadn't been able to do that sooner, then he might still have been on speaking terms with his daughter and his marriage might not have fallen apart.

'I expect you'll be heading back soon, though. It's all over here bar the shouting ... and the trial.'

'Yeah, I expect,' said Jake, but didn't sound convinced. Matt let it drop though.

A match on the TV in the background gave them a chance to change the subject to playing football themselves when they were kids. It seemed a cliché now, but the whole 'jumpers for goalposts' and finding patches of waste ground for a kick around really was how it had been.

'Do you remember, there used to be that really gangly kid who hung around ... what the hell was his name?' said Matt.

'Robson ... Robinson?' Jake suggested.

'We always stuck him in goal because he used to trip over his feet if he was running, would always end up hurting himself.'

'Mind you,' said Jake, draining what was left of his pint at the time, 'he was pretty bloody good as a goalie, wasn't he? Could get to the ball wherever you kicked it. No wonder we never really scored many. Whatever happened to him?'

Matt shrugged. 'Probably ended up playing professionally or something.'

Jake chuckled and it was nice to see. Nice to be able to cheer his friend up, to lighten what had probably been one of the blackest days of his entire life.

'We were always trying to get Jules to be the crowd, stand on the sidelines and cheer us on,' Jake said.

'But she just wanted to play. Bit of a tomboy when all was said and done, wasn't she?'

Jake nodded and smiled, recalling the days when everything had been so simple. When they didn't have a care in the world outside of saving spending money for sweets (or nicking them, Matt reminded him at one point), playing out till the sun went down.

'Even sometimes after that,' said Matt. 'I remember your mum having to come and drag you back home a few times.'

'It seemed safer back then somehow,' Jake said.

'Yeah ...' Matt had changed the subject again before it got too maudlin. 'Hey, do you remember that really hot summer? Not sure what year it was, but people were passing out in the class-rooms at school, during exams.'

'Oh, right!' said Jake. 'I do ... I lost my virginity that year!' he said with a laugh.

'What? You never told me that!'

'Why would I?'

'To show off, why else?' said Matt with a grin.

'Yeah, well ... some things are kind of private, aren't they?'

'I guess they are.' Matt tried not to think about who Jake had lost it with, Jake and Julie together that summer and what they'd got up to behind his back. Hiding things ... A time when he'd thought he still stood a chance with her, when they were the Three Musketeers, or Amigos or whatever, Jake had snuck in there first.

*No, she only ever thought of you as a friend, remember?* He'd known it all along, but had kidded himself. Hadn't stopped him being jealous when he found out, of course. Didn't stop him feeling jealous now. Stupid, because it was so long ago, and things were different today; a lot of water under the bridge and all that. He also remembered feeling like it was a kind of judgement on them, that it served them right when Julie had fallen for Jordan. All the trouble it had caused ... But they'd come through it stronger than ever. Built a family together and been happy for a long time (*happier than* you've *ever been?*).

Knowing all that had been ripped apart didn't give Matt any pleasure. It just made him sad, felt like such ... such a waste.

'If I remember rightly, though, you had a bit of thing with that twin.'

Matt came back to the here and now, but had no idea what Jake was talking about. 'Twin?'

'You remember, she had a brother who was always looking out for her. Helen, I think her name was ... Yeah, Helen and Carl.'

'Oh bloody hell, yes. I remember her now! We never had a thing, though.'

Jake frowned. 'Didn't you? I could've sworn ...'

'She liked *me*, I think. But you could never get her away from Carl. And he was a big bugger, I remember that. I remember him chasing me once until I lost him down by the canal. She's probably living somewhere with him now, and he's still seeing off the potentials. Poor cow.'

'God,' said Jake. 'Funny how things turn out, isn't it?'

'Yeah,' Matt agreed.

'I mean, I never would've pegged you for the force. Far too shady a character.' Jake smirked.

'And I never would've thought you'd be the next Steven Spielberg, yet here we are.' Matt raised his glass. 'To unexpected outcomes.'

Jake raised his own drink and chinked it against Matt's. 'To unexpected ...' The smile fell from his face. Once again the spectre of why he was back here had reared its head. The unexpected outcome of his daughter's death. Maybe this hadn't been such a good idea, after all.

Matt went up to buy more drinks, clapping his friend on the shoulder as he passed by. When he returned, he had with him two large glasses of whiskey with ice. He sat down and raised his glass again. 'I said we'd toast Jordan's memory, so ...'

Jake nodded, his eyes watering as he clinked for a second time. 'Cheers mate.' He knocked back the drink, then got up to buy another. They continued with the spirits, only now the topic moved back to the case, the investigation into Jordan's death – not that there seemed to be one anymore.

'It's like I said, all over bar the shouting,' Matt told him, slurring slightly and sipping the fiery liquid he had in his hand. 'Don't worry, Bobby will be going down for this for a long time.'

'Sam ... Sam thinks he's innocent,' Jake told him, slurring himself.

Matt flapped a hand again. 'Nah. We got him bang to rights.' He narrowed one eye and looked at his friend. 'And what do you think? You're the one who went for him when you saw him. Don't tell me you think he's innocent, too?'

'I ... I ...' Jake shook his head. 'It's just that she seems so sure, in spite of everything. In spite of what I read.'

'Yeah, well. Maybe she's got a thing for younger men,' Matt offered, and noted the way Jake bristled at that. *Definitely just friends, my arse*, he thought to himself. 'You should stick with your first instincts, not let other people get you turned around.'

'I am.'

'Hold on, hold on ...' Matt raised his hand, realising he'd missed an important part of the conversation. 'Back up a bit. You said "in spite of what I read". What do you mean? In the papers or whatever?'

Jake looked sideways, sheepishly. In fact, he looked anywhere but at his friend, and didn't say a thing.

'It's not Sam's notes, because she doesn't think Bobby's guilty. So, come on ... Where did you read something about him, Jake?'

Silence again.

'Is it the same place those numbers came from?' asked Matt. He might not have intended to join the force, had surprised his friend by doing so, but he was a detective after all. 'Channing was going on about those for ages after we brought you in. Like a dog with a bone. Where did you get them from, Jake?'

He looked up then. 'I ... I found Jordan's diary, Matt.'

'What?' His eyes went wide then. 'But ... but our people checked her room, they would've—'

'She hid it. She hid it really well.'

'Fuck,' was all Matt could manage.

'Yeah ... that.'

'But you can't ... Why haven't you told anyone about this?' He leaned back on his seat in the booth. 'You can't ... Jake, do you realise how much trouble you'd be in if—'

'Please,' said Jake. 'You can't say anything about this. It's ... the diary's kind of private.'

'Of course it's *private*, it's a diary!' Matt couldn't believe what he was hearing. 'Does Julie know about it?'

Jake gave a shake of the head. 'And I'd rather she didn't. Not yet. I know it was wrong to take it, but ... Look, I've been getting to know her in those pages. That might not make much sense to you, but—'

'It makes all the sense in the world,' Matt told him. 'Doesn't stop it from being highly illegal.' He knocked back his drink in one, another double. Maybe he could just keep on drinking until he forgot that Jake had told him this. 'And there's stuff in there that points towards Bobby in the run-up to the attack?'

Jake nodded. 'She says she's frightened of him, his mood swings. He was also quite jealous of other guys apparently.'

'Holy shit!' Matt wiped a hand down his face. 'Jake, you have to turn that in.'

'I ... I can't. There's other stuff in there, Jordan wouldn't—'

'We can say you just found it, or you were scared to hand it in because you took it without thinking.'

'I'm not *scared* to,' Jake told him, lip jutting out.

'You're not thinking clearly, you weren't when you took it. Grief can do strange things.'

'Matt, please don't tell anyone about this. I need to work through it on my own.' His hands were clasped together, almost like he was praying to his old friend.

'I can't believe you're asking me to do that … No, wait, I can. You asked me to put you within strangling distance of Bobby Bannister, didn't you?'

'And you did it,' Jake reminded him.

'For you!' Matt said, jabbing his finger across the table. 'But this is too … It's evidence, Jake.'

'You said yourself, it's all over bar the shouting. It's not like anyone needs this to see him go down.' Jake sighed.

Which was technically true. They had everything they needed to put Bobby away for a long, long time. Put him inside where he'd never see the light of day again; the diary would just make the whole thing a lot … cleaner. It was motive, pure and simple – why couldn't Jake see that? 'That's really not the point. There'd be no way Sam could argue reasonable doubt if we had that on record.'

Jake frowned. He obviously hadn't considered that. 'And do you think she could get him off on reasonable doubt?'

Matt opened his mouth, then closed it again. Shook his head, answering honestly: 'No. Not a chance. But that's—'

'Not the point. Yeah, I know. Look, I wish I could make you understand …'

Understand what? How crazy he was acting and had been acting since all this began? Matt actually, really did. Was trying to at any rate. People could go a little nuts sometimes, they just needed the right trigger. And he was trying to help his friend as best he could. But there were limits, there had to be. He was a policeman for heaven's sakes – there were enough compromises already on the force for his liking. Too much looking the other way, too many sacrifices …

That was when he looked up and noticed the time, when the bell for last orders went. 'Let me get us one more, for the road,' Jake insisted.

Matt let out another long breath, but nodded. He knew Jake was only trying to stall, to get him to agree to say nothing about this. Even the drink felt like a bribe now, instead of how it was probably meant. He accepted it anyway, drinking half practically straight away. 'We'd better think about ordering a taxi soon,' said Matt. 'They get booked up, and I'm not dragging Linda out of her bed to run us back again.'

'Wasn't expecting it.'

Matt knew he wasn't, didn't know why he'd said it. 'So …'

'So …' Jake threw back at him. 'What are you going to do?'

'I don't know yet. I really don't.'

'Look, just give me a little more time,' Jake said.

'To do what?'

'It's … Matt, just give me a bit of time. That's all I ask. Then I promise I'll do the right thing. You can forget I ever told you in the first place, nobody would ever know.'

'Apart from me.'

'Yeah, apart from you.' Jake looked sad about that; he knew what he was asking. How big the favour was … again.

Matt finished his double and got out his phone – started to punch in the numbers. He saw Jake shift about, looked like he was about to say something when Matt spoke up: 'Hi, could I order a taxi, please. The Peacock …' The person at the other end queried where it was. 'Yep, that's the one,' Matt told him.

Jake finished up with his whiskey, too, then followed Matt as he headed for the door to wait outside. The air was chilly, sobering up the DC a little as he stood there, rocking back and forth on the balls of his feet, hands shoved into the pockets of the jacket he'd tugged on. If he remembered rightly, he had a bottle of brandy at home in one of the cupboards. He might just continue with this session at home, on his own. Katherine would probably be in bed when he got back anyway; she had work in the morning.

His friend stepped forward at that point, looked like he was about to say something when the taxi crested the hill and made its way towards them, stopping right outside the pub.

181

The driver, wearing a flat cap, opened his door and half-climbed onto the roof to shout over the top of the car. 'Newcomb?'

'That's us,' Matt answered, getting into the front and leaving the back for Jake – same as he had on the way here. He made conversation with the driver on the journey back to the hotel, various topics including the match that had been on in the pub ('They was robbed tonight, I tell you … robbed.') and, eventually, events in the city of late ('I told our girl, you want to stay in for a while. Getting too dangerous to be out at night lately. Getting as bad as that there Graffitiland over in Granfield, it is …').

Every now and again, Matt's eyes would flick over to the rear-view, which threw back a reflection of Jake in the back, slumped in the corner, staring out of the window.

'It's the parents I feel sorry for,' the cabbie was continuing. 'I mean, young people they don't see the danger, do they. The parents are the ones who end up suffering when all's said and done. Don't ya think?'

'Hmm? Oh, yeah,' answered Matt, still staring at his friend in the back. 'Definitely.' The cabbie had obviously not recognised Jake, one of the very parents he was talking about.

Then, abruptly, the vehicle halted and they were at Jake's hotel. 'Here we go then, squire.'

'I'm staying on, need to get to Hallow Crescent – on the Bradbury estate, if that's okay?'

'Sure,' said the man, clearly relishing the prospect of more scintillating conversation. 'Whatever you want.'

Jake was getting his wallet out, fishing for notes. 'It's all right,' said Matt, 'I've got it.'

He looked like he was about to argue over it, but then Jake just got out of the back. Matt thought about leaving him there without saying goodbye, but then he got out too.

'Thanks for … Thanks for tonight,' said Jake when he joined him. 'I needed it.'

'Yeah, well …'

182

'Think about what I said, will you, Matt?' He said nothing. Couldn't come up with anything *to* say. He'd be thinking about nothing else probably until Jake woke up, realised what he was doing. Then the man leaned in and said quietly: 'It's all I have left of her.'

Matt's mouth fell open. He hadn't been expecting that, a final entreaty which really would make him think. About how Jake had lost his daughter, not just the other week but a long time ago. About how the diary was his lifeline, a connection to her now she was gone forever.

Then Jake leaned in further, and suddenly he was hugging Matt. Hugging like they used to do when they were in their teens, as close as they'd been back then. Brothers. For a moment or two, Matt wasn't quite sure what to do with his hands. Then he was patting Jake's back, returning the bear-hug he was giving him.

And as quickly as it had started, it was over. Jake was heading into the hotel, leaving Matt on the street staring after him.

The horn made him start. 'You ready?' the cabbie called over, having clambered out again to hang off the frame of the car – his favourite position aside from being in the driver's seat.

'Yeah,' said Matt, getting back in. 'Yeah, I'm ready. Take me home.'

# Chapter 18

She'd given him some time, a day or so since the funeral. Hadn't wanted to disturb him now even, but figured he'd want to know this as soon as possible. He'd been distant, though; not quite with it. Another sleepless night perhaps? Hardly surprising.

'Is this a bad time?' Sam Ferrara had asked.

'A bad ... No, no. What's up, Sam?'

'Well, you know the sets of numbers you gave me ... I thought I should ring and ... I've figured out what they are.'

There was silence at the other end, and for a moment she'd thought Jake had lost signal on his mobile. Then he replied: 'Tell me.'

Sam knew how important this was to him, that's why she hadn't left it. It was getting to the stage where she was doing this just as much for Jake as she was for her client, Bobby Bannister.

Bobby ... The last time she'd seen that poor kid had been the worst yet. Escorted into that cramped interview room at Redmarket nick, because there still wasn't room for him elsewhere – and she'd been stonewalled at every turn trying to get him transferred. It was almost as if they wanted to keep the lad close, keep a watchful eye on him because he'd murdered one of their own (they thought). Bloody Redmarket folk, she'd encountered the same kind of resistance when she'd moved here herself; that same *League of Gentlemen* 'You're not local' mentality. All she'd wanted was somewhere quiet after spending years in the capital and getting burned out, becoming jaded by the horrors she'd seen.

Only to end up here, representing a young man who'd allegedly committed one of the worst crimes this town had seen in recent years. The image of the brutal killer – and Sam had seen her fair share in the past – didn't really tally with what she'd seen sitting across the table from her, handcuffed to the wood. Just a scared youth, terrified in fact. Lonely and lost after being locked up here for so long, the days and nights blurring into each other.

He'd looked at her with eyes that were a combination of red and black, sore from crying and dark from lack of sleep. 'How're you doing, Bobby?' she'd asked.

'I …' Bobby had hung his head, shook it. This was more than just remorse, more than guilt about what he'd done – Sam knew that. She *felt* it. She'd hadn't been bullshitting Jake that day when she'd told him she could read people, really read them … sometimes, anyway, if she concentrated hard enough.

*Didn't work in your private life though, did it, Sam? Don't even go there …*

She could read Bobby at any rate, knew he was a decent person. Knew he wasn't laying this on for sympathy or because he thought it might get him off the charge. She could also tell when someone was genuinely grieving for a person they loved as well, and Bobby *had* loved Jordan Radcliffe, there was no mistaking that. Had that love turned to hate? Sam didn't think so. Had it caused him to become uncontrollably jealous and commit what they were calling a crime of passion? Sam didn't think that either, in spite of what Jordan's father – and the rest of the population – obviously believed.

'All right, you just hang in there,' Sam told him, reaching over and giving his hand a squeeze. If she'd thought she could get away with it, she might just have gotten up and gone round to give him a hug. He looked like he desperately needed one.

They'd gone over everything once more, and his story hadn't changed. Hadn't wavered in all the time they'd been discussing it. Wasn't like he was going over a script either, just saying the words as if he'd learned them parrot-fashion. Every single time they'd got to the part where he found Jordan, he'd practically broken down. Sam could see him reliving that moment, seeing her covered in blood on that market stall, going to her and gripping the knife – not thinking, not really caring how it looked at the time – then realising it would do little good to pull it out. Even if she'd been alive, she would have bled out, but she was already dead by the time he reached her, that much was obvious.

'S-She ... Her eyes,' Bobby had said. 'There was nothing there. No life, you know what I mean?' The exact opposite of his own, so full of life and emotion, wet with tears that were threatening to break free again. 'Jordan was always so ... When we were together, she was full of energy, wanting to do this or that.' Bobby had pinched his nose, causing the first blooms of saltwater to break free. 'She'd dance the night away in those clubs, like a force of nature she was.'

Sam recalled when she'd been the same, a youngster so full of get-up-and-go she hadn't needed to sleep. Would study all day and dance all night herself, or do ... other things. Before life had intruded, before she'd been hurt so many times. Before she'd become weary and had been worn down by the very life she'd been full to the brim with. She could relate.

Bobby had realised too late, when he'd heard those sirens, how all this would look to the police. Had woken up from the daze he'd been in (but not the daze he'd committed the murder in, not that) and fled the scene – only to be picked up not long afterwards, covered in Jordan's blood. So, *of course* his prints had been on the knife – he'd handled it, thought about trying to pull it out. Didn't mean he'd put it in there in the first place ... although his had been the only set, Sam had to admit.

Didn't look good, she had to admit that too. Looked pretty

damned awful, but she hadn't passed that on to her client. She didn't want to give him false hope, but at the same time didn't want him going off and doing something silly either. He wasn't stupid, though, he knew what kind of trouble he was in. Yet all he seemed to care about now was that he'd lost someone he thought could have been 'the one'. Yes, he was young and she remembered how many guys she'd thought that about back when she was naive enough to think it was possible – but that didn't stop this hurting for him, didn't stop it feeling that way. And, she had to remind herself, it actually was possible; look how long her mum and dad had been together and they hadn't been that much older than Bobby and Jordan.

Then there was the flipside of that, Jordan's parents. They'd got together when they were even younger, had been childhood sweethearts, and look how that had turned out. There was still love there, she'd seen that for herself only the other day at the funeral, seen it in the jealous way Julie had been staring across at her when she was anywhere near her ex-husband. If they hadn't fallen out about Jordan, maybe they'd still be together – maybe they would be again at some point if Julie ever saw that arsehole of a current partner for what he actually was. For what was written all over his face, as far as Sam could see (even without knowing some of the stories about him).

It would not be a good idea to get in the middle of that, one of the reasons she'd headed off before the wake. But still … her mind kept going back to Jake, thinking about him when she least expected it. At first, she'd put it down to just feeling sorry for him because, you know, who wouldn't? That was partly why she'd sorted out getting Jake released in the first place that Monday morning; something that seemed so very long ago now. She'd also wanted an ally, of course, someone who might have the same goal as her: uncovering the truth. Jake Radcliffe thought he had the 'who', he just didn't have the 'why' – probably because, in her humble opinion, there wasn't one. It was what was driving him on his quest, getting him into all kinds of trouble of his own.

Since she'd got him out of his last predicament – fighting with that guy Drummond because Jake figured he'd had something to do with the 'why' – and she'd bought him breakfast or brunch or whatever, they'd seen each other a few times. Enough to call themselves friends? Sam would've said so, she wasn't sure about Jake. Enough that when all this was over, whatever turns the case took, they might see each other some more …?

Dangerous thoughts, but they were definitely there. He didn't even live in this town, she reminded herself. They both had busy jobs. *Don't jump into anything too quickly*; traditionally that was one of her biggest problems. And the complications this time were staggering. So, for now she would help him – they'd help *each other* as she had suggested that first time they'd met. And what better way than what she was doing now, how she'd cracked what those numbers he'd given her were all about (though it was still bugging her where they'd come from).

Who'd cracked it again? Well, she'd had help herself on that score, and more than a bit of luck. A happy coincidence that a colleague, Martin – who'd been at their solicitors apparently since it had set up shop, or close enough – had been working on a boundary dispute. The border between two farms, which had shifted over time without anyone noticing – until one of the farmers had claimed that a section of land was his and had run into issues (something to do with a grab for a well a hundred years back). Sam just happened to be passing Martin's desk, which was strewn with papers and maps going back years, all part of his ongoing investigation which he was moaning about to anyone who'd listen, and something she'd seen had struck her. Something about the numbers he'd been checking and re-checking …

'Tell me,' Jake had said when she'd called him, and so she did. Sam had worked it out, joined the dots when no one else had.

'It's not a code, a bank account or whatever. The numbers are coordinates,' she'd explained. 'It was just that no one had spotted it because they needed to be put together ...'

'Coordinates?'

'You know, latitude, longitude. A map reference, Jake.' Another pause as he took that information in. Again, she wasn't sure whether he was still there so she broke the silence this time. 'Easy enough to find online once you understand what they are. It's a location: a place not that far away.'

'What place?' he asked her.

And that's when she'd made the arrangements, once he'd confirmed he was up to it, to call and collect him.

Jake had been waiting for her outside the hotel when she pulled up in her Audi. There was no one there to bother him today, and probably wouldn't be now until the trial. The funeral had been the big one after the initial reports on the murder, and media-wise things were calming down a lot now. She'd seen it before: the frenzy once news broke, like sharks after chum in the water (not that she could talk about professions and sharks), then pieces about the family, coverage of events as they took a turn or two – like they had done when Jake had been arrested – and now ... nothing. People had short attention spans, readers and viewers especially, and there was always another news item vying to catch their interest, particularly in this age of social media.

It meant they could go on their little mission without hindrance, that nobody need know about it. Jake climbed in and Sam thought to herself how similar he looked to Bobby, how tired and emotionally drained they both appeared. Jake wouldn't have cared for the comparison, but it was there nonetheless.

'You okay?' she said to him as he climbed into the passenger seat.

'Yeah, I'm fine,' Jake told her, not even turning – just gazing dead ahead.

'Fair enough. Right then, let's go, shall we?'

189

'Go … where?' Now he did turn, giving her a questioning look. 'You still haven't told me, Sam.'

She just smiled, put the car into gear, and set off. As they drove she tried a few times to engage Jake in conversation, even making a joke about lending him the car, but he wasn't biting. Sam wondered what had happened since she'd last seen him, something at the wake perhaps? A falling out with someone? He'd been quite volatile; if Matt hadn't stopped him Jake would have gone after Drummond. Matt … maybe a row with him? Or Julie? Or Greg … not that it would be difficult to row with him. Sam had done her best to wheedle the information out of him, it was her job after all and she was very good at it, but no dice. She was also worried about upsetting him, treading a fine line between looking out for him and appearing like she was sticking her nose in where it wasn't wanted.

They'd been on the road a while, heading out of the town, when he asked her again where she was taking them. Before she could answer, they were already there and she was pulling up by the side of the road, next to what looked like a broken gate on a wire fence.

'What is this?' asked Jake, peering through the windscreen. 'Where are we?'

'It's one of Redmarket's old abandoned slaughterhouses,' she told him finally. 'It was picked up by a businessman back in the mid-2000s, when the writing was starting to be on the wall for the industry, but then he went bankrupt himself when the banks crashed.'

'So now it's not owned by anyone?' said Jake.

She shook her head. 'Not that I could find out, which explains why the security's pretty lax, doesn't it? Question is, what's all this got to do with your daughter, Jake?' Sam was hoping then he might open up about where the numbers had come from, but Jake remained tight-lipped about that.

'I'm not sure,' was all he would give her.

'Okay then, what say we have a nose around and see if we can find out.' She got out of the car, putting on her raincoat, and Jake followed as she led the way through the gate and locked the car remotely over her shoulder.

Hitching up her handbag over her shoulder, she wandered down the path that had overgrown grass on either side, trying to avoid her work trousers getting caught on thorns. 'From what I understand, when this place was first abandoned it used to be a bit of a hangout for ravers – do people still call it that? I'm showing my age a bit there. Partygoers, anyway. Might still be, for all I know,' said Sam. 'Could that be the reason Jordan had those numbers? Maybe she came to a secret party here?'

Jake said nothing, so she assumed he didn't have a clue. Sam made a mental note to ask Bobby when she saw him again, see if she'd ever come here with him at all? To be full of life, to dance the night away …

But God, when she saw the place Sam wondered why anyone ever would – especially when there were actual pubs and clubs in town that weren't on the verge of collapsing. *Drugs perhaps*, her mind answered … away from the prying eyes of the town's police force, not that they exactly kept a tight rein on any of that in Redmarket proper because it would put a crimp on the place's nightlife.

The building was big and square, the main body of it a couple of storeys high, with a pair of 'wings' on either side. It was all grey and faded cream brickwork that looked like it had been attacked by some sort of rot or mould. Arched and square windows alike were boarded up or barred, though two or three of these were also hanging off on their hinges. There had been a handful of attempts at graffiti, but it hadn't really taken; it was certainly nothing like what you'd find in Granfield's notorious Graffitiland, that stretch of empty buildings the budding local artists and transients favoured. A lone bare tree stood sentry next to the building, just to add to the eerie feel of the place. And it not only looked like a place that was dying or had died, it smelt of death too – not surprising when you took into account what its main purpose had been up until a decade or more ago.

'Good Christ,' she heard Jake whisper under his breath. It was then that she realised he had absolutely no idea either what the connection was between his daughter and this location, other than the coordinates had come from her apparently.

Though it was the last thing in the world she really wanted to do, Sam suggested that they head inside. Jake looked at her like she was mad, but nodded anyway. They both needed to see what was in there, to figure out what that connection was if they could.

Jake took the lead this time, skirting past her – and she almost got annoyed then, thinking he was doing it because he was 'the man' and should go first. She could bloody well look after herself, thanks! But then she saw he was pulling back the rotten wood on the door for her, making the way passable so she could, in fact, go on ahead of him; something she was simultaneously relieved (she couldn't stand all that macho cobblers) and disappointed about (because she was suddenly questioning if she really did want to lead the way into that dark space, after all). But she went, didn't want to look weak in front of Jake apart from anything else.

Sam stepped gingerly over the threshold, pulling out her phone and flicking on the torch app, flashing that around. She was in a corridor, the walls made of that same brick as the outside – but she couldn't see beyond this, no matter how hard she squinted. She took one step, two steps, moving hesitantly towards the next opening, but paused when she got there. Jake's hand on her shoulder made her start; for a moment she'd forgotten he was even behind her.

'I'm sorry, I didn't mean to …' he began, then tailed off.

'You didn't,' she told him, which was a lie and he knew it. She was nervous – who wouldn't be, coming in here? She'd never been a big fan of horror movies, had only watched them because some of her friends in uni had been into the things, but this was starting to feel uncomfortably like the premise of one. Any minute now Leatherface would come bounding out of the blackness to cut them into pieces ...

That didn't happen in real life, she reminded herself. *No*, said another voice inside her, *real life is much more frightening*.

Sam swallowed dryly and moved on, into the larger space ahead of her. Here and there were flashes of light, whatever was making it through the windows that were hanging off the hinges. They afforded a glimpse of certain quarters of the room ahead, while others remained frustratingly dark. What Sam was able to see she wished that she couldn't: rusted hooks and chains that did nothing to dispel the whole *Texas Chain Saw Massacre* chic. In fact, there was a large one just dangling down in the middle there that looked like the hook that woman had been placed on in the movie. Littering the floor were more bits of curved metal that had once been used to hang up meat she was sure, railings dotted about and lots of pipes. She traced one back to what looked like a large fire hose still attached to the wall, which must have been utilised at some point in the past to wash down the walls and floors. And, yes, there were troughs that the blood could run down into guttering, carrying away the unsavoury liquids that had been spilled during the working week.

Sam closed her eyes to shut it out, but all she could see was the butchery that had taken place here, her imagination filling in the blanks. All she could hear were the screams of the animals. Men in white with cleavers and such, hacking at the meat. Sam opened her eyes again and saw the results of that, a dark redness that the hose hadn't been able to wash away; the effect of so many years of killing in this place. Old blood splatter coating the surfaces, having built up over time. And ...

She stepped forward, drawn to a patch that was lighter than the rest. Fresher. 'Jake,' she called back over her shoulder. 'Jake, come and look at this ...'

As he joined her, she was crouching to get a better look. 'What is it?' he asked.

She rose again and pointed, training her phone-light on the pattern below. 'That blood, I-I think it was spilled fairly recently.'

He frowned, stared at the redness. Then looked up, across. 'Over there, more of it.'

Sam followed his gaze and saw he was right. There was more of the blood there, standing out from its ancient brethren. He went over, passing a set of scales that would have been used to value the spoils of this place – leaving her on her own momentarily. Looking about her, she quickly joined him, agreeing that the spillage there also looked like it had happened in the last few months or so ... maybe even in the last few weeks? 'What the hell ...?' she said to Jake, as they exchanged glances.

'Let's check out the rest of the place,' he suggested, nodding over to a stairway on their left which led to a walkway which ran around the building. Now she didn't care that he was going first, heading off in the direction of those stairs. Indeed, Sam didn't want to go at all. Quite apart from the fact there were lots of dark rooms there, the way up looked about as stable as the building itself. 'Come on,' shouted Jake, and she found she had no choice. Two sets of eyes were better than one, after all.

The stairs were actually more solid than they looked and soon they were on the next level. More railings skirted the walkway, which was just wide enough for two people to walk side-by-side, but at certain points there were gaps in the barriers where they must have rusted away – or perhaps had never been there in the first place. On this level they found lots of smaller rooms, where meat had probably been prepared after being transferred from the 'shop-floor' below. They ran off into the wings of the building attached on either side. In a few of these they found more blood that looked like it had been spilled fairly recently, some on the floor, some on the walls.

They also came across what was left of an office, which Jake went inside and started to search – his own phone out now, the torch flashing around as he went through filing cabinets and drawers. At some point there must have been a flood here, though, probably rain getting in through the ceiling, because what papers he did discover were useless, the writing transformed into lots of miniature Rorschach tests.

It was while Jake was searching that she heard the first noise. Sam stepped out of the office for a moment and cocked an ear. 'Do you hear ...' she said, but Jake was making too much of a racket himself to notice anything.

There it was again, definitely movement. Down below? Or up here with them? It was hard to tell in this place of echoes, this place of shadows. Left, right? Up or down? Sam bit her lip, trying to trace it. 'Jake ...'

Then, sweeping her torch around, she saw it. Or the tail end of it ... literally. She thought at first it was a cat, the kind they always use to scare the audience in those movies she hated; make them jump in their seats. But in actual fact it was a rat, its tail pink and long – as big in size as those that famous horror authors used to write books about, reality catching up with fiction. Although it was horrible, it had run off away from them rather than attacking – more scared of humans than they were of it – and Sam found herself letting out the breath she hadn't realised she'd been holding.

'Sam ... Sam, are you ... *Look out!*' Jake's warning came too late, and she barely had time to turn and see whatever it was that rammed into her. She crashed back against the wall, winded and sliding down it, dropping her phone in the process. The torch stayed on, however, facing upwards and allowing her to see the silhouette of two figures: one clearly Jake, the other much bigger. The latter had hold of the former and was swinging him back into the office – smashing the door and one of the windows in the process. She heard Jake groan as he landed.

One thought raced through her mind as she shook her head,

tried to gather her wits: that Leatherface was here after all! The only thing that was missing was the sound of that famous chain saw he wielded.

Sam crawled forward, reaching for the phone. Fingers inches away when the huge figure found her again and picked her up, flinging her down onto the walkway where she skidded to a halt a few metres away.

Stunned, she nevertheless knew she had to get up, get moving – or she was dead. This person, whoever it was, wouldn't stop until she was dead. Until they both … Were they responsible for the fresh blood around this place? She wouldn't be at all surprised. Wouldn't be surprised, either, if she ended up dangling from one of those hooks downstairs.

*Get up!* she screamed at herself. *Get up!*

She looked back over her shoulder, saw the shadow of Jake now emerging from the office, trying to tackle her attacker and being shrugged off for his trouble. Being punched, flying backwards with the force of the blow.

Then the huge, lumbering figure was heading towards her once more.

Sam heard the crack even before she felt the kick that was delivered – so hard it lifted her off the floor, sent her sideways. A couple of ribs had definitely gone, she could feel that, the pain tremendous. Another kick and she was rolling almost to the edge of the walkway. Some part of her brain was wondering if this was a section that had railings – probably not, she hadn't seen any – so she'd just go flying off the edge to fall into the space below.

But then she stopped dead, hitting railings that halted her progress; that had saved her, at least for now. Because the monster was still on the walkway with her – that was how she saw the figure now, as a monster that wanted to obliterate her. Could she get up and run? Could she get up and get away, at least get to the phone … and what about Jake? Was he all right? What had the monster done to him?

She had no more time to ponder that, because Sam heard the creaking of the railing holding her up. Felt the weakened metal beginning to give way, no longer able to support her weight as she pressed up against it.

Then it was failing, breaking at the base and allowing her to roll further – over the precipice! Her hand instinctively shot out, grabbed a rail and held on for dear life.

Her life!

But when it tilted once again, jolting her and leaving her hanging over the edge, she found she could no longer hold on. The pain in her side was excruciating, gravity not helping with that in any way, shape or form. And before she knew it, her fingers were uncurling, letting go of the rail. Letting her fall.

Wasn't her life supposed to flash before her eyes at this point? Time stretched out – the moments she spent falling turning into hours, days, years – but absolutely nothing was coming. No memories, no recollections. Just the notion that if she hadn't come here for some peace and quiet, come to this small town, and had stayed where she was down south, she'd probably have been better off. Probably have been safer. Alive at any rate ...

If she hadn't taken this case, if she hadn't met Jake Radcliffe, if he hadn't given her those numbers, and she hadn't called him this morning.

*If, if ... if.*

And then there were no more ifs, because suddenly and violently, her body connected with the floor of the slaughterhouse below.

No more ifs, because there were no more thoughts at all.

# Chapter 19

'This is getting to be a bad habit.'

Channing stood in front of him, leaning down. A face that was just demanding to be slapped, but it would only have made things worse. 'No, not habit … What's the name of that film where things keep happening again and again?'

He looked back over at DC Mathew Newcomb, waiting for a reply, but when he didn't get one turned back to the person he'd originally asked. 'Oh come on, it had Bill Murray in it …'

'*Ghostbusters*?' replied Jake snidely.

'You know fucking well that's not it.' Channing pulled back again, out of slapping distance. 'But, anyway, this is like that. I swear we've been here before, haven't we?' He paused for a moment, clicked his fingers. 'Something Day …' he said suddenly.

'I don't remember being attacked in an abandoned slaughterhouse before,' said Jake from his position on the uncomfortable plastic chair in the hospital waiting room. 'Or waiting to see if my friend, who was also attacked, will be all right.'

That was where he was right now, waiting. What he'd been doing since he recovered from said attack, clambering to his feet to find that whoever had done it was gone. To find that Sam was sprawled out on the level below, having fallen from the walkway

– been forced off it, to be more precise. Jake had rushed down-stairs, checking the unconscious form for a pulse, and finding a faint one. Then he'd called the emergency services, attempting to tell them where he was but realising he had no real idea … suddenly remembering the numbers, the coordinates and giving them those instead. 'You can't miss it, there's an expensive-looking red Audi parked at the gates.'

He'd waited with Sam until he heard the sirens, stepped back as paramedics had done their thing. Checking her over and putting her on a stretcher. 'Looks like you've been in the wars as well,' he'd been told. 'Aren't you two a bit old to be playing around in derelict buildings?'

Jake had ignored the remark, but accepted the treatment – which for him amounted to a few stitches. He'd been lucky enough to walk away with a few cuts and bruises; the same sadly couldn't be said for Sam.

A broken leg, definitely, for starters – but also suspected internal bleeding. She'd been rushed into the operating theatre as soon as they'd hit Redmarket Hospital, at which point they'd asked if there was anyone they should be getting in touch with, family or anything?

'I … Miss Ferrara lives alone,' he'd told them, 'and I think most of her family are back in Italy.' She'd told him that during one of their meet-ups.

So he'd told them he'd wait, wanted to anyway. What else was he going to do? He wasn't going anywhere until he found out how she was doing.

It hadn't been long after that when Channing and Matt had arrived, the incident having been reported to the police. And it hadn't been long after that Channing had started to get in Jake's face again. 'I mean, for heaven's sake – does trouble just follow you around or something?'

'I'm beginning to wonder if someone wasn't.'

'Excuse me?' said Channing.

'Following me around,' he replied.

'Oh, and care to enlighten us as to who that someone might be?' Channing folded his arms.

'Well, I didn't get a good look at his face, but—'

'Of course not.'

'It was dark, and I was too busy being flung around like a rag doll, Sergeant,' argued Jake. 'The same as Sam.'

'Sam now, is it?' said Channing with a smirk. 'Last time I saw you two, it was Miss Ferrara and Mr Radcliffe. Now you're, what, besties and auditioning for the Scooby gang or something?'

'I didn't get a good look, but he was *big*,' continued Jake, ignoring such comments for the second time in a day, at the same time wondering if the paramedic who'd brought them here was somehow related to Channing. 'I'm talking huge. Like Drummond huge, Sergeant.'

Channing whirled around, his back to Jake, and walked the short distance the waiting room would allow before twirling back around. 'Not this again, for Christ's sake! So, you reckon Drummond's been following you, then? Is that it?'

'He was at the church,' Jake threw back, 'the day of Jordan's ...'

Channing looked to Matt again, probably because he knew the DC had been there. Matt nodded. 'It's true, sir. I had to get some uniforms to move him along.'

The DS held up a hand. 'All right, all right. But following you out there to the middle of nowhere. How did he do that, exactly? It's not even like the stupid fucker can drive, let alone owns a car.'

Channing did have a point there. Jake hadn't even known where they were going until Sam told him, until they arrived. And there was no way he could have followed the car ... could he? Certainly not on foot. Or perhaps he wasn't as slow as the police thought, was only pretending so they'd leave him alone to do his perving? 'Maybe he was already there,' offered Jake. Perhaps that was where he hung out, not under a bridge with the other trolls at all, but in an abandoned abattoir?

'Oh, you mean that's his evil lair?' Channing held up both hands and wriggled his fingers, trying to make a spooky sound. 'Fucking hell! This is ridiculous!'

'So, what are you going to do, arrest me for getting beaten up again?' spat Jake, though he realised it was tempting fate. 'How about instead of interrogating me, you go and have a look for him? I've told you before I think he's dangerous. And while you're at it, you should get some forensics people out to that place and have them dig around a bit. Because some of the blood on those walls and floors isn't that old.'

He saw Matt raise an eyebrow at that.

'So what?' growled Channing. 'Could be anything. Some bloody derelicts staying there, knocking lumps out of each other. Could have been one of them that did this to you and ... your new "friend" Sam.' He grinned again when he said the name, the implication plain. Here Jake was, not long after his daughter's murder, and he was mucking about with the culprit's lawyer. 'And, by the way, I still haven't got a proper answer about what you two were doing there in the first place.'

Jake said nothing. What could he say, they were following up a lead from a secret diary he was hiding from the police?

'I'm going to hazard a guess that it's something to do with those blasted numbers, am I right?' Channing came forward again, bending and lowering his voice. 'Would that be why you gave the emergency services the numbers so they could find you?' He said it with satisfied smile, like he'd cracked Jake's code or something. But he still didn't know where they'd come from originally, and he never would. Not unless ...

Jake glanced over at Matt, who looked away. He obviously hadn't spilled the beans yet, and the longer he kept that secret the worse it would be for himself, let alone his friend. Not that

Jake had intended for that to happen, he just couldn't part with that book. Not yet.

'Listen, you've got to admit it looks like something weird's going on here,' said Jake eventually.

'I'm starting to think you might have a death wish, and now you're dragging other people into your fun and games,' Channing answered.

'It was Sam who contacted *me* about going there,' argued Jake.

'But why? What were you looking for, man?' Channing sighed, calming down a little. 'Work with me here ... You say something looks weird, but from my perspective all I have is a guy suffering from extreme grief who's going around starting fights and creeping about in old, abandoned buildings that aren't safe. I'd have been more surprised if you *weren't* set upon. What is it you're trying to discover, Radcliffe?' Jake noticed the niceties of 'Mr' were gone now on their third encounter. 'What possible connection could that place have to anything that's happened?'

'I don't know,' said Jake, looking him in the eye. 'That's what I'm trying to find out.'

It was Channing's turn to remain silent, then he said, 'You're looking for closure, trust me I do get this. But you'll have that when the boy's convicted. All of this you're chasing, whatever it is, that's just to make you feel better about everything. It helps to think there's something you can do, so you invent these little mysteries. Stops you feeling so useless. What's done is done, though, you can't change it no matter what you do. And justice will be done, Radcliffe, I can assure you of that. Bobby Bannister will be punished for what he did. And ...' He rubbed his temples with the fingers of both hands. 'And I can't believe I'm saying this, but we'll look into the slaughterhouse, the blood you mentioned. Just to make sure we've covered the bases. But as far as you're concerned, enough is enough now. People are getting hurt here.'

It was a good speech, Jake had to admit that. The kind

Channing was used to delivering in front of cameras Jake was used to being behind. And he had to admit, Channing did have a point. None of this made any sense, him running around trying to ... to what? Solve a crime that was already solved. Find a 'why' when maybe there wasn't one, when it could just be that Bannister was off his head and had murdered Jordan in a fit of rage over the way other guys looked at her, over Drummond looking at her – following her? What good exactly was he doing here? It hadn't done Sam much good, that was for certain!

At the same time, it made no sense for him to be seeing his dead daughter – did it? (*A guy suffering from extreme grief ...*) Or for him to have promised her he'd find out the truth to her no matter what. (*All of this you're chasing, whatever it is, that's just to make you feel better about everything.*)

It was at that moment the doctor Jake had seen before about Sam stepped into the waiting room, still in his scrubs from surgery. Tall, with an impressive jawline, he looked like he belonged in one of those US medical soap operas rather than at Redmarket Hospital. He looked the newcomers up and down, but before he could say anything Channing explained who they were. 'Well,' said the doctor, still addressing Jake, 'you'll be pleased to know we stopped the bleeding and your friend should make a full recovery, touch wood.' He patted the doorframe. 'She'll be out for some time, however, so I don't see any point in you gentlemen hanging around here. What she needs now is rest, and plenty of it.'

'Understood,' said Channing before Jake could get a word out. 'Thank you, doctor.'

When the medical man exited again, Channing told Matt they were also leaving. 'But we'll need you to come in sometime and make an official statement about all this,' he told Jake, who promised he would.

Matt gave him a tired look as he left with his DS but didn't say anything. Hadn't said a lot during the whole thing – not that

Channing had given him much of an opening. So he still had no idea what was going through the man's mind, whether he might tell someone about the diary. He obviously hadn't yet, but then he had been off work till today.

Then he was gone, and Jake didn't have a chance to talk to him alone and gauge anything. He gave it a few minutes, just so they were clear of the building, and went out into the corridor. Sam's Audi was still back at the abattoir, his own car back at the hotel, so he figured he'd ask them at reception to book him a taxi.

Then he saw her, sitting out there in the corridor and waiting. The same as he had been waiting, but for him. She turned and spotted Jake, held up a hand.

Julie.

And he knew then that he had no need to order any kind of transportation. Knew instinctively that she was here to take him back.

To take him home.

# Chapter 20

That hadn't proved entirely correct.

Julie hadn't been waiting there to take him home, at least not the home he'd known all those years. Where Jordan had been living, but also where Greg Allaway, her husband, lived too. She hadn't come in their car, either, because that man was using it for work – was on late shifts apparently this week. Instead, Channing had been in touch and got someone to fetch her, someone who was also waiting outside.

'He said I might be able to talk some sense into you,' Julie told him after they'd said hello properly in the corridor. 'Doesn't know you like I do, does he?'

Jake had smiled, then shook his head. 'Listening to – or even talking – sense was never my speciality,' he replied.

She'd reached up then, touching his bruised face, the plasters covering those stitches he'd needed, concern etched on her own face. 'What happened?' Channing obviously hadn't gone into that.

He just shook his head again, asked her if they could just get out of there. It was then that she'd said she'd see him back home: his other home, not even the one that he called his home back where he worked, but the temporary one he seemed to be inhabiting at the moment.

Julie had led him out to the unmarked car Channing had arranged, and thankfully Jake didn't recognise this driver. Another lady, plain-clothes, but not the liaison woman Linda or any of the other folk from Redmarket station he was apparently becoming quite familiar with. She drove them pretty much in silence, Julie in the front and him in the back again ... on his own. Keeping the distance there, which was probably wise.

The policewoman had dropped them off at the hotel, Julie telling her not to worry, that she'd get a cab back home in a little while. So off she'd gone, leaving them both to go inside. Jake asked Julie if she wanted a coffee or anything and she'd surprised him then by asking if it would be okay if she had a wine instead. When he led her through to the bar area, she asked if he was having anything.

'They gave me these at the hospital.' He took the pill bottle out of his pocket and rattled it. 'But I can think of better ways to dull the pain.'

They took the wine and a lager over to one of the tables and sat down. 'So, are you going to tell me how you got into this particular scrape now?' She waited, tapping the table.

'It's a long story,' he said eventually.

'And this is a large wine.'

He cocked his head, conceding the point, and went through it all with Julie – omitting the part about the numbers and the diary, instead just saying they were following up a lead.

'You've been working with this woman, this Miss Ferrara?'

'Yeah, kind of. Like I said before, she's a friend. And she's just looking for the truth the same as me.'

Julie took a swig of the wine. 'The truth about what?'

Jake shrugged. 'I just ... Something doesn't smell right here, Jules. I've been around enough newspaper people and TV reporters to know when a story doesn't hang together. There's something we don't know about yet, or aren't being told about all this. I can feel it.'

'She thinks Bobby's innocent, doesn't she? The lawyer woman?'

He laughed. 'Lawyer woman?'

'Ferrara.' There it was again, Julie's hackles going up whenever she was mentioned – and especially now that she knew Sam would be okay.

'She *thinks* you're jealous of her.'

Julie almost spat out her drink. 'What? Don't be so ... I couldn't care less what she ... what you both do! I thought I made that clear.'

Jake nodded. 'Yeah. You did, sorry.' He changed the subject back, quickly. 'But yes, she thinks Bannister didn't do it.'

'How about you?'

He took a drink of the beer. 'I ... I think this Drummond guy might be mixed up in it all somehow. Even if he was only the catalyst for it.'

'But you think ... The *two of you* think there's more to it than that, don't you?'

'I ... I really don't know. If – and I admit it's a big if that I'm not saying I fully believe – Bannister wasn't responsible, perhaps that big bloke was?'

'And you're saying that he was the one who attacked you both this morning.' Julie frowned, processing the information. 'He's the one you were fighting with before, that landed you in jail?'

'That's right.'

'So maybe he's holding a grudge or something? What made you go after him in the first place anyway, Jake?'

'When I spoke with some of Jordan's friends, I—'

Julie held up a hand to stop him. 'Wait a minute, when was this?'

'Just after I saw you at the house,' he told her.

She nodded. 'You have been busy, haven't you?' *You don't know the half of it*, thought Jake. 'Okay, go on.'

'Well, they told me this Drummond guy had been hassling Jordan.'

Julie drank some more, then said, 'She never mentioned that.'

'Jordan never mentioned a lot of things. To either of us, Jules.' He added the last bit to make it plain he wasn't having a go at her. That both of them had been in the dark about so much concerning their daughter. More than even they had thought, he suspected.

'Hassling in what way?'

'Following her, one of them said. Doing that thing he does of just staring at young girls ... Creepy fuck.' Jake was nearly down to the bottom of the glass. 'He was there doing it a couple of days ago, at the ... Well, after we'd ...' He saw Julie's eyes brush the floor, sadness washing over her. Jake reached over and took her hand, squeezed it. 'I'm sorry,' he said again.

When she looked up again, her eyes were misty. 'Honestly, it feels like a million years ago now. But it didn't while it was happening.'

'Yeah,' Jake agreed. 'I've been having the same thing with time lately. Here, let me get you another.'

He rose, and she waved him back down again, insisting on buying this round. Jake watched her as she stood there ordering, that fiery red hair which had dulled with time but still fell on her shoulders like a waterfall. It was the first time he'd seen her standing without her long coat on, as she'd shrugged that off when they sat down, and he took in the shape of her. That still perfect figure, in a blue jumper and patterned skirt. However had he walked away from that, kept away from this woman? Driven her into the arms of ...

Jake smiled as she carried back the drinks. 'Thanks,' he said.

'I never thanked you properly,' she said, sliding back into her seat.

'For what?' he asked, confused, thinking she meant the original drinks.

'For what you did during the service, when I couldn't. For stepping in. And for what you said in your speech.'

Jake nodded, finally understanding. 'Of course. I meant every single word, Jules. You were there for Jordan when I wasn't, when I couldn't be … When she wouldn't let me.' It was his turn to look down now, and he drank a good quarter of his fresh pint.

'I … I did what I could,' he heard Julie say. 'Did my best. It was all I ever did, really.'

'I know,' said Jake, looking up. 'I know. You were a good mum.'

She smiled. 'Thanks. And you were …' Julie struggled to say the words, and Jake couldn't really blame her. He hadn't really been a good dad; he'd been fine when everything was going all right, when he was the only guy in her life, but then … He'd found it so hard to cope with the rest, with what they called that 'transition period' between kid and adult. 'You did the best you could.'

'I appreciate that,' he said sincerely. 'We had some good times, though, didn't we?' He wasn't sure whether he was trying to get a conversation going about that or just seeking confirmation that there had, in fact, been good times.

'Oh yes, lots,' Julie said, beaming now as memories came back to her. 'That time at the zoo for one. I still can't believe she kept that little penguin!'

'Her face when she saw the giraffes, I've never seen anything like that in my life.' Jake grinned too, Julie's smile infectious. 'It was like … like pure joy, y'know? I can't even remember what that was like, couldn't even back then.'

'That's kids for you. So innocent, so excited about everything,' said Julie. 'And take them to somewhere like the seaside, or an amusement park and they practically explode!'

'Yeah,' said Jake, laughing. 'And Christmases, birthdays. I have some really fond memories of those. Do you remember the time we bought Jordan that doll's house, and all she wanted to do was play in the wrapping and the box?'

Julie laughed out loud now. 'I do, I do. God, we paid so much for that thing as well.'

'She played with it eventually, when she was on her own. The wrapping and stuff was just because she wanted to play with us, rolling around in it, hiding ...' The mention of that word made him stop short, thinking about her hiding places. Her secrets. He shook his head, shaking those thoughts away. 'And ice cream, you could always get a big smile out of her with that. Raspberry, if I remember rightly.'

'Ate so much one time she threw up,' Julie chipped in. 'Then went back and started eating more.'

'That's right. Wow, I'd forgotten about that.' Jake took another swig of the lager.

They carried on in this vein for a while, reminiscing about everything from taking Jordan to the park for the first time ('And she fell off the swings, banged her knee, but she still wanted to go back on – crying and laughing at the same time as we pushed her!') to her projects at school ('That damned rocket she had to make that I helped her with. You were supposed to fill it with water and watch it shoot up into the air, but ours just burst and we both got saturated!'). By the time they finished they'd just about covered most of her life, the good bits anyway – the bits before she'd started to have trouble, struggling to find her way in the world.

It was at this point he'd almost, *almost* told her about the diary – but kept quiet. Wasn't the right time, not just yet.

When they began to touch on Jordan's later life though, it was Julie who wound the clock right back to their own time as young-sters, laughing about when Jake and Matt used to try and impress her with their football skills.

'We were only talking about that the other night!' Jake splut-tered, working his way down his fourth or fifth drink.

'You were?' she said, surprised.

'Yeah, he took me out to ... Well, you know.'

Julie looked a bit crestfallen then, as if she'd have come if he'd invited her. The old gang together again, just the three of them.

But what would Greg Allaway have made of that? What would he make of this? Jake couldn't help thinking. Would probably have wanted to be at both, knowing him – and wouldn't have thought a thing of barging in where he wasn't wanted. Where he didn't belong.

'Two nights in the same week chatting about the old days with ... with friends,' said Jake.

Julie looked at him then. 'Is that what I am now, a friend?'

'I-I hope so,' Jake told her. 'I mean, *aren't* you?' He'd thought they were mending fences, or trying to. That was another thing time had taught them recently, life was too short for arguments and grudges.

'After all those years married, I ... think I might be a little bit more than that, Jacob.' She pouted, something she always did when she wanted to get her own way – usually in a silly argument over nothing (not the big stuff, and never at the end). Jake used to think it was cute. Still did, if he was honest. And it always, always got him to cave.

'I ... well, yes, I think we always will be,' he said. 'But—'

'More than friends, more than you are with the lawyer woman.' Julie was running her finger around the rim of her empty wine glass.

'There you go again, her name's Sam.'

Julie snorted. 'What kind of name's that for a woman?'

'It's short for Samantha,' Jake clarified.

Another snort.

'What does it matter, Jules? Why are you so bothered by it?'

'Because ...' She stopped rubbing the top of the glass and looked directly at him. 'Because maybe she had a point. Maybe I am a little jealous.'

Jake's mouth fell open. He wasn't sure what to say to that.

'When I saw you both having coffee, I ...' Julie realised what she'd just said, looked from side to side as if waiting to be found out.

'Having coffee?' Jake frowned. 'When was this?'

Julie pulled a face, then realised she couldn't really get out of this one. 'The other week ... After you'd been to the house, after the weekend. The Monday morning.' Now she was over-explaining, something she did whenever she was embarrassed.

'But how did you ...' The penny suddenly dropped. 'You came here to see me?'

Julie nodded. 'I'm not even sure why, Jake. But seeing you again ... I couldn't get you out of my mind all that weekend.'

He grinned. 'Really?' Then he remembered something, his face turning sour immediately. 'The whole weekend you were with *him*.'

She looked at him sideways. 'He has a name, too. Greg.'

'Don't I know it. Bloody Greg.'

'He's ... he's my husband.'

'I know that, as well.' Jake sighed. 'I just can't ... I don't get it, Jules. Why him? I really don't understand.'

'I-I love him,' she replied weakly as if that was explanation enough. 'He was there for me when ...'

'When I wasn't,' Jake said sadly. 'I know. Trust me, I know.' He leaned back, looking up at the ceiling. 'What a fucking mess.'

'Yeah.'

When he looked back down again, Jake said, 'I'm sorry. I really am. If I could go back and change things ...'

Julie nodded. 'Yeah, I know. But what's done is done.'

'I just thought ... Well, I thought you'd be better off without me around. Thought you hated me. I thought you both did, Jordan especially.'

'Oh Jake, we never hated you. *She* never hated you, regardless of what she said. You were her *dad*.'

He laughed, but there was no humour in it. 'A shit one.'

'She never thought that. All those memories we've talked about tonight ... You were just mad at each other and didn't know how to fix it.'

212

'I always … I always thought there'd be time for that. Later. But then …'

She reached out and took his hand this time. 'It wasn't your fault. It wasn't my fault, or even hers.'

'It was someone's,' Jake said without missing a beat.

'Bobby.'

He didn't say anything, just squeezed her hand as he had before. 'That time was stolen from us, Jules. Yeah, we made mistakes. And so did she, Jordan wasn't an angel.' He paused then, realising what he'd just said, but ploughed on anyway. 'But that time … the future. It was stolen from us all, wasn't it?'

'I suppose so, yes.'

They both lapsed into silence, not sure what else to say. But then Julie suddenly looked at her watch. 'It's getting late, I'd—'

'Jules …'

They looked at each other for a moment, and it seemed to Jake like that lasted a lifetime. Then, without another word, she was rising, scooping up her coat and bag, but not letting go of his hand. Pulling on it, leading him in the direction of the lifts.

Then they were inside, and he was pressing the button for his floor. And as he turned back to her she planted the first kiss on his lips. The first kiss they'd shared in years, yet it felt like no time had passed at all.

They barely made it to the room before their hands were all over each other, tugging at clothes, in each other's hair. Before Jake knew what was happening, they were both naked and on the bed.

The first time was quick, two people eager for each other, eager to become one. Tongues darting in and out of mouths, hands exploring, pleasuring. The kind of lovemaking that only comes from knowing your partner well, from having done this so many times before. Julie let out a gasp as he found his way inside her, then her hands were reaching down, grabbing him, urging him

213

on as his thrusts gained momentum. Then it was over, and they both lay panting in each other's arms.

It wasn't long, though, before they wanted each other again.

* * *

If that moment staring into each other's eyes seemed to last forever, then the rest of the night passed by in a flash.

Julie fell asleep first, and he watched her on the pillow beside him. It felt so right, her being here. It felt like he really was home … Didn't need the house, just needed her; always had.

It wasn't long after that he drifted off himself, the combination of drink and what they'd been doing making for the best sleep he'd had since his return to Redmarket. The best sleep in years.

When he woke again, however, light streaming in through the window, the space beside him was empty. Jake cocked an ear, listening out for the flush of the toilet or running water in the shower. But there was nothing, apart from the usual sounds of people getting up in hotels and stomping around, making sure they didn't miss breakfast.

Jake waited a little while, then raised himself up on one elbow. He waited a little more, until eventually he even called out.

'Jules?' No reply. 'Hey, Julie … You in the bathroom?'

He got up, got out of bed – and that was when he saw it, floating to the floor like a leaf. The note she'd left on top of the duvet. Puzzled, he went over to it and picked it up. Read the words, though they didn't really sink in at first:

*Last night was lovely … But it was a mistake, I shouldn't have let it happen.*
    *I'm so sorry.*
    *He's still my husband and I do love him. I don't want to throw away another marriage, can you understand that, Jake?*

214

*I'll always love you too, but we can't go back no matter how much we might want to.*

*It just wouldn't work.*

*J xx*

Jake read it again, scratching his head. What was she talking about, wouldn't work? Of course it would work, if she let it! If she'd just leave that twat she was with ...

Who'd been there, when he hadn't.

Christ.

He read the note again, then he screwed it up into a ball – slumped back down on the edge of the bed with his head in his hands. He'd been so stupid for believing that everything could just go back to the way it was, should have been the one to stop it, though they'd both had too much to drink ... Wasn't her fault, wasn't his fault.

It was just another mess.

Seriously, what was he still doing here? He'd already put someone he cared about in the hospital, almost ruined another's marriage, such as it was ... (but that was her decision, her choice).

Channing was right, he should leave all this well enough alone. Everyone here would be better off without him, he should just go again.

Go home.

And, thinking that, Jake began to cry.

215

# Chapter 21

He'd been packed, all ready to go.

There hadn't been much *to* pack really, just the stuff he'd bought while he'd been here: a few clothes, toiletries, a holdall for the trip, the new charger. And it was as he was grabbing this, about to head out of the door, go down and check out, that he'd spotted the message that had come in overnight.

He'd had it on silent, but probably wouldn't have noticed even if it hadn't been. Jake had been otherwise engaged, losing himself in the moment. Losing himself in someone he thought wanted to be lost as well. Perhaps she had, if only for a little while. But he should stop thinking about that, because every time he did the tears threatened to come again, and he didn't want to keep crying anymore. Was frightened that if he did he might not stop.

The message definitely stopped them coming, though. The one from a number he didn't recognise, an anonymous message with no hello, no goodbye. It just said one thing:

*You should be looking into the mayor.*

The second note that day he'd had to read twice, was puzzled over. But there was more, a second text that was just an attachment. It had been forwarded from somewhere, but that number removed. Usually he wasn't one for opening that kind of thing,

Alison at work was forever warning him about viruses or whatever, but something made him do it. Something about the tone of the message, about when it had come in, the middle of the night.

Jake pressed on it, and once again couldn't quite work out what he was looking at. Some kind of invitation to an exclusive gathering that promised to cater to 'all tastes'. There was a fancy pattern at the top and bottom, but the address where this gathering was being held had been blocked out.

'What the fuck?' Jake whispered to himself, and just held the phone out – staring at it like it was hand grenade about to go off. In a sense, it was. Someone had just thrown him a grenade here, something that could blow everything wide open if only he could work out what it meant. What they meant by 'looking into the mayor'. Why? About what? Invitations to a party or something? It didn't make any sense ...

And the more he thought about it, the more it had to be some sort of wind-up, or hoax or simply spam. Except both messages, the 'advice' and the attachment had come from the same number, and that didn't usually happen with spam, did it? One phishing mail and you were done, that was how it usually worked, wasn't it?

Jake pressed on the number until it gave him the option to ring, then he pressed that button. Nothing happened, no ringing out, nobody answering. He frowned, took it down from his ear and tried again.

Still nothing.

'Okay ...' he said to himself. Then, as he went back to over to the holdall and began to take out the clothes he'd shoved in there, in preparation for the journey ahead, he dialled another number. This time they answered.

'Hello,' said Jake, putting the phone in the crook of his neck as he flapped a crumpled shirt. 'Directory enquiries. Yes, hello ... I was wondering if you could give me the number for the mayor of Redmarket's office please.'

# Chapter 22

The design of Redmarket's town hall was just as schizophrenic as its church.

Jake thought this as he parked up behind it, putting money in the machine for a ticket. It spat one out, which dangled like a dog's tongue until he took it and placed it on the dashboard of his Toyota.

He kept on staring up at it on approach, taking in the building's turrets and domes, the size of the place out of all proportion to the town it served. It was almost as if they were expecting to be at war with the neighbouring towns and cities at any given moment and the whole of Redmarket would need to hold their last stand here.

However, as he got nearer he saw – or remembered, though he'd had very little need to come here when he was a resident – that it also encompassed the law courts as well. For a second, he had a mental picture of Sam going to work on someone in the dock, arguing the case against them as emotionally as she argued Bobby Bannister's innocence. Jake felt bad then, not simply because thinking of that boy brought to mind thoughts of Jordan, of her death, but also because of what had happened to Sam the day before.

She'd got hurt looking into all this with him, but would have been even more hurt if she knew about what happened later on with Julie. Yes, they'd only known each other a short time, but there was something there ... something more than just friendship, even if it wasn't years of marriage behind them. Something that might have been worth exploring if he hadn't bollocksed that up as well, chasing after a dream.

*It's like you've got the Midas Touch in reverse, Jake. Everything you go near turns to shit! But someone, somewhere doesn't want you to give up on this, do they?* Somebody was actually trying to help him, point him in the right direction. Jake didn't know why, or what any of this had to do with Jordan, with Drummond or the rest of it, but now he wasn't just flailing around anymore, doing the Columbo or Scooby gang thing or whatever the hell else Channing had called it.

Now he had a direction, and he also had an appointment. The mayor, Sellars, had graciously given up some time to meet with Redmarket's celebrity grieving father. He'd pitched it on the phone to Sellars' assistant as a meeting to chat about setting up a possible charity in Jordan's name, to help the parents of those who'd lost children under any circumstances. That had got him through the door that afternoon, the chance to do something ... sorry, to be *seen* to be doing something like that was one he knew no politician in their right mind would be able to resist (and the wait had given him a chance to make his official statement at the station about the day before, some lowly uniform jotting everything down Jake could remember).

He'd seen Sellars on the news just after the events back in the market, giving speeches about how Redmarket was still a safe place for the youngsters to hang out at night – regardless of the evidence to the contrary. Had to do that, a lot of the town's income and economy was based around its nightlife. Certainly wasn't based around the meat trade or markets anymore ... So Jake knew that this would mean more airtime for the mayor, who didn't rely on public votes as such – that particular piece of legislation hadn't reached Redmarket and the mayor was still appointed by councillors – but still wanted to keep the inhabitants onside.

And as appealing as a charity idea was – in fact when all this was done and dusted Jake vowed to actually take up that cause and put the project into effect – he had no intentions of talking to Sellars today about that. No, he had other matters to discuss ...

*You should be looking into the mayor.*

Of course, the thought did occur to him on the drive over that this could all be someone's idea of a practical joke. Get the father of the dead girl, who'd already been in jail for brawling, to go after Redmarket's most powerful person all guns blazing. Let's see if we can't get him banged up again, eh? Which would also have the added benefit of getting Jake out of the way, if he was making too much of a nuisance of himself.

It might also be fuelling his opinion about Sellars, leading him to judge the mayor before they'd even met. But that was why Jake *was* meeting face-to-face, wasn't it? So he could try and get a bead on the politician, form his own opinion instead of just believing some random text message that may or may not be trying to send him over a cliff.

Jake pushed on the front doors, which needed a fair amount of weight behind them to move, and walked into the spacious lobby. There was a horseshoe-shaped oak reception desk in the centre, manned by two ladies who looked so alike they could have been twins or clones. Jet-black hair, tied back, thick eyeliner – a little like those musicians from the video by Robert Palmer.

As he walked towards it, his footsteps echoed; the new shoes he'd bought for the funeral also squeaking and pinching. He was wearing the funeral suit as well, his only suit here – his only suit in general, but he wanted to make a bit of an effort for this. Show Sellars he wasn't someone to be taken lightly, he supposed. It was the uniform of the business world, the world of politics, and he was just trying to blend in.

'Hi,' said Jake when he got close enough, and both of the receptionists turned in his direction, wincing at his bruised face. He thought they were going to answer then in unison for a moment when he told them why he was there, that he was expected, but only one did: 'You need the third floor,' said the woman nearest to him. 'Hang a right when you get out of the lift and carry on down the corridor. You can't miss it.'

'Thanks.'

More echoing and squeaking as he strode over to the lifts, where he waited with a man who had a pencil-thin moustache. Jake smiled at the fellow, but he didn't smile back, and when he got out on his floor he threw back a filthy look at Jake like he was something the man had just stepped in.

Not his world … Not his world at all.

He thought of Sam again, wished she was here with him. Wondered how she was doing. He'd almost called the hospital after getting the mayor's number, then stopped himself. The doctor had said she needed rest, and that meant not being pestered by someone who'd put her there in the first place. Not being pestered by someone who'd been a whisper away from just leaving and not even telling her he was going. Selfish, really fucking selfish …

But then, that's what he'd been accused of all along with this – not thinking of the impact on other people. He was being selfish because he was trying to assuage his guilt over Jordan, it was all about him. Jake shook his head. No, it was all about *her*. Had been since … well, forever. Still was. Finding out the truth might help with that, he reminded himself. Might help them all to move on, if that was in any way possible.

First, though, the meeting. And when the lift eventually reached the floor he needed, Jake got out and followed the directions the receptionist had given him. When he got to door, another expensive oak affair, he knocked on it and was told to 'Come'. Instead of the mayor's office, however, there was another reception area with another desk, this time on his right. There was a man behind it, a man whose voice he recognised as the one on the phone: Sellars' secretary/assistant, who'd set up the time in the first place. He too winced when he saw Jake's face.

'I'm afraid the mayor's running a little late,' said the assistant finally, who looked a little like the women downstairs – or their male equivalent, anyway – which did nothing to dispel the idea there was some factory pumping them out like dolls. 'But take a seat, I'm sure it won't be too long.'

Jake thanked the man, after all it wasn't his fault, and sat down next to a table with a pile of newspapers rather than magazines; just to make sure you knew you hadn't taken a wrong turn somewhere on the way to a doctor's or dentist's. He picked one up, a broadsheet rather than a tabloid, and began flicking through. It was full of political jargon, most of which he either couldn't be bothered to try and work out or just bored him to tears. Jake was glad when finally – half an hour later – the guy behind the desk told him the mayor would see him now, standing and opening the door for their visitor as he did so.

The room Jake then found himself in was huge, bigger than any in his flat or back at the house he'd shared with Julie for so many years. The walls on either side of him were lined with bookcases, and those were filled with dozens on dozens of leather-bound tomes. No files, no filing cabinets; just books, lots of books. It made Jake wonder if the mayor just spent the whole day reading rather than doing any kind of work, whether the wait to get inside this 'inner sanctum' was simply to show whoever was waiting just who was in charge.

Ahead of him was a massive arched window with a cross pattern breaking up the glass, but with the most spectacular view of Redmarket beyond. In front of that was a rectangular desk – oak once more – and a chair, which had its back to him. Jake

222

could just about see the top of a head poking up above that, the mayor obviously looking out at that view; surveying the town.

The assistant coughed, then said: 'Mr Radcliffe, sir.' Then he withdrew out of the room backwards as if being pulled on a set of casters.

Jake walked a bit further in, but the chair still didn't turn. When the door closed behind him, shutting Jake inside, he jumped slightly. Then he did so again as a voice came from behind the chair:

'Beautiful, isn't it?'

At first Jake wondered what the mayor was talking about: the office, the desk? Then he realised it was the panorama in front of them both.

'I'd do anything for this town, Mr Radcliffe. Absolutely anything ... And for its people, as well, of course.' With that, the mayor turned around in the swivel chair, then threw Jake a smile. Did not once wince at his face.

The figure rose, and couldn't have been more than five foot all told – certainly looked much bigger on the TV, though that might have been because politicians were always behind a podium. The mayor's arm was held out in a motion that was so quick Jake hadn't even seen it happen, a person well used to pressing the flesh. The uniform was there as well, the suit and tie ... except on closer inspection Jake saw it wasn't really a tie, but a kind of neck scarf that resembled one tied in a knot. And beneath that, a silk blouse – the whole outfit probably costing more than Jake had made over the last few years in his job.

'Sellars,' said the woman, her lipstick muted, her make-up in general toned down so that people would take her more seriously, Jake guessed. Her hair was curly, a perm that was so tight Jake kept expecting one of the springs to pop out at any moment like on a broken sofa, and the large, round glasses she wore gave her the appearance of a librarian – which was handy, given the amount of books on display in her office. She looked about ten or fifteen years older than Jake, but he could have been wrong: someone who just looked a lot older than they were 'Mayor Veronica Sellars,' she finished, still waiting for the handshake, looking down and nodding slightly at the proffered hand.

Jake stepped forward and took it, was surprised when his own was pumped up and down in jerky motions, Sellars' grip almost crushing the bones. 'Mayor,' he said by way of a greeting.

'Mr Radcliffe, I've heard so much about you, seen even more. Please, have a seat.' She finally let go and Jake nearly fell back into the chair she was waving at. 'Before we get started, let me offer you my sincerest condolences on the passing of your daughter. So young, with her whole life ahead of her. A tragic, tragic waste.' The mayor shook her head from side to side, as sharply as she'd shaken his hand.

'Thank you,' Jake said.

'Now then,' said the woman, sitting and gripping the arms of her own chair. 'What is it we can do for you? You mentioned something to my assistant about a charity ...?'

Jake nodded, just the once. 'Yes, I was thinking something for those who've lost children in the past. They might have gone missing, perhaps an accident, or ...' He left the last bit as they both knew what he was going to say. The parents of kids like Jordan.

'I have to say I think that's a splendid idea, Mr Radcliffe.'

*I'll bet you do.* 'Jacob, please.' He wasn't sure why he insisted on his full name, just because it didn't really feel right that she used 'Jake'. In the same way it wouldn't feel right for him to call the mayor 'Ronnie', though it might have been more appropriate given those massive glasses.

'Jacob it is then.' She gave him another smile.

'Do ... do you have any of your own?' he asked her, easing back into the seat – which was incredibly uncomfortable, unlike, he suspected, the mayor's. Another way of telling you just who the boss was here.

'Children, you mean?' The smile faded. 'I'm afraid my late husband and I were not blessed. I wasn't ...' She whispered the next part. 'I wasn't able to have babies, sadly. Not even when that was a possibility.'

'Oh, I'm very sorry to hear that.'

Sellars waved a hand. 'All water under the bridge, Jacob. Just wasn't to be ... But getting back to your idea, when you say children, what do you mean? Is there a cut-off point? You daughter, for example, she was almost 21, wasn't she? A young woman.'

A muscle in Jake's cheek twitched at that. 'They never stop being your children, no matter how old they get.'

'No, no. Of course not. That's not what I meant, I just ...' She smiled. 'These are things we can iron out as we go along. Now, do you have any strategies in mind for raising money? Have you thought that far ahead? A helicopter view of this, or are we talking grass roots?'

Strategies, helicopters, grass ... Definitely not his world, not his language.

'For instance, I have many friends in the business world, and the world of politics.' *No shit*, thought Jake. 'I'd be happy to ask on your behalf for donations or whatever? I'm sure they'd be more than willing to take part, if I made the approach ...' *Me, not you – naturally*. 'Or perhaps you were thinking of some sort of event, a fundraiser perhaps?'

Jake rested an elbow on the arm of the chair and rubbed his chin. 'That might be good. Something like a marathon, or cycle race, perhaps held in Redmarket itself.'

'Hmm,' the mayor replied, no doubt thinking about the disruption which might be caused by something like that, blocking off roads.

'Or maybe a charity auction, or a ball?'

The mayor clapped her hands together. 'Yes, precisely. That's more like it.'

225

'Or ... I don't know, a more private function?' He looked her in the eyes as he said the next bit. 'Something that might cater to all tastes?'

The corner of the mayor's mouth spasmed. Then a combination of looks flitted briefly across her face: confusion, panic, even fear. It was only a flash, and all took place in a few seconds, but she soon regained her composure. Nevertheless, what he'd said had rattled her. 'All ... I'm not sure I quite follow you, Mr Radcliffe.' So they'd gone back to his surname again. 'What do you mean?'

Jake shrugged, he had no idea. 'How about you tell me?'

'It's ... That's a very strange way of phrasing ... What made you ...?'

'Oh, just something I picked up somewhere,' he told her.

Her eyes narrowed then, the effect magnified by those glasses. 'Right. I see ... Am I correct in saying that you're no longer a current resident of Redmarket, Mr Radcliffe?'

'That depends, I've been here a while now. I came back to identify my daughter, you see. Then there was the funeral and—'

'And you've got yourself into a spot of bother a couple of times, haven't you?' It wasn't a question, more a statement of fact that Sellars already knew. The first one, he could let her off because the media had got hold of it. But as for the second, that only happened yesterday ...

'Seems that way,' Jake responded.

The mayor leaned forward in her chair, which tilted – and placed her hands, folded together, on the desk. A classic defensive bit of body language. 'What exactly are you still doing here, Mr Radcliffe? Because I'm not entirely sure it's to discuss a charity.'

*Perceptive*, thought Jake, but didn't answer.

'Let me tell you what I think, based – of course – on what I've been told. You see, there's not a lot that goes on in my town I don't know about.'

'Does that include the murder of innocent kids? Oh, I'm sorry

226

... *young women*.' There was an edge to his voice that couldn't really be missed, and even if he'd wanted to, he couldn't keep it out of the question.

'A young woman, Mr Radcliffe.'

'Yes, my daughter.'

'And from what I can gather, *was* she so innocent?' The mayor waited for an answer to that, but Jake said nothing. It didn't even deserve an answer. 'Is that what all this is, what you've been doing? Looking for a culprit when, actually, he's sitting in our jail, charged, awaiting trial. Now, I know what Miss Ferrara thinks, but I have to tell you she's no stranger to me and she's gone off on flights of fancy before. In this very building, as it happens. We've had to clip her wings a few times.'

'Is that what happened yesterday, she had her wings clipped?'

'Good grief, Mr Radcliffe, from what I heard you were both poking around an abandoned building when she fell and—'

'Was pushed!' Jake corrected. 'Kicked, if you want to be specific.'

'I can't say I'm that surprised, there are some very unsavoury characters who hang around in places like that.'

Why did he get the feeling Sellars meant him and Sam when she said that? 'People like that Drummond guy,' he said to counter that. 'What's his connection to all this?'

'All *what?*' The mayor's hands flew open then – the opposite of the clap earlier – and she spread them wide. 'What exactly is it you think's happening in Redmarket, Mr Radcliffe? I'd love to hear your theories.'

Jake opened his mouth, then closed it again. He didn't really have any was the problem, but even if he did, he wasn't about to share them with Sellars.

The mayor let out a slow breath. 'Look, I can sympathise.'

'If you've never had children, you really can't,' he told her.

'Would you let me finish!' she barked, and he recoiled as if slapped. If his words had an edge, then hers had the ability to run through you. There was no wonder she'd got so high up in

227

the food chain. 'Thank you! As I was saying, I can sympathise – but I will only tolerate so much. Throwing around accusations and wild conjecture is simply not going to help anyone. We have the boy in custody. Our police know he did it, I know he did it, and I think deep down so do you. Walk away from this, Mr Radcliffe. Walk away now, before someone else gets hurt.'

'That sounded very much like a threat.'

'Merely good advice,' said Sellars and when she smiled this time it had a distinctly chilling quality.

'And what if I don't?' asked Jake.

Sellars rose, making him jump again. It was ridiculous, she was tiny – the exact opposite of someone like Drummond – and yet he was more nervous of her than anyone he'd ever met. *There you go*, he said to himself, *you wanted to get a bead on her, face-to-face. There's your bead.* She pressed a button on a console to her left; Jake braced himself, actually worried he might drop through a trap door or something. 'We're done here,' she stated, and at the same time her assistant came through the door, the button a summons.

Jake got up as well, nodding at her. 'Thank you for your time, it's been very informative.'

She nodded back.

Jake made his way to the door, joining the secretary, but couldn't resist stopping and looking back once more over his shoulder. By that time the mayor had sat down again, turning the chair around.

'Very informative,' he said again, then left.

* * *

When he got outside again, passing the clones on the way, Jake reached into his pocket for his phone.

He looked at the messages he'd received one more time. Someone had definitely been on the ball, there was something

228

very dodgy about that woman – sitting up in her tower (literally), looking down on the kingdom she knew everything about. Very little happened in Redmarket that she didn't know about, she'd told him, and he believed her. What all this meant, and its connection to the invite he'd been sent was anyone's guess. But he was determined now to find out, and no scary little woman with a perm was going to put him off.

Moving to a different part of the phone, he brought up a set of numbers and pressed one as he walked back towards his car.

The call was answered pretty much straight away; she was good like that and more or less permanently chained to her desk. 'Hello?'

'Oh hey, Ali?'

'*Jake!* How are you?'

'I'm ... well, y'know, as good as you can expect to be under the circumstances.'

'Yeah, yeah. I'm really sorry.' It wasn't clear from her tone whether she was saying sorry about Jordan, or about their coverage of the whole thing – especially the pieces about Jake (as tasteful as they'd been). Perhaps a little of both. 'We all are in the office.'

'Thanks,' he told her. 'I ... That's really appreciated, Ali.'

'Sure. So, I mean I'm not prying or anything, but when are you coming back to work? I heard you were taking some time and everything, which is totally understandable, but ... you *are* coming back, right? I mean ... What I'm trying to say is you're missed, Jake.'

That was one of the nicest things he'd heard in a while, especially since he'd been back in Redmarket, and he told her so. It also served as a reminder, if he'd needed one, that his life – his real home – in spite of what he'd thought, was back there with his friends at the TV station. However, he had still work to do here, and that was the real reason why he'd phoned Alison.

'And listen, if there's anything you need. Anything we can do ...'

'Actually, since you ask, there is something you can do for me,' he told her.

'Shoot,' she said, but she probably hadn't been expecting the request that followed. 'Right, okay, so an attachment? You haven't been opening those spam emails again, have you? Because I warned you not to—'

'No, no spam. Least I don't think it is. This is on the level, Ali. A tip-off.'

'A story? Does this have anything to do with your fight, and getting arrested? Are you chasing up a story, because you should probably be talking to—'

Jake transferred the phone to his other ear as he opened the car door, then slid inside. 'I'd rather just keep this between you and me for now, is that okay?'

'Sure,' replied Alison. 'Whatever you want.'

'So I'm okay to fire those over for you to have a look at?'

'Yep,' she told him, then let out a little laugh. 'Trust you to go back home and get mixed up in something ...' She went quiet, realising what she'd said; the reason why he'd gone home, and the fact that he really hadn't been looking for a scoop. 'I'm sorry, yeah. Of course. Send whenever you want and I'll get back to you.'

'Thanks,' Jake said again, 'Appreciate it.'

Then he hung up. But before he started the engine to pull out, he stared up at the town hall once more, locating that window with the cross pattern.

And there, standing now rather than sitting and surveying, was the mayor looking right back down at him.

# Chapter 23

He thought certain things only happened in the movies.

Not the kind he was into, or looking to make, but in action movies, Bond flicks. And, while the mayor *was* a bit like some sort of 1970s pantomime villain up in her lair (and he remembered what Channing had said about Drummond and the abattoir), she was no Blofeld or Drax. Or at least he didn't think so ...

Not until the 'accident'. Not until there was yet another attempt on his life.

Jake had been driving back to the hotel when it happened. He'd taken the long way round rather than cut straight through town. Took the scenic route because it would give him time to think about all this, time to wrap his head around the new information. The course correction ...

Of course, he still didn't have any real evidence that the mayor was up to anything. Playing devil's advocate, the whole meeting could have been read as fairly innocent, nothing suspicious at all. Jordan had died, her killer was in jail; that should be the end of it. So what was all this? From the outside it might well look like his words were nothing more than the rantings of a madman.

Except for the vibe he was getting from her, and except for

the way she'd reacted when he'd used the exact words that were on the invitation he'd been sent. That had definitely not been his imagination ... had it? And someone had definitely sent those messages to him, was trying to steer him in the right direction – whatever that might be, and whatever it might lead to.

Yet he still had his doubts, was still questioning everything. Had been on the verge of packing it all up and heading off that very morning. Doing what both Channing and now the mayor had advised and leaving it the fuck alone. Now ... something was still nagging at him, something was definitely wrong. It didn't necessarily mean, as Sam thought, that Bannister was innocent – but it did mean something. Those numbers in Jordan's diary had led somewhere, the stuff with Drummond was something, the meeting with the mayor had been *something*. He just couldn't work out what. Wasn't smart enough, or didn't have enough information or ... something.

Something again. Something ...

All these thoughts had been rattling around in his brain as he drove, making his way from the busy roads to a smaller one that he knew. Less traffic, less noise. Which meant that he should have noticed the car behind him more easily, and he would have if his mind hadn't been so clogged up, so fogged up with everything. A maelstrom whirling round again.

It had probably been following him since he left the car park, though he hadn't been aware of it. Had more than likely hung back until they were more or less alone on that stretch of road, or was perhaps waiting until they arrived at a few of the bridges that you needed to be careful going under because there was only space for one car from either direction at a time ...

As it was, Jake noticed the nondescript green Escort right at the last minute. Right when it was on his tail. They were doing thirty-five in a thirty zone as it was, so Jake didn't speed up or anything. If it was someone unhappy about how fast he was going, they could overtake.

That's what he'd thought they were doing at first. They indicated to come round him, and he'd expected the vehicle to go shooting off ahead in plumes of smoke like an old-fashioned train; exhaust probably banging at the same time, judging by how ancient the car was. It was dirty too, he noticed suddenly, especially the windows. So dirty Jake wondered how the driver was seeing out of the windscreen, or his side mirrors (he couldn't see the back, so had no idea about the state of that or if it made looking through the rear-view mirror impossible).

The car pulled up alongside him, which he remembered thinking was a bit stupid with a blind corner approaching. But it didn't slow down at all, maybe couldn't see it through all the muck that was caked across the glass.

When the first impact came, it took Jake by surprise – and he almost let go of the steering wheel himself. A second jolt, and he gripped it more firmly with one hand, began flapping the other one for the car to back off.

'You stupid ... What're you ...' he shouted, but realised the driver couldn't hear him. The Escort slid sideways a second time, ramming the Toyota. Then the car's nose was out in front and it was veering *into* Jake's vehicle, directing it; steering him in the *wrong* direction. He wrestled with the wheel, grip loosening as he was forced to let it slide through his hands, had no choice but to go where he was being shoved. There was simply no room to manoeuvre, to course correct. To pull away then try to ram the Escort back and retaliate.

Now he realised why the car was so old, because this was its intended use. And the windows were covered on purpose so he couldn't see the face of whoever was trying to run him off the road. The bend was fast approaching though, and the other car was showing no signs of relenting.

Instead, it barrelled sideways one final time, taking the left-hand side of the road away from Jake and causing him to skid onto the grass verge then up a small hillock where his Toyota came to an abrupt halt. He'd had his seatbelt on, so he fell forward and then back, but the airbag didn't deploy.

He looked up just in time to see the other car disappear around the corner. Not quick enough to get the license plate, though Jake suspected it would probably be obscured anyway, or hard to trace. Maybe even stolen.

For long moments he sat there, playing the whole thing back. Going over what had just happened, the 'accident' or something that had been made to look very much like one. It had played out in seconds, but again it had felt like hours as he'd gone through it. Had it been intended as a warning, to warn him off? Or a more fatal 'accident' that he'd been lucky enough to walk away from?

Eventually, Jake got out of the car, almost falling against it because he was so shaky. He'd never been in a car crash in his entire life – *almost*, a few times, including on his drive over to Redmarket, but never actually involved in one. Looking down the side of the car where the Escort had slammed against it, he saw the damage there: the dints and scrapes. He checked over the front and found it mercifully untouched. Still drivable. A couple of cars zoomed past, but nobody stopped. Not many people would think of doing that these days, unless it was something more serious.

He had to laugh at that. More serious than almost being killed? All right, it didn't *look* very serious then – a couple of skid marks as he'd gone over onto the grass. Might look like he'd been trying to take the bend too fast and lost control … cars going by too quickly to see how banged up the driver's side was. Jake laughed again, a nervous laugh. Going from terrified to delirious.

Then, looking at it, thinking about what had almost happened, he started to feel angry. No, in actual fact, he was furious. Whoever had done this, and on whoever's orders … he was livid. How dare they? But it did mean one thing; whereas before he'd only been suspicious, had nothing confirmed, now he felt sure in his gut that something – there it was again, *something* – was amiss. Didn't hang together right, just didn't fit.

It made him all the more determined, that anger. To get to the truth of whatever was going on. He thought absently about reporting the crash to the police, but they'd think the same thing: just an accident, Jake driving recklessly after leaving his meeting with the mayor. The damaged side? Maybe he'd even hit a car himself on the skid, might be looking at charges himself if the diver reported it (Jake had a funny feeling they wouldn't).

So, there he was by the side of the road, thinking that this kind of thing only happened in the movies, and wondering what his next move should be. Something aside from calming down enough to get back in the Toyota and drive to where he'd been heading in the first place (assuming that Escort wasn't just waiting for him, to try again) when his phone vibrated in his pocket.

He pulled it out, noticing that his hands were still shaking, and pressed the screen button to accept the call.

'Hi ... Jake?' said a female voice. Alison. Jake nodded, then realised she couldn't see him, and said that it was. 'Hi yeah ... Are you all right, you sound a bit ... I dunno, strange.'

Jake assured her he was fine, and it was then that she said it. The words that made him laugh again, or at least smile. 'You know those texts you sent me earlier.'

'Yeah?'

'Well,' said Alison, 'I think I might just have something for you...'

# Chapter 24

He'd been about to turn away and leave, she could see that.

Thought she was asleep, but she was only cat-napping. But Sam had spotted him when her eyes fluttered open, a shape lurking in the doorway, watching her. 'Jake!' she'd called out to him and he'd frozen on the spot. She thought he was just going to go anyway, leave without saying anything to her – but he turned back around, held up a hand. In his other one he was holding a box of chocolates.

He could barely look at her, his gaze like a butterfly not wanting to settle there, his face full of guilt. There was no need, she was a big girl and she'd been the one who'd taken them to that horrible falling-down building in the first place. Based on coordinates Jake had come up with, yes, but she'd driven them both there. Insisted on taking the risk with him of going inside. He had no need to feel guilty …

Unless it wasn't just about the attack?

Didn't matter, she thought to herself as he came over – it was just good to see him. Good to see anyone who wasn't a nurse or a doctor. She'd not even had any visitors from work yet, even thought they'd been notified of the situation. And Sam wondered then just what they'd say about it, the questions they'd ask about what she'd been doing in such a dangerous location. Not that she didn't have a reputation for going off-course from time to time. It was just that they'd probably have a problem connecting all that to the Bannister case. She was having a problem herself, as it happened.

But here she was, alive and ... if not well, then she'd recover. It was more than she'd been expecting when she was kicked off that walkway, when the railings gave and she'd tried to hold on but couldn't. Jake was in a lot better condition, she had to say – for one thing he wasn't laid up in here with his leg in a cast, his ribs strapped up after undergoing surgery to stop an internal bleed. She'd been lucky, they'd said to her. Didn't feel all that lucky at the moment, felt like she'd gone ten rounds with Creed and come off worse. But she *was* alive, that was the main thing. And where there was life ...

Jake had some bruises, a couple of plasters that had stitches underneath. Nothing major, and nothing that spoilt his looks. Now *she* felt guilty for thinking that, about a guy who'd lost his daughter so recently – and she felt guilty about the heat rising to her cheeks, the blush she knew was there.

'Hey,' he said as he came alongside the bed.

'Hey yourself. Those for me?' She nodded at the chocolates he was still cradling.

'Oh, yeah,' he told her, looking down as if noticing them for the first time. He proffered the box like some kind of delicious olive branch. 'Didn't really know what kind you liked.'

'Hmm, well, good choice. They'll help wash down the hospital food,' she said with a small laugh. 'But no flowers?' She regretted that joke as soon as she'd said it, and apologised. Stupid, stupid, stupid! He looked like a rabbit in the headlights ... 'These are great, thank you,' she said, accepting the chocolates and gesturing for him to sit. 'Do you want one?'

Jake shook his head. 'I'm not really ...'

'You are eating though, right?' *Bloody hell, Sam – now you sound like his mother!* But it had been one of the things they'd talked about when they'd seen each other, a running gag about him eating; about her making him eat, as Italians were prone to do, being in love with food and all.

'I ... Anyway, how are you? You're the one in the hospital bed.' A not so subtle change of subject or focus of attention, shifting it back to her.

'I ... I'd be lying if I said I was fine. I hadn't really pencilled in an operation for this week, or ...' She patted the leg. 'Still, it got me a room to myself which in this day and age is a miracle. Or maybe that was because they got wind I was a lawyer, wanted to keep me away from the other patients in case I offered to represent them and sue for negligence. They brought my car back, which is also good – and before you ask, no you can't borrow it while I'm in here ...' She smiled at him, but his face remained the same. 'Feel free to write something on the cast, by the way. I don't have a Sharpie on me, but ...' Jake looked down then. 'Hey, it's okay. Really. Nobody had a gun to my head, I make my own decisions. None of this was your fault. I'd love to get my hands on whose it was though, tackle him in the light and maybe have a baseball bat handy, know what I mean?'

Jake said nothing.

'In fact, sometimes stuff like this, an experience like this, where someone ... It can actually bring you ... Makes you realise how close we all are to that farm.'

'Yeah,' said Jake, and for a moment she sensed he was thinking about something else; mulling it over. Not the slaughterhouse, but another close shave.

'Look at me, it's all right. Promise.' But she could see when he did look up that it really wasn't. 'What is it, Jake. What's the matter?'

He made to get up again, but she grabbed his hand. 'I really shouldn't have come here tonight.'

'Come on, sit down. Tell me.'

'It's ... It's nothing.'

'Jake, I've been lied to by the best of them – and knew before they even opened their mouths – but you're not even particularly good at it.'

He shook his head, sat back down again. 'I guess ... Well, I guess I owe you that much.'

'What are you talking about?'

Jake stared at her, but she wished to God then he was looking anywhere else. 'Julie,' he stated.

'Oh.' She let go of Jake's hand and he looked away again. 'When was this ...?' Sam asked, then suddenly realised she didn't need any more details; didn't want them actually.

'She ... Julie was waiting for me after ... Well, here. We had a few drinks, chatted about old times and—'

'One thing led to another. I get it.' But she really didn't. Inside, Sam was shaking; angry and upset, though she knew she had no right to be. Had no claim on Jake, especially compared with a woman he'd been with since school. A woman he'd walked out on, by the way, and who'd married again, Sam reminded herself, which just made her even more angry. And the evening after she'd had bloody surgery! What the *actual* fuck?

'It was wrong. It shouldn't have happened, it was ... it was a mistake.' Even as he said the words, though, she could tell they weren't his. Not originally. 'It's a mistake that won't happen again.'

'Hey, no biggie. We're just mates, Jake.' She said the words but couldn't hide the hurt. Wasn't sure she wanted to ... Maybe she wanted him to feel bad now, feel as hurt as she was. But then she said, 'We ... we were just helping each other out.' Were? As in past tense? Were they done here?

Jake noticed it as well, nodded. 'I guess ... Well, I just wanted to see you again, I suppose. One last time.'

So what, he was leaving now? He was just going to walk away from her, from the promise he made to his daughter? Why not, he'd walked away from one of them before. But she could see it was more than that. Perhaps he had been thinking about skipping out, but there was something else in his face now, a sort of determination, or resignation, she couldn't decide which. A mixture of both, maybe?

'Jake, what are you … What's happened?'

'I don't know what you—'

'Yes you bloody well do! What have you found out?'

'Nothing.'

'That's bullshit. Tell me.'

He rose at that point. 'It really is time I was leaving, Sam.'

She reached out for his hand once more, but he was already too far away from her. 'Jake, please don't do anything rash.'

He smiled sadly at her. 'I really am glad I met you, that I was able to get to know you a little bit. And I am genuinely sorry.'

Then he walked out the way he came, leaving her lying there open-mouthed, pressing the button to get a nurse. To get them to pull the phone on the armature closer so she could call someone, anyone.

But what would she say? She didn't have the faintest clue what Jake had found out, nor where he was going.

She just knew he would soon be in all kinds of trouble.

# Chapter 25

He was in trouble, serious trouble.

Jake pressed himself up against the wall, could hear the footsteps approaching. Nearly there, nearly. He tried to control his breathing, though it wasn't easy – the threat of being discovered massive. And it wasn't simply trespassing he'd go down for, it would be breaking and entering at this point. Or worse, given the kind of people he was dealing with.

What the fuck had he been thinking? Just what the fuck …

Sam had been trying to warn him, and wasn't there just a part of him that didn't want to visit her because of that? Not just because she would be able to see right through him about Julie – which, if nothing else proved how insightful she was, how good at reading folk – but the rest as well. What Alison had told him on the phone after his close encounter with the Escort.

'I think I might have something for you,' she'd said. The text had been sent using a burner phone, which he'd pretty much figured out for himself when he couldn't get through. Whoever had sent it couldn't risk it being traced back to them, didn't want to get themselves in trouble obviously. But – and it had taken some doing, she told him – she *had* been able to trace where the original message had been sent from. Not a phone at all, but via an email account registered to a Mr R. Auder. 'Now, I couldn't find anything about him at all, but there's an address if you want it.'

Yes, yes he did.

'Just don't ask me how I got all this, or say anything to anyone, because the software, it's ... well, it's not strictly legal. Friend of a friend helping me out and all that.' He promised he wouldn't say a word, because what he was intending to do with that address wasn't strictly legal either. And he got her to promise not to ask him what he was planning ... for now.

He'd thanked her, then said he'd be in touch again soon. But even as he'd hung up, Jake didn't know if he ever would be again. He'd thought the same as he walked out on Sam, but that had been one of the reasons for going there in the first place – manning up, because he wasn't sure how this would pan out. Finally mustering the courage to visit her after what he'd done, what he was about to do.

It hadn't exactly gone the way he thought it would, or maybe it had. Maybe it had gone exactly the way he imagined, ending with Sam getting hurt (again) and being worried about what he was up to. How could it ever have gone any other way?

Jake had got in his car then and headed off to the address, once he'd ascertained he wasn't being followed, that was – he didn't want whoever was driving the Escort finishing the job. The location was a farmhouse in the middle of nowhere, between Granfield and Redmarket; there were fields on either side, so he'd parked some distance away and decided to try and get closer on foot.

*'How close we all are to that farm.'*

He'd thought about calling Matt or even Channing before he set off, but it would be the same old story; they couldn't do a thing without any evidence, and actually he didn't even know what evidence he was looking for anyway. Evidence of what? Jake was hoping the answer lay inside the house somewhere, or why had that invite been sent to him to begin with?

242

And he'd thought then, as he kept low and approached the building which had a couple of lights on, shining through windows, that this was also what they did in those action movies, in Bond films – usually followed by the hero blowing up some outhouses as a distraction. Sadly, he'd left his explosives behind in his other jacket, but when he got close enough a set of floodlights sprang into life anyway.

Jake ducked behind one of two Land Rovers parked on the drive, keeping out of sight ... he hoped. When he peered round the corner of the vehicle, he saw a couple of figures emerge from the house and have a look around. One of them – a tall, thin bloke – asked if the other could see anything, while the second one – smaller and squatter and with a beard – just said something about the motion detectors being too sensitive; that it was probably a woodland animal or whatever. Absently, Jake wondered which of the two – if any – was the mysterious Mr Auder.

Stepping back, he almost tripped on a stone and suddenly he remembered the fight with Drummond; saw an opportunity to create a different kind of distraction. Jake scooped up the stone and threw it – not at the men, but as far as he could in the opposite direction.

'What was that?' asked the tall man when it landed, and before the other one could answer they were both heading off to investigate. Jake ran, making a dash for the open doorway, figuring it wouldn't be alarmed if they'd just come through it, but not knowing if any more people were inside the place.

*Close to that farm ...* Inside *that farm!*

He stepped in and saw a large kitchen with a range running the length of one wall, cupboards and work surfaces filling up the others, with a washing machine and dishwasher tucked underneath. Keeping as quiet as he could, he made his way through to another open doorway.

Poking his head through this one, he looked right (a set of stairs) and left (a hallway with another open door). He could hear the TV in there before he saw it, canned laughter as some old sitcom played out. And he could see the boxes of takeaway chicken meals, only half-eaten, the cans of beer. He'd obviously interrupted their supper ...

But he didn't have any more time to ponder that, because he could hear the men's voices now returning – the bearded man saying, 'I told you so' to his mate about the animals and vowing to have a look at the lights again in the morning. They'd be coming through the kitchen door any moment, so Jake had no option but to head right to the bottom of the stairs and scoot up them. Making his way quickly, but hopefully without making too much noise. The men were quite loud anyway, carrying to where he stood paused about halfway up the stairs. They were still talking about the lights, and then started nattering about the programme they'd been watching.

'Classic, this one!' said beardy.

'If you say so,' replied the other, mouth full of chicken.

Jake let out the breath he'd been holding, then carried on up the steps to the top – distributing his weight so they didn't creak so much. The volume on the TV was turned up and he heard the end of a joke about not mentioning the war, then both men guffawing.

He continued on up the stairs, treading on the floorboards carefully. Gingerly making his way along the landing. Jake had a flashback then, suddenly, to his old home. Heading for Jordan's old room, trying not to look at Julie and Greg's bed (what would that twat think if he knew where his wife had been last night?). He'd snapped out of it, should be concentrating on what he was doing ... *where* he was going tonight. Where to start the search, not that he knew what the hell he was searching *for* – definitely not small animals, though.

The room closest to him was open, and Jake could see there was nobody inside; just a bed and a wardrobe with a mirror. The same was true of one on the opposite side. Ahead of him was the toilet and bathroom, and again the door was open, the room empty. He continued along slowly, towards a door that was open a fraction on the far side, and one that was completely shut nearest to him.

Then he heard it. The noise ... The sound at the bottom of the stairs.

'That stuff always goes right through me, I've told you not to buy it!' the squat man called back to his friend as he started to head up the stairs. Jake swallowed, hard. Pressed himself up against the wall and tried to control that breathing. He had seconds, at most, before the man was on the landing – about to head to the toilet and relieve himself.

*Close to ... inside ...*

Seconds before he was discovered up here with no excuse whatsoever. It was like that sitcom they were watching, where they'd be in and out of the hotel rooms, making shit up; farcical, but not funny in the slightest at the moment.

There was no retreating to the empty bedroom on his side now, he'd run straight into the guy. And Jake didn't have time to get to the rooms on the opposite side of the landing. Which just left the closed one closest to him, pretty much behind him. Checking, searching all of the rooms would have to wait. Right now he needed to hide.

Just like he'd done with Jordan when she was little, just like she'd hidden things back then – and now. He had no choice, the man was almost at the top of the stairs. Jake turned the handle of the door beside him, hoping against hope it wasn't locked. For a fraction of a second he thought that was the case, but it was just sticking and turned eventually, allowing him access to the room.

He opened it, slipped inside and closed it again. The room was in darkness, everything in shadows. Which at least told him nobody was using it right now. Jake heard the man on the landing, not even trying to be quiet as he plodded along towards

245

the loo. Then the sounds of him urinating; he hadn't been wrong about the brand of beer going through him, it sounded like Niagara Falls, especially as he hadn't even bothered to close the door.

Then there was the flush, but no sound of taps. Just the man on his return journey down the stairs.

Jake slumped against the door, just as relieved as he was.

*Well, if I'm going to search this place I might as well start with the room I'm in*, he thought. So he reached around to see if he could find a light-switch, so he could see what kind of space he was in. Another bedroom, perhaps?

But no. When he finally found the switch and flicked it downwards, he found he was in quite a large space, bigger than the bedrooms, and it was filled with metal cabinets rather than wardrobes. Jake frowned, recognising what they were immediately. They were the sorts of cabinets you kept film in, or used to back when film was used.

He walked over to the nearest one, which was open a crack, and opened it even more, gritting his teeth at the squeaking sound the hinges made. He'd been right: inside, on the shelves, were rolls and rolls of photographic film and sheets of photographic paper. Not just the kind Jake had used when he was first starting out, but even older than that – the kind his mother might have used, or his grandmother. There were cans of film as well, and boxes of slides, labelled with dates that went back to the 1950s, 1960s and 1970s, all in neat little rows. He picked one of the boxes up, marked 1973, and opened it.

Taking out one of the first slides he came to, Jake held it up to the light. It was a room, a bit bigger than this, and a handful of men were inside it. A couple were in shirtsleeves, grinning, others were still in their Seventies-style suits. He replaced the slide, got out another. This time one of the men who'd rolled up his sleeves was bending over, looking at something Jake couldn't quite make out because the image was tiny. He squinted, but still couldn't see what was going on. Written on the slide itself, in faded biro, was a name.

Still frowning, he took out another. It was quite plain what this one showed: it was a knife, blood dripping from the weapon. The background, though it was hard to tell, looked like it could be pale, pink flesh. The next one showed the damage the knife had done, what looked like stab wounds, the skin torn and ragged around it.

Jake let out a slow breath this time, and felt quite light-headed. He couldn't help thinking about Jordan on that market stall, stabbed, left for dead ... Was that the connection here, were these killings that were being documented? Had Jordan's been? Like the photo that had been taken of him and the policeman there?

Leaving the slides for a moment, he found photo albums on lower shelves. Also dated, these went back to the 1940s, the 1930s, even the 1920s. Carefully, Jake opened one up and found sepia-toned pictures inside that were similar to the slides he'd seen. Men gathering, knives and other implements used on skin and the whole thing recorded frame by frame, names written in fancy handwriting in the white spaces beneath the photographs. But were they the names of the people perpetrating the acts or the people they were killing?

Jake paused when he flipped over one page and was granted a view of one of the victims, a boy who couldn't have been more than about 14 or 15, looking up at the camera frightened to death. A man was standing behind him, holding a cleaver high. The boy's arm was being gripped by someone out of frame, his torso held down by other hands. It was quite clear what was about to happen, but the next photo in the sequence left nothing to the imagination. The arm, cut off at the shoulder, hacked at until it had come loose – and the boy screaming in agony. Jake went from feeling light-headed to physically sick, closing the book so he didn't have to see any more.

Forcing himself, he opened up a few of the other cabinets.

Inside these he found video tapes, all labelled with names, all dated. There was no player that he could see around, but he could hazard a guess as to what was on the tapes. They were making some kind of snuff movies, surely? Were these being sold on the open market, available to the highest bidder? Christ almighty, it was like something from a bad dream ...

He began to think then, the men in these things were obviously enjoying themselves – clearly having a good time. Were they being paid to do this, like actors in the porn industry? Maybe they *were* actors? he thought suddenly. Nobody seemed to be trying to conceal their identities, in spite of the fact if what they were doing was real, they could be arrested for it. Hell, back when some of those photos were taken, they'd have swung for it – hanging still a punishment for crimes like those.

Was all that shit just special effects? He was starting to hope so, but could it have been that good back in the 1920s and 1930s? They'd taken that lad's arm off for heaven's sake? All smoke and mirrors?

Or was it real and the perpetrators were being paid anyway. Had Bannister been paid to do this, but got caught?

There were more albums accompanying the videos and in spite of himself, he looked inside a couple. They were filled with Polaroids this time, but no less lurid. No less gruesome in what they depicted. They didn't look fake, but ...

Jake put them down, checked inside another cabinet – this one filled with DVDs and Blu-rays. It was like some kind of warped museum of film and television, showing the ways people had captured images over the last century or so. But he knew that wasn't the purpose of all this, and it had to culminate somewhere.

It was then that he spotted it, the laptop in the corner of the room, resting on a table. The top was closed, but when he opened it the screen lit up – it had only been on sleep or something. Probably a good job, thought Jake, because if it had been shut down it would have been password protected no doubt. As it was, the homepage was on display, but nothing was saved on the desktop.

Jake moved the mouse using the touchpad, opening up the computer section of the laptop and then going into the saved documents. He raised his eyebrows, because there were dozens and dozens of files. There had been some attempt to scan the old stuff in, because some of them went back to the dates of the photos in the albums; back-ups in a modern age.

He clicked on a folder that was marked last year, opening it up and finding not only jpegs (and the thumbnails of these were bad enough, he didn't need to see the full-sized versions), but also video files.

Finding the volume control and turning that down, he clicked on one. Jake stood back, hand over his mouth as he witnessed two men with salt-and-pepper hair carving something into what looked like a young girl's back, judging from the pigtails. This time her wrists were bound, manacled actually, as the men went to work on her. *Fucking hell ... are those words? Or symbols? Some sort of occult thing?*

He had no idea what he'd been expecting when he came here, but it definitely wasn't this. This was so fucked up, so twisted, he was having trouble processing it all. But he had to know, needed to know if Jordan and Bannister had been mixed up in all this somehow ... It was why he'd come here after all, though he hadn't known it at the time.

Jake went to the toolbar at the bottom of the page and searched for 'Jordan Radcliffe'. He bit his lip while he waited, couldn't help tapping his fingers on the desk, though he stopped suddenly because he realised the noise he was making might carry.

His heart almost stopped too when the message popped up.

There was a match.

His hands shaking, Jake tapped on the display which brought up a folder. He looked inside. There were several photos, and a couple of films. Closing his eyes and opening them again, he clicked on one of the pictures. Again, it was hard to make out, but it looked like the top of an arm – the tip of a blade just moving into view on the right-hand side. Though it was the last thing in the world he wanted to do, he clicked on the next one. It showed the blade slicing that skin, redness running from it as it did so. Another he clicked on showed the finished results, but still there was no face. Even though the marks there matched the ones he'd seen in the morgue, the ones he'd thought were down to self-harm, it could still have been someone else.

That hope lasted until he clicked on the next image which showed the cuts on the arm, and Jordan looking over her shoulder – probably at whoever had done this. Bannister, perhaps? Jake looked at some of the other pictures, all dated just a week or so before Jordan's death, but couldn't see the youth in any of them. A couple of blokes there, faces clearly visible, recognisable if he had to point them out in a line-up, but no Bobby.

Jake stepped back from the screen, rubbed his face. Took a deep breath.

'*Your daughter, for example, she was almost 21, wasn't she? A young woman.*'

'*And from what I gather, was she so innocent?*'

All the rest of it, the guys, the going out and stuff, he was still trying to understand – although the diary had helped in that respect. But this? This he was having trouble with; it was more than he could handle. That she'd got involved with these ... sadists, that's all he could think of. How? Why? Had that been down to her current boyfriend?

It just didn't make any sense.

Jake's eyes flicked down to the toolbar and he saw a symbol for an email program there. Moving forwards again, he clicked on it. There were a couple of emails in the inbox, the most recent he saw was basically telling the people here that operations were to cease and desist until the media circus over the death of Jordan

Radcliffe had passed by, which was understandable. They couldn't just carry on with all this while there were so many journalists around ... But they hadn't counted on Jake sticking his oar in, digging into things.

There was also an email dated a couple of days ago, telling them they needed to get a clean-up crew to the site. To get rid of some of the blood that was still there, and bollocking them for leaving it in the first place.

Some of the blood that was—

Quickly, Jake checked the outgoing messages and found one with an attachment that would no doubt get sent to all the contacts in this email program's address book, making things easy. He clicked on the attachment and there it was, the original invitation that he'd received by text – how Alison's friend with the dodgy software had been able to trace this location. Only now it showed the address of the gathering, the party that was suitable for 'all tastes' (and thanks to what he'd found in this room, he knew just what that meant, or some of it).

The address was a set of numbers, coordinates. The same set of numbers that had been in Jordan's diary ...

He went back to the folder, examining the pictures now not for clues about his daughter or Bannister, but the location. And, yes, he was damned if he didn't recognise some of the background details – the walls especially. This had taken place in one of the upstairs rooms of the slaughterhouse he and Sam had visited. No wonder they'd been attacked! They were getting too close to all this, to the people behind it – whoever they were, and there was still nothing here to connect it all to Sellars though some computer whiz might be able to.

Indeed, there was enough on this computer, probably backed up on some other nebulous system, to bury them all – let alone in here!

Jake closed everything and sandwiched the laptop together again. Now he had to get out of here and report back ... No, first he had to let someone know where he was, and what was here. Matt.

He took out his phone and was about to dial the number when he thought about noise again and opened up a text instead. Fingers working furiously, fumbling over words, Jake told him about the farm, where it was and some of what he'd found. Basically just saying, get someone out here as fast as possible, only people he trusted though ... and at this point in time Jake wasn't entirely sure that included Channing.

He pressed send. Nothing happened. Then he got an error message saying that it couldn't be delivered. Panicking, Jake's eyes scanned the smaller screen in front of him. There was hardly any signal out here, which wasn't really surprising. This place hadn't been chosen for its picturesque surroundings. They had Wi-Fi, but mobile signal appeared to be atrocious. For a second he thought about sending an email instead, but that wouldn't be found until the morning probably – or might be discovered on their system. Plus, he realised he didn't even have Matt's email. Hadn't needed it before.

Signal ... he needed to get a better signal. Maybe outside the door, on the landing? Always worked in his place. So, remembering to switch off the light, he opened the door to the room and quietly stepped out. Tried sending again.

Then Jake looked up, slowly. Opposite him was a bald man who'd stepped out of the room opposite at the same time as, or a second or two after, he'd done the same. It occurred to Jake that if there had been anyone else watching it might have looked like a scene from that sitcom the others were enjoying downstairs.

*Close to ... Inside ...*

And time seemed to stand still once more as Jake took the man in. He was wearing a vest, arms out as he stretched, caught mid-yawn. A tiny blue vein was pulsing at his temple. He was fit, well-muscled, might be able to best Jake in a scrap but would definitely be able to with the help of his friends. Which is probably why Jake had compounded the farcical nature of the situation by putting a finger to his lips and trying to shush him.

The man was just gaping at him, probably wondering if Jake was a figment of his imagination or an after-effect of a dream he'd just had. But time couldn't stand still forever, and eventually the guy realised what he was looking at was real.

'Oi,' he said quietly, then more loudly, '*Oi!!*'

Jake blinked once, twice, and bolted sideways. Bolted left to rush down the stairs, hoping that he might get to the bottom and get out of the house before the man's cries alerted the others down there.

Fat chance of that, because already they were in the hallway grumbling and asking what all the racket was about. Jake barrelled into the bearded man, knocking him over, then ran right into the arms of the other one who was stronger than he looked. Grabbing Jake in a bear-hug, and forcing him to drop his phone, they looked like lovers about to become intimate. But the only kiss Jake was interested in was a Glasgow one, pulling his head back as far as he could and butting him hard.

The thin man let go, sliding down the wall and clutching at his face. Jake looked back over his shoulder, which was definitely a mistake, because he saw the bald man now on the stairs holding a gun.

*Shit!* he thought. *Not so farcical now, not so funny …*

*Close … Inside … Buying the farm …*

'Come back here!' shouted baldy.

There wasn't much chance of that, but the distraction did mean Jake missed the thin man grabbing at his leg from his lower position. Jake tripped, went flying, and landed on the hall floor. Winded, he still attempted to get up and get away, but the element of surprise was gone now and the three men – men Bond or one of those other action heroes would have been able to fell single-handed, but Jake was just Jake – were on him seconds later.

Seconds after that he was hit on the back of the head with

something – the butt of the gun? – only it didn't knock him out. He just felt pain, was aware of his scalp leaking, bleeding. He might even have said 'Ow!' but he couldn't remember. More farce ...

Then it didn't matter, another blow and it was all over.

Cue more canned laughter and the credits rolled over the end music of the show.

# Chapter 26

Even before he woke up, he was aware that his feet were not connecting with the ground.

He was flying then? An angel ascending … And once more those thoughts about seeing Jordan again wafted through his mind. His war against the demons in the stained-glass window was over; he'd tried, done his best, and this would be his reward.

But no, he wasn't flying or ascending, because he wasn't moving. His arms were up over his head, like the bald man's almost had been when he was stretching – except Jake's were held fast. Secured by something … *to* something.

And there was pain. Not just from the back of his head where he'd been struck – twice – but also in his shoulders, which were carrying his weight as gravity did its worst.

Not flying then. Hanging.

Jake shifted that head, which was a definite mistake – as was moving it from side to side, to see whether he still could. Then he opened his eyes, the shapes in front of him blurred at first, but even when he could see, when he'd focused, they were not that distinct. Dark and fuzzy, but there was a reason: the light in here was minimal, coming from a couple of standing lamps. Lamps the figures were behind so he couldn't make them out; at least two, he thought. Beardy and the thin man from the farm, or the bald guy with one of them?

He looked down at that point, expecting to see an abyss below him. Some sort of drop like they also had in those action films when they were interrogating people. But actually his feet were only a few metres off the ground, a floor that he recognised. Quickly Jake looked up and regretted that just as much, but it gave him his answer – the final part of the mystery of where he was.

His hands were bound with plastic ties around the wrists, but he was actually hanging from one of the chains and hooks they'd seen when they first came to this place a couple of days ago.

Meat ready for the slaughter.

Jake wriggled around on the hook, trying to get loose; attempting to haul himself up and hop off it, but he didn't have the strength in his upper arms (could have used baldy's help with that). When he let go again, the strain on his shoulders was incredible and he grunted, then let out a cry.

'Fuckers!' he growled, spittle flying from his lips. 'Let me go!' There was no reply, the shadowy figures remained behind the lights. 'I know what you've been doing here, you're finished!'

There was a laugh, light and breathy like a little girl's. Definitely didn't belong to any of the men he'd run into at the farm.

'Did you hear what I said? I know everything, let me go!' he barked.

'Oh, I sincerely doubt you know *everything*,' said the person who'd laughed. 'And the fact you know this much is the reason we can't let you go, Mr Radcliffe.' He knew the voice, had heard it recently, but more measured. An act, a portrayal of civility. Now it just sounded … evil. There was no other word for it.

'Sellars.' Jake said the name like it was a curse, and really was it too far from the mark to say that? The woman was a curse on this town, a blight. Responsible for so much misery.

She moved forward now, still wearing that suit from earlier

256

when he'd arranged to see her. 'What a thorn in our side you have been recently, Mr Radcliffe. But you've had ample opportunity to walk away from this, not least today. I did try to warn you ... Not even when you had your little run-in, or should I say run-*off*, on the road did you back away. Now, sadly, we're going to have to take certain steps to make sure our secrets remain ... secret.'

'Fuckers!' he snarled again.

'Language, Mr Radcliffe. Such language.' Sellars tutted.

'That's what you do, isn't it? To people who get too close to the truth, too close to all this? You get rid of them?'

'Actually, we find blackmail usually works. You've seen the pictures, I assume, the footage. Who'd want all that lot exposing? We certainly wouldn't. It's never really an issue, trust me.'

'So, what, you've been doing this shit all these years ... Why?'

'Why else, Mr Radcliffe. Power!' Sellars clapped her hands together as he'd seen her do before, but then rubbed them. 'I don't expect a man like you to understand, but this is bigger than me. Much bigger than one person.'

'But you're ... Those people, you're killing kids!'

She frowned then, behind those massive glasses. 'I thought you said you knew everything, that you understood?'

Jake gazed at her, open-mouthed.

'You really don't understand a thing, do you? We don't kill anyone. Not if we can help it.'

'What? What the fuck are you talking about? Those girls and boys, they—'

'They're paid for services rendered, Mr Radcliffe. And paid well, I might add. Much better than working in a supermarket or burger shop ... In exchange for partaking in, ah, certain activities.'

So payment was involved, he'd just got that bit wrong. It was the kids taking part who were paid? No, he didn't believe that ...

'We have physicians on hand, but there are accidents, I grant you. Sometimes one of our members gets a little carried away, but—'

'I saw a boy get his fucking arm chopped off!' argued Jake. 'You call that carried away?'

'This would have been one of the older photographs, yes?' Sellars folded her arms, stepped a little closer. 'Back then things were a little more … fast and loose. There weren't as many public records kept, that sort of thing. Sometimes children … young people … went missing without a trace.' She shrugged. 'What're you going to do?'

'Children *still* go missing,' he pointed out.

'Occasionally we draw on the pool of homeless, youngsters who have run away from home. But even then we pay them, unless they get … difficult. We prefer to think of it as a business transaction these days.' Sellars stopped, smiled that chilling smile of hers. 'Oh, wait, is this the bit where I explain my wicked schemes? I expect you think all this is a bit melodramatic, like something from a film or TV show? I'd have thought you'd approve of that, Mr Radcliffe, given your background.'

'I don't approve of any of this crap. You're warped in the head, all of you!'

'If we are, then we're not alone I assure you. There are so many of us, and this has been going on so long that—'

'Back to the 1920s, I know,' he butted in.

She released one of her hands to jab a finger at him. 'But you see, there you are again. You really *don't*. The things you've seen, they don't go back to the beginning of all this. We keep the really early photographic records in the vault, that goes back to when photographs were first being used – and then before that paint-ings, sketches. But not even those go back to the start of all this; far from it. Just be thankful we don't do what they did back then to appease them. There's no cannibalism these days, not on my watch. Well, not much anyway.'

Jake thought he really was going to throw up. Then he thought about those carvings, what those men were doing to that girl with the pigtails. 'Appease *them*, you said. Rituals,' he blurted out. 'This is all occult stuff, isn't it?'

Sellars cocked her head. 'Well … yes and no. Personally I don't really believe in all that nonsense, but some of the members do like to keep with certain traditions dating back to when Redmarket was founded. Back then, of course, it was commonplace. Went hand-in-hand with the town's trade at the time. Our church, for example, that started out as a site of pagan worship. But it was the Vikings who really kicked things off, I can tell you!'

'Mad … This is all fucking crazy,' stated Jake.

'Depends how you look at it. There was a period not so long ago when all of this died down, one of the previous mayors didn't really have the stomach for it. And look what happened? Our town nearly died, our industry certainly did. Then, when we started again, when we found this place … Oh, we haven't always held our gatherings here – they've been in old warehouses, packing plants, the farm you were nosing around, even in people's homes sometimes. But, well, this seemed quite appropriate don't you think? Easy enough to conceal all those hidden cameras … Et voilà, suddenly the town comes back to life. Not our particular industry, I'll grant you – that suffered from the general global economic downturn – but we bucked the trend and survived. No, not just survived: we thrived! Became *the* place to come for the nightlife. For business opportunities, investments … Of course, some of our clients needed a little persuasion, but they saw sense in the end. When I said I felt sure they would have donated to that charity you were talking about, I meant it. They would have had no other choice.'

'You would have blackmailed them,' said Jake.

Sellars grinned. 'Of course! That's how all this works, Mr Radcliffe, don't you see? Everyone has their weak spots.'

'So someone, somewhere, has got dirt on you too,' he surmised. She didn't answer that, but there was another twitch of the mouth, the same as there had been in her office, and she got back to her original tack: 'I suppose it's up to you whether you believe the "sacrifices" worked, the spilled blood. Or whether it was just good business sense on our part, moving those pieces around the chess board so to speak.'

Jake grimaced. 'And that's it, just a little spilled blood, eh? "All tastes" it said on that invitation, what the fuck do you mean by that?'

Sellars sighed. 'Occasionally there's a sexual element involved, I'll give you that. Wouldn't be my first choice, but ... It's totally consensual, however. None of the recipients are forced into anything.'

'No, they're bribed ... or blackmailed again. You said yourself that was how it worked,' snapped Jake, throwing her words back at her.

'No, no ... Not the same thing at all. It ...' Sellars let out another weary breath. 'You don't understand anything about this, do you? Not really.'

'What's to understand? A bunch of sicko perverts are carving up kids ... or young people as you call them, and having sex with them. It's been going on for as long as anyone can remember, and apparently the infrastructure of Redmarket is inherently corrupt. Did I miss anything out?'

The mayor stared at him through her thick glasses. 'This is pointless. I'm trying to explain things to someone who will never understand them, and who is also a dead man.'

'Dead ... Like my daughter, you mean? How involved in all this was she? How involved was Bannister?'

'Again, you know nothing.'

'I *saw* her!' he screamed. 'I saw the pictures from here! I-I saw the scars on her arms when ...' He stopped, tears threatening. 'How the fuck did she get wrapped up in all this, why would she—'

'Money!' Sellars shouted back. 'She was paid, Mr Radcliffe. I keep trying to explain that to you. It. Was. A. Job!'

He thought about Jordan's wardrobe, the jewellery and make-up he couldn't fathom how she afforded. This was how, sadly. This explained everything. But Christ, if she'd needed money, why hadn't she gone to her mum? To him. But then he knew the reason why she hadn't come to him, didn't he – they were barely speaking. It had forced her to turn to these people, these lunatics …

'But I will tell you this before you die, she got cold feet about it all. Wasn't a particularly willing participant to begin with and in fact refused to attend after her first time.'

Jake took in the words, what that meant. She'd got mixed up in something she didn't really understand, and how could she – how could anyone understand this insanity? But hadn't gone too far with it, wanted out, and that had got her killed. They'd orchestrated it all, and the police …

'So, I'm guessing Channing's involved in this up to his neck. He's the one who kept telling me to back off at every turn. What, is he back there behind the lights with you?'

Sellars shook her head, beckoning the man back there to move forward. And even now Jake could see the size of that figure wasn't right for Channing. Too big. Definitely none of the guys from the farm, more like …

'Drummond,' he whispered. So he *had* been involved in all this.

The mayor laughed again, but it was a cackle rather than that whiny noise this time. 'Drummond? That simpleton. Why are you so obsessed with that man? I really don't understand. He's harmless or we would have done something about him ages ago. No, let me introduce you to someone now, Mr Radcliffe.'

A massive shape stepped past the light at that point, somebody who could easily have been mistaken for Drummond at a glance. *Or in the shadows, as you were being attacked*, thought Jake. But on second glance, or even third, there was absolutely no mistaking this fellow dressed in black for Drummond. His eyes, which darted

261

around the place as if weighing everything up, were too keen – and his senses probably were as well. This was a trained man, and Jake had a feeling he knew what the guy was trained *in*.

'This is Mr Ketley. He tidies things up for us when they go wrong, if there are any of those accidents I referred to earlier. You've met him before, but I can see you're probably piecing that together right now. Yes, it was him you encountered here when you were snooping around. And how exactly did you find out about it? From Jordan somehow, I'm guessing? She wrote it down somewhere, didn't she? This location? That's how you had those numbers on you when you were arrested … Oh, and in case you were wondering, it was also Mr Ketley you encountered on the road. It was left up to him as to how he handled that, so I suppose he gave you one last chance. Now you have none left.'

A fixer, thought Jake. That's what this man was. And he'd fixed their little problem with Jordan as well, hadn't he? For the first time since all this began he started to wonder if Sam had been right, that Bobby Bannister was totally innocent. That he'd simply gone along to meet up with Jordan at the time they arranged, only to find her slumped back on a market stall with a knife sticking out of her chest.

'And,' continued the mayor, breaking into his thoughts, 'it's not a bad thing he resembles your arch-nemesis, seeing as we're going to blame your demise on him. The halfwit getting his revenge and all that, eh Mr Ketley?'

The massive man nodded, but said nothing.

Jake spotted that Ketley's hands were gloved, as he looked around and scooped up a piece of metal piping from the floor.

'A spot of bashing the head in should do it, don't you think?' Another nod from the fixer.

Jake started to wriggle again, but had as much success as the last time. Then, panicking, his mind searched for possible ways out of this mess. That's when he said: 'People know what's going on here! You won't get away with this.'

'Who? Who knows?' The mayor looked about her, as if expecting an audience suddenly, then stuck out her bottom lip and shrugged. 'Ah ... I understand. You're talking about the text to your friend, DC Newcomb?'

More panicking. They'd found his phone then, back at the farm – but he didn't know whether the text had actually sent or not, whether he'd been able to get signal on the landing or even when he got downstairs again.

'Now, I know what you're thinking,' said Sellars. 'Did it send? Is he on the way with the cavalry? Well, I can answer the first question for you easily enough ...' She looked behind him now, past his shoulder, and Jake frowned. Then he heard someone stirring, someone who'd been so quiet up to now Jake hadn't even known he was there.

Suddenly, another figure was walking past him. *Bloody Channing*, thought Jake – *he was here after all*. There wasn't any confidence to the stride, though – if anything it was apologetic, hesitant. Seconds later, the man was standing with his back to Jake. He didn't want to believe it, to believe his eyes, but when the figure turned around and faced him, he had no choice.

'I'm sorry, Jake,' said Matt, hardly able to even look at him.

Jake shook his head, even though the pain at the back was still there. 'No ... no, it can't ... Not *you*. Anyone but you!'

*Didn't know the bloke anymore. Not really.*

'I'm sorry,' his friend repeated.

*Far too shady a character ...*

'So, you see, he did get your text after all,' the mayor said with a smirk. 'As for the second part of the question, is the cavalry on the way, DC Newcomb?'

He shook his head. 'No. No cavalry.'

'But ... but you have a son, Matt. How ...'

'Don't be too hard on him, Mr Newcomb. Remember what I said, even if they can't be bought, everyone has a weak spot.'

His family, that had to be it. They were threatening Matt's son, his wife ... It was the only thing that made any sense. But that still didn't excuse this, didn't excuse Matt being involved – even indirectly – with the death of his daughter. 'You bastard,' was all he could muster.

Matt looked genuinely sad when he said that, as if he was disappointed that Jake couldn't forgive him. 'Look, you couldn't possibly ... I ... You just don't get it, you weren't here. I did what I had to. What I thought was ...' But the words dried up, he was trying to defend the indefensible.

And now Jake had to wonder just *how much* of a part Matt had played in Jordan's death. After all, Jake knew he wasn't averse to bending the rules – smuggling him in to see Bannister, for example. And the CCTV in there! Channing's remarks:

*'I'm assuming there's no footage of what took place back there ... You're definitely not that stupid, Newcomb.'*

*'So, it's just the kid's word against ours, right? Wouldn't be the first time.'*

They'd taken out the cameras at the market square as well, made it look like vandalism. It all got him wondering about the DS again. When Sellars had shaken her head, perhaps she'd only meant that it wasn't Channing back behind the lights, it had been Ketley. Didn't mean Channing wasn't part of all this. How far did it all go, how deep?

*'What if ... what if none of this had ever happened, eh?'*

'You fucking bastard,' Jake repeated.

'Now now, I warned you about your language before, didn't I, Mr Radcliffe? And there's really no need for name-calling. DC Newcomb didn't know about Jordan's ... involvement with us until very recently,' the mayor continued. 'Did you?'

Matt said nothing, just hung his head.

He'd known about the rest of it, though. Didn't get him off the hook – didn't get any of them off the hook.

If only he was, though, Jake thought. Off this bloody hook so he could ...

What? Do what? He was no match for Ketley, especially with Matt helping out … Matt? Christ!

*Face it, Jake, you're just as useless as you ever were. Just as much use to Jordan as you were back when you left. Just as much use to yourself.*

'It … it will be quick, right?' asked Matt, looking from the mayor to Ketley and back again. 'He won't feel anything?'

'Matt,' said Jake. 'Listen, you don't have to do this. There's still time …'

Time.

The policeman rounded on him: 'There's no time, Jake! Don't you understand, there never was … Time's run out!' Matt calmed his breathing down. 'You were so desperate for answers, you wanted the truth – well, now you have it. Now you know the truth … about all of us.'

In spite of himself, Jake shook his head once more.

'As touching as all this is, time *is* ticking on and we can't stay here all night.' Sellars waved a hand for her fixer to step forward. 'Mr Ketley, I believe you have some work to complete.'

Ketley nodded, gripped the piping more tightly. He approached Jake, who tried to swing back on the hook. The first didn't get him very far, but the second swung him back far enough for him to get his legs and feet up – adrenaline coursing through him. Gave him enough momentum to swing forward and kick the huge man with the soles of both feet.

It was like kicking a rockface, the man barely moved an inch. Instead, he grabbed hold of Jake's legs, wrapping his free arm around them, and lifted him up and off the hook. He landed on the floor of the slaughterhouse with a thud, all the air exploding out of his body. Ketley let go of him, raised the piping. He had to make it look good, make it look like something Drummond could have done so he'd take the fall.

The simpleton, the boyfriend. All wrapped up in a nice little parcel with a bow on top. Like so many things that had probably been swept under the carpet, covered up or forgotten about. When all this had started, there wasn't even the need – it was only in the era of records and systems of government or police forces that it had been necessary in the first place. All to keep Redmarket alive, while his daughter lay dying on a market stall.

Fuck that!

Jake rolled out of the way of the blow, and the piping connected with the floor – clattering uselessly.

'Don't fight it, Mr Radcliffe,' the mayor advised. 'You're only making things harder for yourself. Though I suppose that's what you've been doing all along, isn't it.'

'Go to hell!' he managed, bringing up a foot and aiming for Ketley's privates. He half-missed, half-hit his target but it didn't seem to deter the man either way.

And then he was looming over Jake, piping aloft once more.

This was it, there was no more fighting it – not for Jordan, not even for himself. If he died, then at least he'd see her again … he hoped. Or would his punishment for not being there when she needed him be the opposite? The pitch black of oblivion?

There was no more time to think about it, no more time at all. Never had been, according to Matt.

The piping was coming down. As the mayor had rightly pointed out …

Jake was a dead man.

266

# Chapter 27

Jake closed his eyes, hearing the crack of his skull as it was bashed in, but not feeling it.

He wondered why. Then Jake blinked his eyes open again and understood. Twice in the space of the last ten minutes or so, or however long it had taken Sellars to have the conversation with him (seemed like yet another blink of his eyes, but that was time again for you), he'd thought he was dead. Thought he might be sent on his way to be reunited with Jordan.

But that wasn't going to happen, at least not yet, because he hadn't had his head caved in at all. Looking up, he saw that Ketley had paused mid-lunge. Again, he wondered why. It was difficult to see at first, because his clothes were so dark – clothes that made it easy for him to blend into the shadows – but there was a wetness at his chest. Small at first, it bloomed and spread, then dripped.

A bit splashed on Jake's cheek and it was warm, and some dripped off to the side of him. He risked a sideways glance and saw that, yes, it was red.

It was Ketley's blood.

The man was turning now, reaching across to feel at the wound. There was another loud crack and this time Jake recognised it for what it was: a gunshot.

*The cavalry*, thought Jake; it had come after all. Maybe not because of the text, but for some other reason: information he wasn't privy to at that moment. Didn't matter, the only thing that did was the fact that Ketley now had two bullets in him.

Three! Because as he turned fully around, another one struck the man and this did force him back a little, caused him to shift sideways a fraction. Before he fell over sideways, crashing to the ground like some sort of demolished building. Revealing the person who had done this, the person standing there with a smoking pistol.

Matt.

*'It ... it will be quick, right?'*

Jake thought of the question, but Sellars was the one who said it out loud: 'What are you doing?'

He didn't answer her, and instead walked across to Jake, bending and putting his hand in his pocket to take out a small knife. Matt jammed the gun under his armpit and opened up the blade, then proceeded to cut the ties that were holding Jake's wrists together.

Jake studied his face, trying to find some sort of explanation in it and failing. Before Matt could give him one, he was struck by something. The pipe that was meant for Jake's head, whacked sideways into his instead. Matt rose, staggering, then dropped to his knees. The gun had fallen to the floor with a clatter and Jake scrabbled across for it.

Ketley, still bleeding from various places, was raising his weapon again – about to hit Matt a second time. Jake scooped up the pistol. He knew nothing about guns at all, other than this looked like an automatic. But it had been fired already so the safety probably wasn't on ... and there were probably more than three bullets in the clip. Jake aimed it at Ketley, but froze. He'd never shot a gun before, let alone shot a person. Those action movies he kept thinking about made it look so easy, but when push came to shove it really wasn't.

That hesitation cost Matt dearly, the pipe descending and catching him a glancing blow off the forehead.

*What's wrong with you? That's the man who more than likely killed your daughter,* thought Jake. That was it, enough motivation to do this. He squeezed the trigger, not once but twice.

One of the bullets missed completely, but Ketley was too large a target for both to do the same. It struck him in the neck, a fountain of blood jetting out. The big man dropped the pipe and staggered about, clutching his throat before collapsing yet again.

Jake crawled over to where Matt lay; there was blood pouring from his head wounds, but he was still pointing at something beyond them both, trying to speak. In the end he managed to get one hushed word out: 'Mayor.'

Looking over his shoulder, Jake saw Sellars had gone; heard her footsteps as she made a run for it. He nodded, rising at the same time and going over to the free-standing lights. Jake turned one around and started scanning the space ahead for the woman, like prison guards looking for an escaped convict or searchlights looking for bombers during the war.

He caught the back of her disappearing around a corner, heading for the doorway – and Jake gave chase. Running as best he could, his feet still numb from hanging above the ground, he got to the place where he'd last seen the mayor and rounded the corner ...

Only for her to come flying out at him. Jake hadn't been expecting that at all, thought he'd be chasing her down the driveway to this place in the pitch black. Instead, here was the small woman raking his cheek with her nails, then trying to wrestle the gun from his grip. She still wanted to end this, fixer or no fixer. Wanted to see Jake dead. That was why she'd come along personally ...

She was also a lot stronger than she looked, and Jake found himself being forced backwards, her snarling face inches from his own. Sellars was like a thing possessed, a million miles away from the smart businesswoman he'd visited that afternoon – cool, calm and collected. Now everything in her world was under threat and he saw the real mayor come out, vicious and primal. She was still grabbing for the gun in his hand, forcing it up, then down.

And it was at this point it went off again. Both of them paused, neither knowing who'd been shot – if indeed anyone had. But it was the mayor who let go now, screaming out in pain, hopping backwards before losing her footing and crumpling to a heap. The material of her trousers was torn, and seconds later it was wet, blood pumping out of her thigh.

She clutched at it, shouting obscenities at him. Now who needed to watch their language! Jake gritted his teeth, stepped forward and raised the gun so that it was in line with her head. At this range he couldn't possibly miss.

'Nobody would know,' he said to her. 'In the struggle, it just went off again. One in the leg, one ... Nobody would know.' He wasn't sure whether he was trying to convince her or himself. Sellars' expression changed; she was no longer the one in control and she looked scared. Could obviously see the determination in his eyes, light from the lamps reflecting off them. See the hatred he was feeling boiling away inside.

His finger was twitching on the trigger, about to pull it when he saw movement. Something out of the corner of his eye, a figure ... At first he thought the mayor must have brought more people, that the guys from the farm had tagged along after all. That she was trying to reach them when she escaped. But why attack him herself if that was the case? Why not leave him to them?

As the figure stepped closer, stepped into the light from the shadows, he saw exactly why.

It was Jordan, appearing as she had done in his hotel, in the cell at Redmarket station. Pale and wan, exactly as she had been in the morgue. Jake's mouth dropped open and he blinked. 'Sweetheart ...?'

Sellars frowned, looked back to where he was staring, then returned her gaze to Jake, confused.

But the girl was definitely there ... wasn't she? Had come to a stop not three feet behind the mayor. And she was shaking her head, just like she'd done the previous times he'd seen her. 'I don't know what ...'

Jordan shook her head again and pointed, just like Matt had done to warn him the woman was running off in the first place. Now he knew what she was getting at, what she wanted him to understand. Jake blinked, nodded and looked down at Sellars. When he looked back up again, Jordan was gone. But then her message had been delivered, hadn't it.

'My daughter wouldn't have wanted me to kill you,' he said to Sellars, who was still looking baffled. 'It's too good for you, too ... quick. You should be punished for what you've done.'

'Fuck you!' Sellars growled at him.

Jake reached down and grabbed her by the collar, dragged her back across the floor of the abattoir. Back to where Matt and Ketley lay; there had already been enough bloodshed in this place, and not just that night.

He dropped the woman next to them and looked over at the man who'd saved him, the man who'd also been involved in all this. He was unconscious, head covered in redness.

Jake checked the pocket Matt usually kept his phone in and found it straight away. It was locked, but there was the emergency call option on the screen. There was also a decent signal, just like there had been when he'd been here with Sam. Jake pressed it, saw 999 come up – but also saw the mayor grinning.

'Hello ... Yes, could you put me in touch with ... the police in Granfield, please? Yes, this is an emergency.'

That wiped the smile right off her face. Of course, Jake had no idea if her influence stretched all the way to that city – probably – but it was a better bet than Redmarket station.

He didn't go into details, just told them to get there as quickly

271

as possible and also to send an ambulance to that location as well. Then all he could do was wait until they showed up.

But wait, safe in the knowledge that this time he'd finally done right by his little girl.

# PART THREE

Redmarket's colourful origins, its early days, remain shrouded to some extent in mystery and rumour. Some say that the old religions were practised, pagan rituals and also rites adopted from invading forces such as the Anglo-Saxons or the Vikings. Some have also linked the town to witchcraft and Satanism, although all of this was thoroughly stamped out of course by the time Christianity became the prevalent religion in Britain. Nevertheless, it is interesting to speculate about what was going on in the formative years of the town, and the exciting events that might have happened back in the mists of time.

# Chapter 28

Jake stared through the glass.

Watching the monitors and the many machines that were keeping the man alive. The pumps breathing for him, the dials and drips. Katherine and Ed had been here earlier, visiting, but she'd had to take the lad out because he was so upset. Jake had spoken with Katherine for a little while, passing on what he'd found out about Matt – not medically, but what had been discovered outside of all that. To her there probably *wasn't* anything outside of this, though.

The investigation was still ongoing, Granfield police uncovering more and more about the web of corruption in Redmarket every single day – not that Sellars was helping any, keeping tight-lipped about the whole affair. Quite a lot of police had already been taken into custody, along with politicians close to her, and the day-to-day handling of operations had been temporarily taken over by the next city across. Remarkably, Channing was so far in the clear – hadn't been recruited yet it seemed, regardless of all his friendships with people in high places. Perhaps the mayor thought he was better left out of it, or was keeping his talents in reserve … or just plain didn't trust him? Or his smile? Maybe he'd known something was going on, but not what exactly.

But Matt, he'd known about so much. Whether they'd been

blackmailing him or not, or even threatening his family, money had been traced to a private account set up in his name. Or had that been part of the blackmail, set up without his knowledge?

*'Remember what I said, even if they can't be bought everyone has a weak spot.'*

There was no evidence to suggest, however, that he'd known about Jordan's involvement, or about her murder. Jake liked to think he didn't anyway, that what the mayor had said about Matt back in the slaughterhouse was right. That it had been down to Ketley alone.

After all, Matt had been the one who'd sent that text from the burner phone, which the Granfield coppers had found in a bin not far from his house. It had been Matt who'd pointed Jake at the mayor in the first place, had sent him the invitation. Might have been to put him right in the lion's den, all part of a plan to manoeuvre him into position so Sellars could get rid of Jake once and for all. But, if that was the case, why help him at the end? Had that been the intention all along, was that why he'd brought the gun (which had been stolen from evidence apparently, part of a haul from a drugs bust)? Or had there been another reason, perhaps he was frightened for his own life? Or maybe his conscience had just got the better of him?

*'To unexpected outcomes.'*

One thing was for sure, Ketley wasn't saying anything either – he'd died in the slaughterhouse. And Matt might as well have done, the blows to the head catastrophic. Once he'd lost consciousness that was it, he'd never come around again and there was minimal brain activity now. Even talk of turning off all that equipment.

*'There's no time ... Don't you understand, there never was ... Time's run out!'*

Had Matt known how all this would go, but was just sick of the lying and the secrets? Wanted to blow the whole thing wide open, make sure his family were no longer under threat?

Or had there been enough of his friend left that wanted to see

Jake get justice once Matt discovered what had happened with Jordan? But *when* had he found out, after the numbers? Because of Jake's investigations?

'He saved my life,' Jake had said to Katherine, who was also having trouble processing all of this. Remarkably, she was a lot calmer than she had been when she'd first found out, crying and screaming, an emotional wreck. When someone that buttoned-up loses it, they really lose it. Apart from a few tears, though, she was more or less back to that 'prim and proper' person Jake had seen at the funeral. 'That has to count for something.'

'But ... but what he did ... I just can't ...'

He wanted to say what he'd been thinking at the time, 'I guess you don't really know anyone', but that would just have been rubbing it in and this poor woman had suffered enough. They'd *all* suffered enough.

*'She makes her own decisions, her own choices ...'*

*'You'd be surprised how many grown women make the wrong ones.'*

Jake was aware of someone coming up behind him and turned.

'Thought I'd find you here, but so much for the element of surprise. These blasted things.' Sam nodded down at the metallic crutches she was using, her leg still in its cast. 'I'm like Robo-lawyer ... Though, it could have been worse.' She looked beyond Jake inside the room in the ICU department, through the window he'd been pressed up against.

'Yeah,' said Jake. 'Could've been worse.'

There was silence for a moment or two, then Sam broke it. 'I see you've been all over the news again. Hero dad avenging his daughter and all that.'

'Thankfully it's calming down a bit now. But I'm definitely no hero,' was Jake's response to that.

'No, you're a bloody idiot going off to that farm on your own without telling anyone. Without telling *me*.'

'I'm sorry,' he said, and not for the first time. Though when he'd seen her just after the events at the abattoir he hadn't been able to get much of a word in edgewise for the yelling. Then she'd surprised him by just giving him a massive hug and telling him she was glad he was okay.

'Well … you're flavour of the month with my firm, that's for sure. We're part of the team sorting all this mess out, and I will be too when I finally get discharged. I was speaking to the detectives they've put in charge this morning, Burton and Wright. And you're pretty popular with Bobby Bannister and his folks as well.'

Jake nodded. It was good news that he'd been released, no point in two young lives going to waste – although he still wasn't sure what to make of the lad. Wasn't sure how he felt about some of those things from Jordan's diary. He realised he'd missed something and asked Sam to repeat it.

'I said: so what next?'

Jake wished that he could go back to when he hadn't heard the question. He had absolutely no idea what to say to it. What next? He hadn't even thought about that, everything had just been such a whirlwind.

'I expect you'll be heading back home soon, right?' she ventured when he looked like he wasn't going to answer. Home, he thought, rolling the word around in his head. Home.

'I guess I should be heading back there at some point, but I'm in no rush to get to work. I'm still owed some time, so I think I'm going to take it.'

'Good for you,' said Sam with a smile. 'And if you find yourself back in this neck of the woods while you're doing that …'

'But I thought … Aren't you going to be snowed under with work? What you just said …'

She shuffled about on the crutches, repositioning them under her armpits. 'Never too busy for a spot of brunch … or maybe even dinner?'

'But, what about what happened with—'

She shushed him. 'Quit while you're ahead, buddy. Besides, it's just a dinner.'

'Right,' he said.

'Since you brought it up, though ... Do you have any plans to see her?'

'Who?'

'Who do you think?'

Jake was starting to feel a little awkward, discussing this just outside Matt's room, given both what had happened to him and how he'd felt about Julie himself. He waved a hand for them to start walking down the corridor away from ICU.

'I already said at the time and after, it was a mistake. Shouldn't have happened; she was right about that. I was just ... neither of us was in a good place.'

'But you are planning on seeing her, aren't you?'

'I ... We have ... had a daughter together.' He said it like that was both an answer and an explanation, but even Jake could see it was a pretty weak one.

Sam looked down sadly, pretending to be watching the crutches as they propelled her along.

'I owe it to Jules to at least tell her I'm going.' Plus, thought Jake, he'd already decided he was going to tell her about Jordan's hidey-hole, give her the diary. She'd be mad probably that he'd kept it from her, but might at least see that without it he'd never have found out the truth about her death.

'Okay,' said Sam softly.

'But I can be here to pick you up when you get out, if you like? Give you a lift home?'

She looked up then and beamed. 'I'd like that.'

'There's one condition,' he said to her.

Sam frowned. 'What's that?'

'You let me do it in the Audi.'

She laughed and it was a nice sound, the best sound he'd heard in a long while.

And before he knew it, Jake was laughing with her too.

\* \* \*

279

It had seemed like a good idea at the time.

No, not a good idea – but the right thing to do. He'd thought it even as he was telling Sam, but here, now, he wasn't so sure. Especially when Greg had been the one to answer the door to him.

Greg's car hadn't been there, so Jake had assumed it was safe to knock, skirting past the few reporters who were still camped out here for some reason – though they hadn't really bothered with him. There was only so much mileage left in this now, and even they were getting bored.

However, as he'd soon found out when that prick opened up, Julie had taken the car out herself to run some errands. That had left Greg in the house, alone.

'Do you mind if I … Can I wait for her? I've got something for her.'

'I suppose,' said Greg, who seemed even snappier than usual that day. Then Jake found out why. 'But I'm on the phone, so …'

Jake nodded, then was allowed into the hallway where he could see the phone there was off the hook, resting on the table. Greg jabbed a finger in the direction of the living room as the man picked up the phone again, and Jake could tell from what he was saying he was talking to his son. Something about a parking fine he'd got and how the lad didn't have the money to pay it. Of course he didn't, he was a student – they were always broke, weren't they. In debt before they'd even started their courses these days; it was one of the things that was in Jake's short film about them.

He wandered around the living room while he waited; it didn't seem right to sit down without Greg or Julie present. In spite of the fact it had once been his house, that he'd once had every right to sit. Those days were long gone, and you couldn't get them back. He'd been a moron to think he could that night. But oh, it was incredibly tempting to wipe the smug grin off Greg's face by telling him. If he didn't think it would hurt Julie (not that she'd cared about hurting Jake when she slipped out and left that note), he'd do it.

But she'd been right, it would be yet another marriage in the toilet. What was the point? And he was tired, so tired. It was time to move on with his life …

When he spotted the paper and envelope on the couch, Jake couldn't help catching the header. The car parking bill that had obviously arrived at this address instead of the uni one; the car and its driver was probably registered to there. That wasn't the unusual thing, though. What was strange was it had come from Redmarket council. Jake paused, staring down at the letter.

He picked it up then, noticed the date the fine was issued at the same time he heard Greg say on the phone: 'Don't worry, we'll sort it out Billy-Boy.'

Everything seemed to happen simultaneously in slow motion and speeded up time after that. Greg finished on the phone, and joined him in the living room, saying something about the fine and one day his son being able to clear up his own messes. Jake had turned, letter still in his hand, and Greg had caught the look in his eye – swallowed dryly.

*William. Billy-Boy. BB … Lightning strike!*

And suddenly he was on the man, dragging him in and shoving him down onto the couch. Greg tried to fight back, but Jake pinned him to the furniture – letter screwed up in his fist, being thrust in Greg's face. 'What did you do?' he screamed at the man. 'What did your son do?'

Greg gaped at him, the first time Jake had ever seen real fear there – though whether it was because of what Jake was doing, or what he'd found out was unclear. 'I-I don't know what you're talking about!' he argued, but there was very little conviction in his voice.

'The ticket!' Jake was still screaming. 'He wasn't away at uni that night, was he? He was here … He was in fucking Redmarket!'

'I …' Greg shook his head, attempted to get up again but couldn't.

'You knew, didn't you? You son of a bitch, you knew – and you covered for him!'

Now Greg's mouth was just opening and closing, like he was searching for words, and failing. Still in a state of shock.

'Jesus Christ! My daughter ... *My Jordan!*' Jake was half-bellowing, half-whispering the words, tears of anger, of pain, escaping.

A bang then made both men jump, that reminded Jake of the gunshot which had saved him back at the slaughterhouse. Only this time it was the front door, Julie back home and rushing in when she heard the ruckus.

'Jake! Jake let him go!' Her hands were on him, trying to pull him back, pull him off Greg before he did something else. 'What the hell are you ...'

He rose, frightened she was going to hurt herself more than anything – but what he really wanted to do right at that minute was throttle Greg. Put his hands around the man's throat and choke the life out of him.

'Are you ... Have you gone mad?' Julie was gazing at Jake, trying to comprehend what was going on, perhaps thinking this was about the night they'd spent together, that her marriage was over now. And it was, just not in the way she thought.

Jake's mind was in a whirl, he needed to call the police. Needed to get them here, get them over to William's uni as well before his dad could warn him. He wasn't going to get away with it – not this time.

'What's ...' Julie was still staring, needing an answer.

So he gave her one. 'Ask him,' Jake snapped at her. 'Go on, ask him, Julie. About how he lied, about how he covered everything up!'

'I don't ...' Her gaze now was flitting from Jake to Greg.

'Ask him,' Jake repeated. 'Ask him about how his son murdered Jordan!'

282

# Chapter 29

A different day, looking through a different window.

This time through a two-way mirror in Redmarket police station. A room he was more than familiar with himself. Now, however, William Allaway was sitting on the side of the table Jake had previously occupied. William's lawyer was next to him, a stuffed shirt from a different solicitor's to Sam's. The guy kept telling his client to keep his mouth shut, that he was only getting himself into more trouble, but the lad wasn't really listening.

It had been going on a few days now, the questioning. Jake had been around for some of it, especially at the start – allowed as a courtesy to watch. If it had been up to Channing, he wouldn't have been anywhere near the place, but luckily Sam had pulled a few strings with the detectives she'd been dealing with. One was with William right now, DI Wright – a woman he really wouldn't want to get on the wrong side of. Dressed in a smart suit and blouse with straight auburn hair, she was making mincemeat of that boy, much to Channing's chagrin. That man's patented fake smile was nowhere to be seen, and he was uncharacteristically quiet as he sat next to the superior officer taking the lead.

Wright was drawing the information out of William, pandering to his ego about how clever he'd been, thought of everything. Had even disabled the CCTV cameras in advance.

'Wasn't hard to make it look like vandals,' William told her.

'I'm sure,' said Wright, nodding. 'So, you knew Jordan was meeting up with her boyfriend and followed her.'

'I wanted to talk to her before she met up with that drip Bannister,' said William. 'We had ... unfinished business.'

'But you knew before you ... talked to her that if it didn't go your way you were going to kill her.'

'I hoped it wouldn't come to that, but she just wouldn't listen.'

'So you made sure the cameras weren't working, wore the gloves. Had the knife on your person?' Wright looked up at William.

'I loved her!' said the boy, getting slightly agitated. 'But she didn't want to know.'

'She was your sister, William.'

'Step-sister. Doesn't count.'

'It does in the eyes of the law.'

'I knew how I felt. I told her ... But she ... And then there was Bannister getting in the way.'

'If you couldn't have her, nobody else could, right? And you saw a way of framing Bobby at the same time.'

'He's so fucking stupid. Who sees a knife and grabs hold of it, puts their prints on it?'

'Someone who was trying to help. Someone who loved Jordan and wasn't thinking clearly. Certainly not in a pre-meditated way like you were.' Wright flashed him a tight smile. 'You see, I don't think you even know what love is. You wanted to own Jordan, right? Possess her? That's not the same thing.'

William stared at her blankly.

'Good, isn't she?' Jake felt the nudge, looked over at the man standing beside him. DS Burton, who looked like he'd walked out of the fashion pages of some magazine with his blond, tousled hair and good looks. 'Like a dog with a bone when she gets going, is our Erica.'

Jake nodded. 'Channing doesn't seem too pleased about it.'

'That tosser,' said Burton, folding his arms. 'He's only in there because it's better than all the earache.'

And Jake recalled now the way Channing had bitched and moaned about Burton and Wright's questioning of Greg Allaway – the way they'd played off each other seamlessly, like tag-team wrestling. The way they actually got results.

Jake wanted to see Greg's point of view, he really did. A father, like he was. He'd argued he'd just been looking out for his kid, same shit he'd said to Julie eventually. 'I didn't find out till a couple of days afterwards, until he called me at work in floods of tears asking me what he should do. Well, what would you have done? He's my son! I told him to keep his mouth shut … Let Bannister take the fall. It was an accident, after all. He's just a stupid kid.'

Watching him in the interview room now, William seemed anything but. And it had been far from an accident … Made Jake wonder if he hadn't got some of this from Greg himself.

*'Are we sure he's Greg's?'*

As for Julie, she was barely able to look at Jake now. Hadn't had a clue any of this was going on under her nose. Hadn't had an inkling her husband was lying to her, or at the very least hiding the truth. An accessory …

*Saying something about the fine and one day his son being able to clear up his own messes.*

This whole thing was one big mess, and was just as much his fault as it was anyone's. If he'd been more forgiving, if he hadn't walked out, none of this would have happened. It had ruined so many lives. Without that, there would have been no Greg. No William, with warped fantasies.

He was telling Wright about them now, how he felt sure he and Jordan would be happy one day. That they could live together

285

and how well he would treat her, in spite of the fact she wanted nothing to do with him romantically.

Wright got up, stretching her legs, and wandered over to the glass, the mirror on her side. She raised her eyebrows, knowing that her DS could see her, as if to say, 'What a nutter!'

'Yeah, don't worry. He's going down for this for a long, long time,' Burton said and clapped Jake on the shoulder. It reminded him of how Matt used to do that. Matt who'd been hiding his own secrets, but who'd saved him. Matt who was now gone, disconnected from those many machines that had kept him going.

'Unexpected outcomes ...'

'Thanks. Do ... do you have any kids of your own?' Jake asked him then.

Burton looked horrified at the very suggestion. 'Not ... not that I know about, no.' Which suggested he might have a few he didn't, and he did have that look about him: a bit of a player. 'Not planning on any anytime soon.'

'Well, if you ever find you do at some point, look after them, won't you? Love them and try not to judge them, DS Burton. Because you don't get that time back again.'

The man with the tousled hair nodded. 'You got it, Mr Radcliffe. And it's Chris,' he told him.

'Jake,' he said, holding out his hand for the DS to shake. 'I'm just Jake.'

# Chapter 30

She stood on the platform, waiting. Wondering …

Wondering again whether it was possible to love someone and hate them at the same time. It wasn't about Jake now – she'd barely seen him since all this kicked off, just couldn't … Could still picture him when he found out. The hatred, the blame again.

She probably owed it to Jake to tell him she was leaving, but simply couldn't face the man. The one she'd hurt by leaving him at the hotel, by marrying Greg – letting him and his bastard of a kid into their lives.

*'Ask him about how his son murdered Jordan!'*

'I'm sorry,' Julie whispered again, as she'd done so many times lately. Feeling numb once more, but fighting back more tears. 'I'm so sorry, Jordan.'

If you traced it back, of course, it all began when Jake left. If he hadn't, then maybe … But what was done was done. She'd made a huge mistake, had no words to defend it.

And now she was doing exactly the same thing Jake did all those years ago, the irony not lost on her. Running away because she couldn't stay here now.

She'd had no idea where she was heading when she got here, dropped off by the taxi she'd ordered. Even as she'd stepped up to the ticket office, she'd had no clue. Then she'd looked sideways at the screens showing departures, and one destination had caught her eye. Somewhere they'd taken Jordan when she was little, a family holiday at the coast.

Julie bought the ticket quickly, then headed out onto the platform with the couple of cases she'd hastily packed.

Waited for the train to arrive, wondering. Was still wondering as it pulled in and she let the passengers get off, then boarded herself.

Was wondering if you could love and hate someone at the same time. Love, hate. But mainly hate ...

With Greg Allaway firmly in the middle.

# Epilogue

As the man walked forward, he had one name on his mind.

He paused when he reached his destination, where all this had begun. Where it would end. Autumn was giving way to winter, there was even the threat of a snowflake or two, so it wasn't wise to stand out in the freezing cold at night – and yet he did. He stood looking at the square ahead of him, the rows of wooden skeletons looking like the carcasses of long-dead monsters.

Monsters like the ones she'd been so afraid of when she was little, like the ones he'd sworn to protect her from. But the real monsters had come later, they'd been all around her in this town.

And, of course, she'd been living with two of the worst.

Jake stepped forward again, laid the flowers down on the stall where Jordan had passed away. He hadn't seen her again, not since the slaughterhouse, and to be honest he wasn't even sure he'd seen her then. That all the times he'd seen her hadn't just been, as Channing had said, one of the side-effects of grief. In any event, he hoped wherever she was, Jordan was at peace. Hoped also that he might be able to find a little of that for himself.

There was movement off to the side and he thought he'd spoken too soon, that Jordan *had* been watching him from the shadows – pale, sad face looking on. But no. As the figure came closer, Jake could see it was male. Not the policeman, either, the one he'd met the last time he was here, but someone around his age.

'Mr … Mr Radcliffe?' came the croaky voice, unsure of himself. Unsure whether the man just wanted to be left alone. But didn't he also have the right to be here, on this night? Perhaps even more right than Jake …

'Hello Bobby.'

The youth, who had a beanie on today covering his spiky hair, joined him. He too had a bunch of flowers with him and he held them up as if asking permission he didn't need. Then he stepped forward and placed them on the stall.

It wasn't a coincidence, of course, them being here at the same time on the same evening. The one-month anniversary of Jordan's death. Had it only been a month? Jake still couldn't believe it.

'I miss her,' said Bobby, stepping back and joining Jake – but not getting too close. Probably remembering the last time they'd met, when he'd wanted to kill the lad. But a lot had happened since then. So much.

'Yeah,' replied Jake.

'You know, she talked about you a lot.'

'Yeah?' said Jake, turning to face him, genuinely surprised by that.

Bobby nodded. ''Course. You were her dad. She … She hated the way it had gone with you two. I know she wanted to sort it somehow one day, but …'

'But we just ran out of time,' Jake finished for him.

'She didn't … She wasn't as bad as you thought, you know.' He could see Bobby bracing himself, as if expecting a whack, but he continued on regardless. 'We … we hadn't even—'

Jake held up his hand. Too much information, but he appreciated what the kid was saying. 'I know she thought a lot of you, Bobby. Wanted to be sure …' And he still had to remind himself every now and again that when Jordan had been talking about mood swings, about someone acting weird, it had been William – Billy-Boy – she'd been referring to. When she'd written about Bobby being nice, being lovely, it had been this youth she meant.

'I really did love her,' Bobby told him, and Jake didn't need Sam's skills to hear the truth in that. To see that he had.

'I think she loved you too, Bobby,' he replied. There was just one last thing nagging him, and he needed to ask about it. 'While you're here, I heard that you had a row with Jordan about that guy, Drummond?' It was something that had set him off on completely the wrong path back at the beginning of all this.

Bobby looked puzzled for a moment. 'Oh, *that!* Wasn't really a row, her mates like to blow things out of all proportion ...' Jake thought about Becky and nodded; it was more than possible she had done that when he spoke to her. 'I was just worried about Jordan spending too much time with him. Don't know if you've noticed but he's ...'

'A bit creepy? Yeah, I had.'

Bobby shrugged. 'Jordan reckoned he only hung around those places because he was trying to get back the family he'd had and lost ... They used to look after him, see? He used to have a younger sister as well, I think.'

'What happened to them?'

The youth shrugged again. 'Dunno, some kind of accident I think. But it left him on his own a while back. The authorities are shit around here, they should have been keeping an eye out for him. But Jordan ... I think she was trying to help him. She was kind like that.'

Another stray, lost and in need of help; that sounded about right. If only she could have found her way herself before it was too late. 'I'll have a word with Sam, see what we can do about getting him that help.'

'Miss Ferrara? Sure! She's cool.'

'Yes. Yes, she is.'

A silence descended that seemed to last an age, and Jake

291

couldn't help thinking as he looked at the stall again: *If I could just go back. If I could just see her one more time.*

The cough at the side of him reminded Jake he wasn't alone. He regarded the lad again, nothing like the monster *he'd* imagined. Maybe even the best of the bunch as far as Jordan's boyfriends went. Might even have stayed with him, had a family. Who knows, he and Bobby might have become friends someday.

Jake surprised himself then by saying, 'Hey, do you fancy grabbing a pint or something? My round.'

The lad looked terrified suddenly, but then smiled. Nodded. 'Yeah, I'd like that.'

'We can talk about Jordan,' said Jake. 'You can fill me in on some of the blanks. Some of the ... happy memories I missed out on.'

'Be glad to,' he said.

So Jake led the way, not to the noise of the clubs ahead of them – but to find somewhere a bit quieter where they could talk. A bit brighter than this market square. Because it was time, finally time.

Time to walk away from the dark.

## Want more?

To be the first to hear about new releases, competitions, 99p eBooks and promotions, sign up to our monthly email newsletter.

# Acknowledgements

My heartfelt thanks to Belinda Toor who read this and liked it enough to commission it, and who has been so brilliant to work with. A massive thank-you also to Abigail Fenton and the whole HQ Digital/HarperCollins team. If I start to thank everyone who has helped me during my time as a writer, I'm bound to miss someone out so I'll just say a big 'words are not enough' thanks to all of my dear friends in and out of the business; you know who you are. Lastly, but never leastly, I need to thank my family for their support and in particular Marie, who has always had my back. Love you all 3000.

Dear Reader,

Thank you so much for choosing to read *Her Last Secret*.

For a while now I've wanted to write a story about a character who's investigating the death of a loved one. Not a cop, but just an ordinary person who – if anything – is being hindered by the authorities. Someone driven by guilt because they weren't there for the person who'd been killed. In fact, might even be estranged from them.

So I started to think about possible combinations, like husband and wife or mother and child, and the one I kept coming back to was father and daughter – which, as everyone knows, can be an incredibly strong bond. So, what if the generation gap arguments of growing up drove these two characters apart, but something fatal happened before they could reconcile? That's the basic jumping-off point for this novel, but it also focuses on the disintegration of a family – as Jake Radcliffe has to deal not only with the fact his daughter Jordan has been murdered, but also the mixed feelings about seeing his ex-wife Julie once more. Especially as she's remarried.

This seemed like the perfect dramatic background for a man on the edge trying to get to the bottom of what happened, to the truth of the situation – something that will put him in all kinds of danger. Set against the backdrop of the fictional northern town of Redmarket, which I've tried to make a character in itself, this is definitely Jake's story but also shows the other points of view in this complex situation. A family tragedy, a murder mystery with plenty of twists and shocks. I hope you enjoyed reading *Her Last Secret* and, if you did, perhaps consider leaving a review … even just a line or two would be fantastic.

Warmest wishes,

*P.L. Kane.*

Dear Reader,

We hope you enjoyed reading this book. If you did, we'd be so appreciative if you left a review. It really helps us and the author to bring more books like this to you.

Here at HQ Digital we are dedicated to publishing fiction that will keep you turning the pages into the early hours. Don't want to miss a thing? To find out more about our books, promotions, discover exclusive content and enter competitions you can keep in touch in the following ways:

## JOIN OUR COMMUNITY:

*Sign up to our new email newsletter: po.st/HQSignUp*

*Read our new blog www.hqstories.co.uk*

🐦 *: https://twitter.com/HQDigitalUK*

📘 *: www.facebook.com/HQStories*

## BUDDING WRITER?

*We're also looking for authors to join the HQ Digital family!*
*Please submit your manuscript to:*

*HQDigital@harpercollins.co.uk*

*Thanks for reading, from the HQ Digital team*